If You Don't Have Anything Nice to Say

LEILA SALES

FARRAR STRAUS GIROUX

NEW YORK

Farrar Straus Giroux Books for Young Readers
An imprint of Macmillan Publishing Group, LLC
175 Fifth Avenue, New York, NY 10010

1 3 5 7 9 10 8 6 4 2

fiercereads.com

Library of Congress Cataloging-in-Publication Data

Names: Sales, Leila, author.
Title: If you don't have anything nice to say / by Leila Sales.
Other titles: If you do not have anything nice to say
Description: First edition. | New York : Farrar Straus Giroux, 2018. |
    Summary: After word-loving seventeen-year-old Winter Halperin
    thoughtlessly posts a racially offensive remark, her comment goes viral,
    turning her life into a nightmare.
Identifiers: LCCN 2017042317 | ISBN 9780374380991 (hardcover)
Subjects: | CYAC: Social media—Fiction. | Interpersonal relations—Fiction.
    | Conduct of life—Fiction. | Prejudices—Fiction.
Classification: LCC PZ7.S15215 If 2018 | DDC [Fic]—dc23
LC record available at https://lccn.loc.gov/2017042317

Our books may be purchased in bulk for promotional, educational, or business use. Please
contact your local bookseller or the Macmillan Corporate and Premium Sales Department at
(800) 221-7945 ext. 5442 or by e-mail at MacmillanSpecialMarkets@macmillan.com.

For Emily Heddleson, my constant partner,
the closest I'll ever come to having a big sister of my own

"We tend to relentlessly define people by the worst mistake they ever made."
—Jon Ronson

"That is not what I meant at all;
That is not it, at all."
—from "The Love Song of J. Alfred Prufrock," by T. S. Eliot

"But what one 'means' is neither important nor relevant."
—from *Between the World and Me*, by Ta-Nehisi Coates

1

I'm seventeen years old and I have already been famous twice in my life. The first occasion was a dream come true. The second occasion was a nightmare from which I still cannot wake up.

Fame seems from afar like one of those things that's inherently great. Like owning a pony! It's only once you get it that you realize your pony is in fact a wild stallion. It will turn on you. It will wreak havoc. It will run away. It cannot be contained.

My fame arrived, both times, because I love words. I love the sounds they make, the funny and surprising ways that the same twenty-six letters work together in infinite different combinations. I love the stories behind words: where they come from, where they're going. I love piecing them together like a puzzle.

You get punished for loving something too much. That is the truth of it all.

This sounds stupid now, but I used to want to be a writer. I thought that writing might be a good place for all the words I have rattling around in my brain. And it was, for a little while. Until someone read what I had written.

That's supposed to be the best, right? You work hard on something, you practice and execute and refine it, and you claim, "It's just for my own enjoyment. As long as I like doing it, that's all that matters." But even as you say that—because you know it is the noble thing to say—what you *really* hope is that outsiders who know what they're talking about will see this thing you have produced and say, "You're a genius!"

So I'll own up to it: I didn't *just* want to write. I wanted to write, and I wanted people to read what I had written, and to like it, and to like me by extension.

This obviously did not go the way I had envisioned it.

I don't know what the moral of this story is. That's how you know it's not a good story. Good stories have morals. The moral is that there's no place like home, or the moral is that love conquers all, or the moral is that love actually conquers nothing of consequence. You should come away from a story thinking that you at least kind of understand what the point of it was. That it wasn't just a bunch of made-up people doing made-up things to no purpose.

What *is* the moral of my story? Don't aspire to make anything of yourself? Don't try to do anything? No one will ever understand you? Shut up and sit down? Whatever the moral is, it's clear that I haven't learned it yet. I am no wiser for my errors. Wounded, but no wiser.

The best I can hope for is that my story isn't over yet. That the moral will show up sometime much later.

Before we go any further, I want to make sure you understand this: I am not a good person. If that's important to you, to only read things by good people and about good people, where all their conflicts are unfair things that happened to them despite their pluck and kindness, then you should stop reading right now. I am not the girl for you.

I'm sure you know what I did. Everyone does. You might not *remember* that I did this. Or you might remember that *somebody* did it, but not that the person in question is *me*. I will jog your memory because I don't want our relationship to be founded on any pretense. I want you to know who you're dealing with here.

Pretense. If you trace its origins way back, it comes from the medieval Latin word *praetendere*, which later turned into *pretend*. Use it in a sentence: *I have no pretense to innocence.*

I am Winter Halperin. I'm the one who went online after the National Spelling Bee and posted, "We learned many surprising things today. Like that *dehnstufe* is apparently a word, and that a black kid can actually win the Spelling Bee."

That's what I wrote. And I put it online for the whole world to see.

You can stop reading now, if you want.

2

Who would say such a thing? What kind of racist, insensitive, attention-seeking, sheltered, clueless bitch would say something that basically amounts to, *Wow, I didn't know black people knew words!*? That's what everybody wanted to know.

Well, no. They didn't actually want to know. If they had, they would have asked me. I have this fantasy sometimes where CNN or NBC has me in for an interview, and the whole world is watching, and the news anchor asks me in a very calm way, "Winter, do you want to explain why you did it?" And I respond in an equally calm way, and I explain myself, and then the whole world understands and is satisfied.

This would never happen. The nightly news doesn't care what I have to say. Nobody does. And if I were given the opportunity to explain myself, I would somehow screw it up, my words would get twisted again, and whatever I said in my defense would be used to make me look even more racist, insensitive, and bitchy than I already do.

However, this doesn't stop me from sometimes explaining myself to my mirror. Like if anyone ever asks, I want to make sure I'm ready. Like I need to say it aloud sometimes, even if I'm the only one who can hear, just to remind myself what the truth is. It sounds good, I think, when the only person listening is me. But what do I know? Lots of things sound good to me. I can't trust myself.

It was close to midnight on a Thursday in late May, four weeks before my high school graduation, when I wrote and posted that: "We learned many surprising things today. Like that *dehnstufe* is apparently a word, and that a black kid can actually win the Spelling Bee." I brushed my teeth and then checked to see if anyone had read my post. Already Corey had liked it and Mackler had reposted it, and that pleased me, that in only five minutes two of my friends had given their approval. Then I went to bed.

I silenced my phone, as I always do. When I first got it, I used to leave my phone on overnight. But then the screen shattered. (Technically, this was my fault, since I threw it against the wall. In my defense, it was beeping with a notification of a new crossword puzzle's availability at four a.m.) I never bothered to repair the screen, but I did start silencing the ringer while I slept, figuring that anyone who needed to reach me could wait until the morning.

What I didn't realize is that a life can be destroyed in the course of one night.

When my alarm went off, I looked at my phone for the weather, which is what I do every morning as an excuse to stay in bed for an extra minute. But I couldn't even get to the weather, because my phone was filled with notifications. And I don't mean that Corey had texted me minute-by-minute updates of the old *Star Trek* episode that he was watching, or that I'd gotten an automated traffic alert or whatever. I mean *hundreds* of notifications. Maybe thousands. So many notifications that my phone couldn't handle them; it kept shutting down and then restarting, like it had forgotten how to be a phone.

It was hard to read any of these notifications, because new ones kept coming in on top of them. So I knew that something bad had happened, but my first instinct was that a bad thing must have happened to *everybody*. Maybe the president had been assassinated or an earthquake had wiped out the entirety of California except for my house. What else would I possibly need to know about with so much intensity?

I finally managed to get one of the notifications open, but without context, it didn't make any sense. "I can't believe you still haven't apologized," it said. It was from someone whose name and face I didn't recognize, an adult, and I didn't even wonder why I'd need to apologize to this woman, but instead wondered who she had mistaken me for.

The next message said, "Winter Halperin is a racist bitch who deserves to burn in hell," and that was the moment at which I panicked. I jumped out of bed and ran downstairs to where my mother stood, resting her hands on the countertop, leveling a bleary-eyed gaze at the espresso machine as it whirred.

"Mom," I said. "Mom, Mom, Mom."

She turned, looking alarmed—probably as much by the fact

that I was awake and downstairs so early as by the horror in my voice.

"Winter? What's wrong?"

I shook my head and thrust my phone into her hands.

"I don't know what . . ." She trailed off as she started to read. "What is this all about?" she asked, her voice shrill. The espresso machine started spurting out coffee, but my mother didn't even seem to notice. "Who are these people?"

"I don't know," I said. "I don't know. I think they're playing a prank on me."

"Playing a . . . Why?" She started poking randomly at my phone.

"Mom," I said. "Stop it, you don't know how to . . ." My mom isn't *that* old, but she is old enough to be terrible at technology. She somehow managed to turn on the ringer, which resulted in about a hundred consecutive beeping sounds.

"*Oy gevalt.* What did I do? What did I do?" she asked, frantically jabbing at the screen.

"*Mom.*" I tried to wrest it out of her hands, but she was still trying to fix the situation by pressing buttons, so she wasn't letting go, and I pulled the phone toward me, and she pulled it toward her, saying, "Just one second," and then my phone went flying up into the air, crash-landed on the floor, and went skidding under the refrigerator, knocking down a magnetized finger puppet of Mozart as it went.

"What is your *problem*?" I yelled, even though I knew that whatever this problem was, it was far too big to be my mother's fault.

"At least that beeping stopped," she pointed out. "Maybe all those terrible messages have stopped, too."

"They were on the internet, Mom. If we looked on my computer, they would still be there . . . Oh my God, *why*? How can we make this go away? Where is Dad?"

"He already left for Portland," Mom said absently.

My father is a sales representative for a toy company, so he spends a lot of time on the road, visiting toy stores or attending conventions, with his car packed full of puzzles and glow-in-the-dark bouncy balls and, sometimes, magnetized finger puppets of famous composers.

"Where's my phone?" Mom asked, feeling around on the counter as if maybe her phone were right there but she was for some reason unable to see it.

"Probably still charging in your room," I answered. "Mom. Drink your coffee. I need you to be helpful right now." My mother gains roughly ten IQ points for every sip of caffeine that she downs in the morning.

She drank her coffee. "Can we just tell them that they need to stop? This is harassment. You're a minor. I don't even think this is legal. I'm going to call my lawyer."

I nodded vigorously. Even with my phone silent, maybe destroyed, under the fridge, I could still picture those messages that had lit it up: *You are such a bitch. You are such an idiot. What is Winter Halperin's PROBLEM?* Mom must be right. That couldn't be legal stuff to say, not to a seventeen-year-old.

"I'm going to get my phone," Mom told me. She strode forward, and I stuck to her like a burr. I didn't want to be alone.

There was a banging at the front door, and I grabbed my mom in a panic. Could it be that one of those crazies had somehow tracked down where I live and was outside right this minute?

Mom seemed to have the same thought, because she said, "Stay here. I'll find out who it is."

I stood alone in the kitchen, knotting and unknotting my hands. Without really thinking it through, I grabbed a chef's knife from the drying rack. In case whoever was at the door came for me, I'd be ready to . . . what? Cut them? Yeah, right. I'd never hurt anyone in my life. I couldn't even manage to spar when I took karate in first grade. If a crazy from the internet was here to kill me, I'd have more luck winning a debate than a physical fight.

Then my sister, Emerson, came flying into the kitchen, her blond topknot bouncing up and down on her head. Mom was right behind her.

"Oh, it's you." I breathed a sigh of relief, set down the knife in what I hoped was a casual manner, and gave her a big hug. "I thought you weren't getting home until later?" Emerson had just finished her freshman year in the University of Oklahoma's musical theater program.

"Apparently she decided to drive all through the night so she could get home earlier," Mom said drily. "You can imagine how her mother feels about this."

"That's why I didn't tell you in advance," Emerson said, "because I knew you'd worry. But look, here I am, I'm safe and alive—"

"*Kina hora,*" Mom muttered.

"—and the person you really need to be worrying about right

now is Winter," Emerson went on. She turned to me. "Winter Leona Halperin. What the hell is wrong with you? Did you actually tell the entire world that African Americans *don't know how to spell*?"

And *that* was when I put two and two together.

"Oh," I said. "Oh my God. Is *that* what this is all about?"

"Is *what* what this is all about?" Mom demanded.

"My friends have been texting me about this since, like, three a.m.," Emerson said. "I *tried* to reach you. Don't any of you people ever look at your phones?"

"My phone's under the fridge," I answered.

"Emerson, you were texting while you were *driving*?" Mom exclaimed.

"Of course not," Emerson said, which I immediately took to mean *yes, definitely*. "But Brianna just sent me this Yahoo article a second ago, and I had to . . . Look, it's easier if I read it to you." She cleared her throat. "The headline is 'Spelling Bee Champ Disses Minorities.'"

"'*Disses*'?" I repeated. "What kind of reputable news source uses *disses*?"

Emerson kept reading. " 'If you haven't gotten caught up in the general societal bashing of one Winter Halperin (yes, her name really is Winter), you must be living under a rock. To bring you up to speed—last night, after the final round of the annual Scripps National Spelling Bee, the California teen took to the internet to post the following: 'We learned many surprising things today. Like that *dehnstufe* is apparently a word, and that a black kid can actually win the Spelling Bee.'

"'Ms. Halperin was referring to the victory of Sintra Gabel, the eighth grader from Queens, New York, who took home the gold in this year's spelling bee by correctly spelling the word *dehnstufe*, which means 'a lengthened grade' and derives from the German.

"'When asked for her opinion on Ms. Halperin's statement, Ms. Gabel declined to comment, but her father said, "My daughter is terrifically smart and hardworking, and as of tonight she is the best speller in the nation. It's unfortunate and hurtful that this has been turned into a conversation about her race rather than her intellect and her accomplishments. Winter's thoughtless remarks show just how far America still has to go before we reach true equality."

"'Ms. Halperin's original post has, in the few hours since she wrote it, been reposted and commented on more than twenty thousand times. "It's the very definition of viral content," explains Dr. Orlando Beaudrault, professor of media studies at Northwestern University. And where will it stop? "Who knows," says Dr. Beaudrault. "As the internet grows, so too do its viruses. It seems like every time we see an explosion of outrage like this one, it gets bigger and bigger. How far will this specific one go? As far as I can tell, the sky is the limit."

"'If you're wondering why so many people are reacting so strongly to a teenager's post, all you need to know is who Ms. Halperin is: she herself was the champion of the National Spelling Bee five years ago, when she was in seventh grade. Her winning word was *ptyalagogue*. Now a high school senior, Ms. Halperin will be attending Kenyon College starting this fall.'"

Emerson clicked off her phone and crossed her arms.

"I don't understand this," Mom whispered, steadying herself on the wall.

"I'm going to delete that post," I said. "Right now."

"It won't matter," Emerson said gently. "You're already cruci-fied. It's too late."

And, of course, she was right.

3

What else happened on that first day? I can't give a full account; even as the moments unfolded, I didn't know what was happening to me. I felt like I was drowning, like I kept losing consciousness and then regaining it only to find myself further and further underwater.

I stayed home from school, which was unprecedented. Some people, like my friend Mackler, have a pretty laissez-faire relationship with school attendance: a poor night's sleep or the first warm day of spring is reason enough to stay home. But in my family, you follow through on your commitments and show up at school or work unless you are on death's doorstep. But maybe I *was* on death's doorstep, because Mom and I didn't even discuss the idea of my leaving the house. It was as if school didn't exist, as if nothing in the real, tangible world existed, and the only world of consequence was the one on the internet.

My name went from getting no more than a few search results, all five-year-old news pieces about my spelling victory, to being the first result to pop up when you typed the letters *W-I-N-T* into the search bar. Let me repeat that: "Winter Halperin" preceded even *the season of winter* in Google search results. BuzzFeed ran an article of "20 Perfect Responses to Winter Halperin's Racist Post." I remember them all, and I imagine I always will. Number seventeen: "We learned many surprising things today. Like that just because someone is a good speller, it doesn't mean she's not a bigot." Number nine: "Hey, Winter Halperin, do you know how to spell 'white supremacy'?"

I'll just explain myself, I thought. *I need to explain myself.*

I didn't understand, then, that this is not how the world works. When we decide someone is an angel, she is an angel only until she falls from the sky. But when we decide someone is a villain, she is a villain forever. Everything she says or does is only more proof of her villainy. She cannot be redeemed.

Yet I wrote and posted my defense as though the internet was some fair court of law. "This is Winter Halperin," I wrote, "and there's been a big mistake. I was definitely never trying to say that white people are in any way smarter or better spellers than African Americans, or people of any other race.

"In fact, the National Spelling Bee is disproportionately won by kids from Southeast Asia. I'm one of the few white winners from the past decade, because so many of them have been of Indian or Pakistani descent. Black kids almost never win the Bee—even less often than white kids. I don't know why that is, and I certainly don't believe that it's right or good. I was just trying to call attention to that situation.

"It's not that *I* was surprised that Sintra Gabel was the country's best speller. It would be like if a short person won the NBA championship and I said that was a surprise—not because *I* assume short people aren't good at basketball, but because *society* assumes short people aren't as good at basketball as tall people.

"I promise I'm not a racist. Two of my best friends in the world are African American. I was trying to make a humorous commentary here, but obviously it fell flat, and I sincerely apologize if anyone's feelings were hurt. Sintra's an amazing speller and she deserves this victory. I give her my wholehearted congratulations."

I worked really hard on that explanation. I was proud of it, especially the basketball analogy. I honestly, idiotically thought that might be the end of the whole thing.

But it took only seconds—hardly enough time for anyone to even read and process what I'd written—for the rebuttals to start pouring in.

"Oh, look, White Winter speaks at last."

" 'I sincerely apologize if anyone's feelings were hurt'—can you even *imagine* a more passive way to apologize?! Like, '*If* anyone's feelings were hurt—which maybe they weren't, who could say!—then I'm sorry that they feel bad, even though I'm *not* sorry for my actions, which totally have nothing to do with people's hurt feelings.' WINTER, YOU ARE THE WORST."

"omg I can't believe she's parading out the old 'I can't be a racist, some of my best friends are black!' shtick. If I were her right now I'd be so mortified, I'd literally kill myself. Can anyone explain why this bitch is still alive??"

"I just want to be clear that I am a guy and I'm only 5'8", and my basketball team has never lost a match. Short people can be great athletes. Black people can be great intellects. Sorry to ruin your tiny little understanding of the world, Winter."

"I hate that this is the sort of bullshit we have to put up with, even in the twenty-first century, even in what is supposedly the greatest nation on Earth. There are only so many black stereotypes: you can be the athlete or the drug dealer, you can be the baby mama or the ho. And if you deviate from that in any way—like if you're a smart, kick-butt little girl who's a spelling bee champion—people's minds are blown. They're all, 'Whoa! Where did she come from? Is she a unicorn?' Nope, she's not. She came from the same place as the rest of us—it's just that she hasn't learned yet that there are certain things she's not 'supposed' to be able to do."

"Someone should steal *her* away from her home, enslave her, beat her, rape her, tell her she's three-fifths of a person at best, and see if any of that helps her understand what she did wrong."

"Ooh, let's see what Winter says. 'I was definitely never trying to say that white people are in any way smarter or better spellers than African Americans.' Why do you think that we care what you were *trying* to say? I don't give a rat's ass if you were *trying* to say, 'Let's have peace on Earth' or 'I want pancakes for breakfast.' What you *actually* said was that you were surprised a black kid was smart enough to win the National Spelling Bee. Do or do not, Winter—there is no *try*."

"Is Winter hating on Southeast Asians now, too? My dad is

Pakistani and he's one of the worst spellers I've ever met. (Love him, though!) RACE DOESN'T EQUAL SPELLING ABILITY. How does she not get this??"

And on and on and on. They didn't stop. They never stopped. For every individual out there who grew tired of my story or had to take a break to go to school or work or take a shower or a nap, there was some new person seamlessly moving in to take their place, as if this were a relay race that everyone in America was playing and the baton of Hating Winter could never touch the ground.

The morning faded into afternoon, the afternoon into evening. Emerson went out for a while, then returned with reports from the real world. "You were all anyone could talk about," she said, jumping onto the couch where I had been sitting all day, searching for my name again and again. "Katharine said everyone is making a mountain out of a molehill, and Brianna said she's known you since you were four years old and obviously you're not a racist, and Tyler said his cousin who lives all the way in *Toronto* e-mailed him to ask if he knew you. Everyone is on your side." Emerson held my hand in hers. "They know you well enough to know that you just made a stupid mistake. You're not the terrible person that all these idiots online seem to think you are."

Of course I wasn't that terrible person. I couldn't be. I was a good girl. Vacationing neighbors trusted me to feed their cats. Overworked teachers counted on me to monitor the class if they had to leave for a moment. I didn't get in trouble. I'd never once gotten detention. I didn't even run in the halls. I was nothing like the person being described online.

"Did anyone you talked to say I should be raped and murdered?"

I asked—because those were the comments that frightened me most, the ones that said, "Why doesn't White Winter do us all a favor and go die," followed by, "We should just kill her and put her out of her misery," followed by, "Death is better than she deserves. Someone needs to rape that bitch," followed by, "Not it. She's way too ugly to fuck."

Emerson blanched. "*Obviously* not. Who the hell would say something like that?"

I gestured limply toward my computer.

"That's horrible," Emerson whispered.

"I know." It was scary, too. I didn't really believe that one of these commenters was going to track me down in person and torture me the way they said I deserved—but they *could*. Saying that sort of thing would get you kicked out of school, but what happened to you if you said it online, to a person you didn't even know? Nothing. There was no principal or police force of the internet. No one could stop you.

Later that afternoon, some enterprising asshole found a photo of me at age eleven, competing in my second National Spelling Bee. That wasn't the year I won. This photo was from the year before that, when I was in full-on middle-school awkwardness: colorful braces, too-long split-ended hair, a headband with a ridiculously big cloth daisy on top. It doesn't matter; nobody expects an eleven-year-old to have figured out how to get the most out of her hair and wardrobe. Still, if there was going to be a photo that everyone in the world associated with me, I wished it had been taken after I'd shed some more of my baby fat. In this photo I'm standing at the microphone, my mouth open, my eyes mostly closed. I don't remember the exact moment this shot was taken, but based on my expression, I'd say I was in the process of spelling a word aloud as I visualized it in my mind.

At first, the internet had a lot of commentary on my physical appearance. "No wonder she's lashing out at other people," said one post. "I'd do the same if I looked like *that*. Whatever it takes to feel better about yourself, am I right?" And, "How am I not surprised that White Winter is a fatty?"

Here and there I would see a post saying something like, "Come on, she's just a kid in this photo. I'm sure none of us were gorgeous prepubescents. Lay off." But even those posters would hastily add, "Not that I am in *any way* defending her completely inappropriate remark." As if they were worried that by suggesting I wasn't a monster through and through, someone might suspect *them* of being the racists.

Within a few hours, the use of this photo morphed. People started posting it with their own writing on it. This picture of me—innocent, hard-at-work, little-girl me—became a meme. "We learned many surprising things today," said one iteration of my photo. "Like that 9/11 was an inside job." Or, "We learned many surprising things today. Like that my cat just peed in my shoes." Now it wasn't only when you typed in *W-I-N-T* that you got search results about me. If you typed in "surprising things," up popped hundreds or thousands of versions of this same photo, each one with a different stupid surprising thing to learn. And I saw them all. I clicked through every last one.

That evening faded into night. We'd had plans to take Emerson out to her favorite Greek restaurant in honor of her first night back, but now no one even mentioned it. My dad came home, cutting his business trip short to be with me. He held me in his arms for a long time, crushing me toward him, as if by keeping me close he could keep everyone else away.

But he couldn't, of course. As soon as he left the room, I checked the internet again, desperate to know what I had missed, and this time I saw a statement that came to my defense—in the worst way possible. "We here at the Aryan Alliance stand in full support of Winter Halperin and the truth she espouses," it said. "If you are a believer in white superiority, then you will stand with us and stand with Miss Halperin."

My stomach roiling, I clicked on their profile. I could get through only half of their description of the Aryan Alliance as an organization devoted to the principle that the white race is smarter, braver, kinder, and altogether better than any other race in the world before I had to close out of that window, pressing my hands to my stomach, trying not to throw up.

How could those people possibly think that I was one of them? I was *nothing* like them. That was in no way what I believed. That wasn't ever what I meant. Didn't it *matter* what I meant?

Eventually the rest of my family went to bed. It was one o'clock, two o'clock, three o'clock in the morning, and it did not even occur to me to try to go to sleep. Basic systems in my body had shut down. The parts that demanded food, hydration, sleep, and bathroom breaks had all gone silent. It was as if I didn't even have a body anymore, just an online persona.

And I was scared to go to sleep. I remembered too clearly that the night before, I'd closed my eyes and everything was fine, and when I woke up, everything would never be fine again. What *is* the moral of this story? Is it *don't fall asleep*?

Sometime early on the second morning, my eyes burning from too many hours spent open, I started seeing a new sort of photo. These ones weren't of me (though that humiliating photo persisted, too, don't worry). These new photos were of all different people: old, young, male, female, smiling, stern. What every one of these individuals had in common was that they were all black, and they were each holding a sign that said SURPRISE: I CAN SPELL. Almost immediately, a website sprang up to collect them. I spent the early hours of the morning, with all the world dark and silent around me, clicking through page after page of strangers' faces and their handwritten signs.

I just wanted this to stop. I wanted this to disappear. I wanted to rewind thirty hours and make one simple, different choice. I wanted anybody's life except for my own.

And then things really fell apart.

4

My friends tried to help—most of them did, anyway. Corey and Mackler kept up a running commentary of normal-sounding messages all day long. **I showed Fiona the hamster video and she almost peed herself laughing IT IS COMEDY GOLD YO.** And, **Are you sure you don't want to come to the movies with us? Mack will even give you free popcorn, think about that.** And, **Jason and Caroline are fighting AGAIN it's hilarious.** It took all my energy and focus to reply with a smiley face.

But the mention of Jason jabbed at me like a knitting needle, because he himself—the final member of our crew, our other best friend—hadn't said a word. And as the day went on, and then the evening faded into night, and still I didn't hear from him, I grew more and more concerned. Surely he knew what was going on. Everyone in the entire world knew.

So where was he?

I messaged Jason a dozen times over the course of the day, starting with **Hey** and going all the way to **Please just reply to let me know you're alive.**

He didn't write back.

Is Jason still with you? I asked Corey and Mackler after a family dinner that I couldn't bear to eat.

Nah he's out with Caroline, Corey responded. **Why?**

Nothing, I said.

Around twelve thirty, I slipped out of my house and walked over to the Shaws'. Jason and I live in the Berkeley Hills, and to drive between our houses takes a lot of winding through the streets, but fortunately there are steep staircases cut through the hills that lead straight from my street down to his. The staircases are poorly lit and poorly maintained, and late at night it's easy to convince yourself that you're going to run straight into a dead skunk or a murderer. Our parents always asked us to stick to the roads, but I never did.

When I reached the bottom of the stairs and Jason's house, I saw him through the living room window, reading a book on the couch. I paused for a moment before making my presence known, just watching him. I almost never saw Jason alone. He was always with Corey and Mackler or the guys on his basketball team or his girlfriend of the month, so I never had the opportunity to admire the confident sprawl of his legs, as I did now, or the way he unconsciously rubbed his hand across his stubbly black hair, or the way he bit down on his bottom lip when he was thinking.

Snap out of it, Halperin, I told myself. It's hard when one of your best friends is stupidly good-looking. People who are your friends shouldn't be allowed to be so beautiful.

I approached the living room window and stood on tiptoe to tap at it. Jason's head jolted up from his book, then stilled when he caught sight of me. For a moment we stared at each other through the glass. Then he stood and crossed the room to the front door to let me in.

"Thanks," I said once I was inside. "I didn't want to wake up your parents, and you weren't answering your phone. Are you okay?"

"Yeah," he said, not quite meeting my eye.

I waited for an explanation, received nothing but silence, and tried again. "What did you and Caroline get up to tonight?" I asked brightly.

He shrugged. "I dunno. Turns out she's kind of crazy."

This is how Jason describes all his exes and soon-to-be-exes. If you ask me, he *drives* them crazy by asking them out and then being completely emotionally unavailable. But that is simply my opinion.

"Crazy how?" I asked, just to keep him talking.

"She gets jealous. It's weird."

It wasn't weird at all. To really get to know Jason, to become part of the fabric of his life and have him woven into yours, took a herculean effort. Mackler, Corey, and I came closest out of everyone, and I suspected that even we had access to only about twenty-five percent of Jason. Any girl who he was dating got far less than that: a Saturday-night date to the movies, a perfunctory pre-bedtime text, as much physical affection as she wanted—but emotionally, she was always cordoned off and penned in. I couldn't blame Caroline for feeling jealous of all the sides of Jason that she couldn't know and could never have.

"What are you doing here?" Jason asked at last. He hitched up his flannel pants, and it occurred to me that even this—my being here alone and late at night when he was in his pajamas—was infringing on his firmly marked territory.

"I don't know if you heard," I replied, "but I'm having kind of a rough week."

"What do you want from me, Winter?" he said.

"I just need you to act like my friend," I replied in a low voice. "I need to know someone is on my side. This is so scary, and I don't know how to make it stop. Or if I can *ever* make it stop. I said I was sorry and tried to explain myself, and nothing changed. I don't know what else to do." I flopped down onto his couch.

Jason's voice was heavy. "Look, I believe that you're sorry you said that thing because it made people act like jerks to you. I believe that you're sorry you got in trouble. It goes without saying that you're sorry.

"But here's the thing: I don't believe that you're sorry you actually had those thoughts in the first place."

I stared up at him. Could this really be the reason for his silence—silence at the time in my life when I most needed support?

He went on. "I don't believe that there's anything that would stop you from saying the exact same thing again if you knew that next time, no one would care."

"I was just trying to make a joke," I whispered.

I could imagine—sort of—how strangers might not know that,

might not understand my tone and might assume the worst of me. But if you *knew* me, how could you fault me? And how could Jason at this point *not* know me?

"Should my life get destroyed over the fact that I made one bad joke?" I asked, my voice stronger now. "I get it, okay? *I'm not funny.* It wasn't funny. It was supposed to be, but it wasn't. But should I be punished because I'm not as funny as I thought I was, because I'm a worse writer than I wanted to be?"

"This isn't about *your* punishment or *your* writing skills," Jason snapped. "Have you even taken *one second* to consider how this might make anyone else feel? Let me spell it out for you: you said it's a shock for a black person to win a competition that requires intelligence."

"I did not," I argued. "Do you really think that's the sort of thing I would say?"

"It's what you *did* say."

"That's obviously not what I meant. For starters, as someone who once spent, like, five hours a day spelling words, I can say that spelling is not even really a test of intelligence. A lot of it is just rote memorization. It takes mnemonics and hard work, it's not *easy*, but it's not like the world's smartest people are also the world's best spellers."

This was one of the things that bothered me often. I'd been one of the best spellers in the country, but you couldn't *do* anything with that skill. It didn't translate into better grades or a greater understanding of the French Revolution or organic chemistry or anything, really. As it turned out, it didn't even make you a better writer. Because even if you had access to almost every single word in the English language, as I did, the trick was in how you used them. And no matter how good your words were, there was still no guarantee that anyone would understand your meaning.

"Are you really taking the side of all those crazies out there?" I demanded. "The strangers saying I should be lynched, I should be whipped, I should be raped and then have my children taken away from me and sold into slavery so I could pay for what I've done? Are you going to take their side over mine?"

"Of *course* not," Jason said, flinching. "I'm not associating myself with any of those assholes. But if there are sides here, I'm not taking yours, Winter. You betrayed me."

"In what way did I *betray* you? Are you really going to try to make me feel guilty about this? Do you think I don't feel guilty enough?"

"I just want to know if, at any point in the past two days, you ever stopped to think about how it would make *me* feel," Jason said, "finding out after all these years that you think I'm an idiot."

"I don't think that." I was astonished.

"I am black," Jason said. "In case you didn't know."

I didn't speak for a moment. Yes, Jason was black. But it was not anything we ever *discussed*, because what was there to say? Like, "Hey, what do you think about the fact that our skins are different colors?" We didn't talk about any of that stuff: how I was Jewish while Mackler was Methodist; how I was female while the rest of them were male; how Mackler was so large and Corey so scrawny. What was there to say about any of that? It was all just stuff we'd been born with, the backgrounds to who we really were.

I was so flustered that Jason was bringing this up now when he never had before, not once, that I blurted out, "I don't care that you're black."

He grimaced. "Clearly."

"That came out wrong. I'm sorry. Look, Jason, I don't believe that all white people are smart or all black people are stupid. You *know* I don't believe that, because that is an insane, irrational, backward, horrible thing to believe." I thought of the Aryan Alliance and shuddered.

"Nobody *says* they believe that one race is better than another," Jason said, starting to pace the room. "But when a security guard 'casually' trails me at the mall, or a woman crosses to the other side of the street when I'm walking behind her, or when my pediatrician told me that when I started high school I shouldn't get involved in any gangs, do you think it makes any difference what they *meant* by any of that?"

"Is that real?" I asked, horrified. "I've never seen anyone treat you like that."

"Do you think I'm making it up?"

"No! I just can't believe it."

"You don't notice it because they don't do it much when you're with me," he said. "Because you look so safe. You look like the stereotype of a person who would *never* shoplift or drag someone into a dark alleyway and pull out a switchblade. If you're with me, then I *must* be safe."

And yet of the two of us, I was the more radioactive. I didn't know how people thought they could see that in his skin color when they couldn't see it in me. That was irony.

Irony. A truly great word. From the Greek, obviously, as so many great words about literary technique are. It has a bunch of different meanings, and yet still people use it at the wrong times. *Irony* refers to the difference between the expected outcome and the actual outcome—like here, apparently one would expect the danger to be Jason and not me, when really the opposite is true. And it can also mean something more like sarcasm: when you use words to express the opposite of their literal meaning.

How do you tell people, though, when you want your words to be understood *ironically* rather than *literally*? How do you convey that? Why isn't there a special font we can use that means "just kidding"?

Jason sat down beside me and looked at me, his brown eyes soft and sad. I understood so badly what drew girls like Caroline to him. He was handsome and inscrutable. He had vast wells of emotion, and maybe, if you tried hard enough, someday you would get to the bottom of them.

"Corey's black, too," I reminded him, feeling supremely uncomfortable to be calling attention to this fact, as if I were revealing a secret. I'd never *announced* somebody's race like this, and I hated doing so now.

"I've noticed," Jason said drily.

"I'm just saying, *Corey* doesn't care about my post. He thought it was funny—or, I don't know, if not funny, at least not any sort of *problem*. He liked it."

"Good for Corey. He and I don't have to have the same opinions, any more than you and Mack are going to agree on everything just because you're both white."

"I didn't say that," I said, my voice growing louder with frustration. "Stop trying to tell me what I believe. I said it's surprising for an African American speller to win the Bee simply because *that almost never happens*. It's surprising because it's *unusual*. And that's a fact. I didn't say that I thought that was a *good* thing. In fact, I think it's a *bad* thing. But it's what happens, year after year."

"And why do you think that is?" Jason asked bitterly. "Do you have any possible ideas about *why* they almost never win?"

"Because they're . . . not as good spellers."

"Because we're stupider," he supplied.

"No! That's obviously not true. Look at Sintra Gabel."

"Oh, sure," Jason said. "There are exceptions. There are always the exceptional ones who prove to the world that the rest of us could succeed, too, if we just worked really hard, like they did. But on average—*disproportionately*, as you said—there's a whole goddamn race of people who are worse spellers. Why? Do you think they're born that way?"

I shook my head, though it actually didn't seem entirely irrelevant—there *were* things that each individual was born to be better or worse at. It mattered what you did with them, of course: I was born good at words, but probably that wouldn't have come to anything if my parents hadn't encouraged me. And on the flip side, no matter how much training I'd been given, I probably never would have turned into a truly gifted athlete, because I wasn't born with whatever it is good athletes are supposed to have. (Reflexes, I think. Maybe reflexes.)

"I can't believe I have to explain this to you," Jason said. "I *hate* that I have to explain this to you. *Not everyone has your privilege,*

Winter. Not everyone has parents with college degrees, who are around all the time, who talk to them with big words, who listen to what they have to say. Not everyone has money to throw at coaches and after-school enrichment programs and books and computers. Not everyone even knows all those things are options in the first place. Not everyone has spent their whole life in a good town with a good school system. Not everyone is trusted like you, or given the benefit of the doubt like you, or expected to do great things like you. A lot of people are fighting a seriously uphill battle just to get treated with the basic respect you go through your whole life assuming you're entitled to."

Jason had never said anything like this to me before, but he wasn't telling me anything I didn't know. I knew I was fortunate to have a loving family and good education and health and people who believed in me. I knew lots of people all over the world didn't have half of that; it wasn't a guarantee. I was grateful for it all. But how did any of that make me a racist and a bad person?

"Can you even try to understand what it's like to *not* be you?" Jason asked, frustrated. "My mom used to tell me that I had to be twice as good as the other kids in school—twice as polite, twice as hardworking—just to get half of what they got. I knew that was true before I even thought to ask *why*. Then I started seeing all this black activism stuff online, and it was like . . . I woke up.

"When I started middle school, my parents had all these rules for me: never run or shout unless you absolutely have to, keep your hands out so everyone can see that they're empty, don't wear hoodies so people can see your face, don't be on the streets late at night . . . a hundred ways to make other people feel safe around me so *I* don't get in trouble. When your mom was so busy teaching you how to spell, Winter, did she ever have to teach you any of that stuff?"

My mouth had fallen open. "I'm so sorry, Jason," I said when I found my voice. "I had no idea. Why didn't you ever mention any of this before? I could have . . ." But I didn't know what I could have done. How could I—how could *anyone*—have changed that?

There was so much of Jason I had no idea about. His grandmother lived with him, and somehow I'd only met her once. When he passed his driving test, we found out weeks later, and then only because Mackler wrested his wallet away from him and discovered a driver's license in it. I didn't even know Jason's middle name. None of us did.

"You know what the *really* funny part is?" he asked. His voice was bitter. "I actually used to think my parents were wrong. Like, okay, maybe when *they* were my age, people were racist, but surely by now society has moved on. Or maybe in some parts of the country it's like that, but not *here*. I even used you and Mackler as proof. I told my parents they were ridiculously old-fashioned and overprotective, and why would you be friends with me if deep down you thought you were better than me?"

"I don't think I'm better than you," I said. "You know I don't."

He kept going. "My dad said, 'They might be your friends, but they will never truly understand where you are coming from. They might like *you*, but they will always view you as an exception to the rule.' I thought he was wrong, but he was right." Jason rubbed his hands over his face. "And I don't know, maybe I'm not even mad at you. Maybe I'm mad at myself for convincing myself that you were different."

"I *am* different," I told him, reaching out for him. "You can't blame me for all of the world's problems."

But he moved out of my reach. "I think you should go home now, Winter," he said. He blinked slowly, crossed the room, and held open the door for me. So there was nothing for me to do but head back into the night again, alone.

As I walked slowly up the dark, steep stairs toward home, I let in a thought that I'd barricaded myself against for the past forty hours. What if I wasn't the innocent victim after all? What if Jason was right? What if *everyone* was right and the bad guy here . . . was me?

5

The rest of the weekend I did not change out of my pajamas, and I did not leave the house. I sat in front of the TV and watched Cartoon Network for about twenty hours straight. My mother spent most of her weekend on the phone with her lawyer. "Isn't there anyone we can press charges against?" I heard her say from my nest in the living room. "This BuzzFeed list, for example . . . Oh, I see. Oh . . . I understand. *Oy*. What if we made a list of these commenters who are calling her names? There's this one person, his username is Troll1776, and he describes her as 'an ugly excuse for a human, both inside and out.' That must be defamation of character. Can't we go after him? . . . Really? But couldn't we track down who he is? Find his IP address or . . . something?"

If I were in a different sort of mood, I might have giggled to hear my mom throwing around references to BuzzFeed and IP addresses, as if she were some sort of internet genius when I know for a fact that she can't even find the folder where she keeps her MP3s without enlisting help. But I wasn't in that mood, and I didn't know if I ever would be again.

"Can we send cease and desist letters?" Mom asked, her voice rising. I turned up the volume on the TV. "Tell Google to stop listing these sites? . . . Jerry, you're not helping! . . . Are you seriously telling me there's nothing we can do except *wait it out*? What about when she starts college in the fall? What about my *business*?"

Some amount of time passed. The Powerpuff Girls stopped saving the world, and the Scooby-Doo crew started solving mysteries. My mother came into the living room and clicked off the TV. She moved aside a fuzzy monster prototype that my dad had brought home from work so she could sit on the couch next to me. "Do you even understand how serious this whole situation is?" she asked.

I blinked at her. "Yes?" How much more serious could this possibly be?

"Yet you're just going to sit there and watch TV all day?"

"What should I be doing?" I asked. "What else can I do?"

"Do something productive. Try to show people that you're a good girl, that this was all a big misunderstanding."

"I wrote an apology, Mom. I explained myself. I tried."

"Keep trying. Do some volunteer work. Donate money to the ACLU."

"Sure," I said listlessly. It's not like these were bad ideas. But they wouldn't be enough. Nothing would be enough, nothing, *nothing*, so there wasn't much point in trying anything.

"Do you understand what your actions have done to the family?" Mom asked.

I didn't say anything, just stared at the blank television screen, trusting that she would tell me exactly what I had done to the family.

"You've made me look like a fraud," she said. "You've made me look untrustworthy. My publicist says I need to release some sort of statement, and right now, frankly, I don't even know what to say."

My mom is neither a fraud nor untrustworthy. In fact, if there were some kind of mom contest, she would probably win it. She's, like, a *professional* mother. For a few years, starting right after Emerson was born, she was a mommy blogger, which is the vaguely demeaning term applied to mothers who write online about being mothers.

My mom's blog was called *Turn Them Toward the Sun*, and it became a really popular parenting site. She'd originally intended to go back to her job after having me—she'd been a strategy analyst for a health-care company—but then she discovered that, one, she loved writing about parenting and, two, thousands of other people loved reading what she wrote. When I was four years old, she published her first parenting book. The back cover said, *If you want to teach your child to sleep through the night or eat his veggies, this is not the book for you. But if you want to teach your child to be* extraordinary, *then read on!* Since then she's published five more books of parenting advice and has established a career as a parenting consultant, which means that she gives inspirational speeches on how anyone, with the right love, commitment, and strategy, can raise extraordinary children.

And now here we were.

"Maybe people won't know that I'm your daughter," I suggested, grabbing the monster prototype and hugging it to my chest. She had kept her maiden last name, after all—surely that would help.

"They figure these things out," she said. "It's not that hard to put together the pieces, and nothing is a secret on the internet if you're looking for it."

"But it's not *your* fault," I tried. "It was me. You didn't have anything to do with it."

"How are they supposed to know that? People always blame the parents." She sighed deeply. "Please help me understand. Why did you post that comment?"

"It was stupid," I said. "I shouldn't have done it."

"So why *did* you?" she asked again.

"Because . . . well, it's true that the Bee is almost never won by an African American speller. So it surprises people when it happens. I didn't mean that I think that's fair or right."

Mom shook her head. "I understand what you *meant* by the comment. That's not what I'm asking. I'm asking, why did you put it up on the internet?"

And this was the humiliating part. Because there was no good reason for it. "I just hoped people might think it was funny," I mumbled.

"I cannot understand it," she said. "I don't understand your generation's impulse to share everything you think or do the instant it happens. Where does that come from?"

I shrugged. I didn't know. And was that only *my* generation?

Or was it everyone who understood how the internet worked (i.e., everyone except my mother)?

Mom pulled me in for a hug, and I breathed in the lemony scent of her shampoo as I buried my face in her shoulder. "I wish everyone in the world could just see the Winter who I see," she murmured. "A caring, beautiful young woman who would never purposely hurt anybody."

I wished that, too. I didn't want to cause any problems for *Turn Them Toward the Sun*, which had been so important to my mom—to my whole family—for my entire life. I'd been an anxious little kid, and one of the big things that used to worry me was that I would let down my mom's business by not being sufficiently extraordinary. Emerson was, probably from the minute she was born, though obviously I wasn't present for her birth so I can't say for sure. But pretty much from the time she could talk, she could sing, in this expressive, weirdly husky voice that sounded out of place on a child but totally mesmerizing. And she had no stage fright, no fright of anything, as far as I could tell. She was recruited to play every kid role at the community theater—they were desperate to have her.

And that was, in part, why I was so *relieved* when I discovered that I had a knack for words. Emerson was a fine speller and a serviceable writer, but she was busy with other things that seemed more important to her. She hadn't claimed words yet. So I claimed them instead, because I could. I made them my own. All of them. Every word I could find.

After my spelling bee victory, there had been a big article about my mother in *The Pacific*. It was called "Darlene Kaplan: The

Inventor of Modern Parenting?" (That question mark was key, and the reporter's answer seemed pretty clearly to be "no.") Most of the article focused on my mom, of course: the reporter sat in on some of her seminars and counseling sessions and described how the Turn Them Toward the Sun approach functioned. But she also came over to the house briefly to meet me, Emerson, and Dad.

Usually Mom kept us out of any media about her. Even on her blog she had just referred to us as W, E, and The Dad. This was both because she didn't want us to get kidnapped and because part of the Turn Them Toward the Sun approach was encouraging your kids to pursue activities for the sheer love of them and not for any external reward. Therefore you weren't supposed to pay your kids for good grades, or give them a medal if they participated in an athletic event, or give them name recognition if they did something cute. But Mom let the *Pacific* reporter meet and write a little about us, I think because the woman was suspicious of my mother's parenting techniques and Mom wanted to prove that they really did work, and we were proof.

The reporter's name was Lisa Rushall. I remember thinking she looked surprisingly schlumpy—not in a bad way, just not how I'd imagined a big-deal reporter would be. Her hair hung in a loose ponytail, and she wore an oversize flannel shirt over the rest of her outfit. She talked to me about winning the spelling bee, and I told her that in the months before my victory, I'd been studying words for thirty hours a week. "How do you find time to do your homework?" she'd asked, and my mom frowned and said, "Homework always comes first in this house." Then the reporter asked me to spell a few words, like *idiosyncratic* and *chicanery*, which I was used to at that point: as soon as you qualify for the National Spelling Bee, it seems like the only thing adults can think of to ask you is whether you know how to spell different things.

Then she talked to Emerson about how she had started dance classes before most kids could even stand, and began method acting classes when she was eight, and had the starring role in the high school play as a mere freshman, and all that. Emerson told her she was Broadway-bound in a calm, almost patronizing tone that left no room for debate. There aren't many fourteen-year-olds who can be patronizing to adults they don't even know, but Emerson was one of them. "Would you girls say that Turn Them Toward the Sun has worked for you?" Lisa Rushall asked.

"Definitely," Emerson said.

"I wouldn't be national champion without it," I said.

All of which was completely true—I stood by it then and I stand by it today—but the reason we said it wasn't that it was true, but that we knew Mom wanted us to. She needed us to make her legitimate, and so we did.

And now I'd gone and ruined it all.

6

I awoke with a gasp on Monday morning, my alarm like an ambulance siren in my ear. It had been past three in the morning by the time I'd managed to fall asleep, which meant I'd gotten in less than four hours of nightmares. That wasn't a lot of time, but it was long enough for anything in the world to have happened. It is dangerous to stop googling your name, even for just a few hours. You should never stop searching for yourself.

Lying in bed, my head throbbing, I did a quick pass through the internet. The "Surprise: I Can Spell" photos had multiplied. The "We Learned Many Surprising Things Today" meme had jumped the shark ("We learned many surprising things today," read one entry. "Like that my boyfriend is the cutest in the whole world!!! xoxo"). There was an article about me on the *New York Times* homepage.

"Do I have to go to school?" was the first thing I asked Dad as

I walked into the kitchen. He was sipping tea and examining the underside of a robot figurine, which he set aside when he saw me.

"You love school," Dad reminded me. "Remember when you had to miss a week because we were in Cleveland and you said that you were 'school-sick'?"

"I was nine," I pointed out. "And it was easier to love school before hundreds of thousands of people hated me."

"So what's *your* idea?" Dad asked, setting down his mug and leveling his gaze at me. "Just stay in hiding forever?"

"Is that an option?"

He sighed. "Look, Winter, sometimes bad things happen. They're hard to deal with. Everyone experiences that. When your grandmother died, I didn't want to get out of bed ever again. But as you know, I got past that."

"How?" I asked. "How did you get past that?"

"Simple," he replied. "I got out of bed."

This was different, though. What my father was talking about was a bad thing happening *to* him. But this time, *I* was the one who had done the bad thing. How do you get past *that*?

"When Grandma died," I said, "we *needed* you to get out of bed. Emerson and Mom and I and everyone who you work with. You didn't have the option of staying in bed forever. But nobody cares if I show my face in the world ever again. In fact, I'm pretty sure most people would prefer if I didn't."

"*I* would care," Emerson announced, snapping shut her purse as she walked into the kitchen. She was heading to her first day of her summer internship at the San Francisco Theatre, and she was fully dressed for the part: high heels, slim-fit slacks, a statement necklace. There seemed a good chance she'd be president of the place by the time the day was out.

"It doesn't matter, though," I appealed to Dad. "We only have a few more weeks of school, anyway. Nothing's going to happen except exams, and I can do those from home. I can stay here all summer, let everyone forget about me, and then start a new life at Kenyon in the fall. I don't need to go to school now."

"You have to keep living your life, babycakes," Dad said gently. "That's all you can do. You don't have to win every fight or make everyone love you or be the cleverest person in the room. You don't even have to raise your hand or answer every question on a test or get to every class on time. You just have to keep living."

Emerson and I exchanged a narrow-eyed look, because this was *not* the gospel of Turn Them Toward the Sun that Dad was quoting. This was some kind of half-assed strategy that he definitely seemed to be making up on the fly, and if Mom hadn't already left for a meeting, there was no way she'd let this stand.

Turn Them Toward the Sun is actually a pretty straightforward approach to parenting—though, shh, don't tell anyone or they won't spend hundreds of dollars buying books and webinar sessions about it. The name comes from a conversation that Mom once had with her sister, who was freaking out about having a baby, and what if she raised it wrong, etc. And Mom told her, "You'll be fine. Children are like plants. Just water them twice a week and turn them toward the sun."

What this means in practice is: Don't get too involved in your children's lives. Don't tell your kids what to do; just foster the right worldview in them so that they will choose to do the right things.

If your child shows an aptitude or a passion for something, encourage her toward it and do whatever it takes to allow her to continue pursuing it. Give her all the resources she needs, but let her decide how to use them.

This was how I became the nation's best speller. At an early age, I'd shown an interest in words: I compulsively named things as I saw them, starting with *car* and *dog* and later moving on to *palm frond* and *ramekin*. Obviously my mom played along with me, because this was what I was into, so that meant she was into it, too.

The first time I won a spelling bee was in third grade, and that was just luck: I went to a small Jewish elementary school, and I read more books than anyone else in my class did. I lost in the all-school bee to the fifth-grade competitor; not a surprise. But I was hooked. I wanted to do another spelling bee, and next time I wanted to win.

My mom kept spelling with me. Casual practices on long car rides or while we waited for our food to come at a restaurant turned into marathon sessions with dictionaries and flash cards. I started studying English words' origin languages: German, Latin, Greek. Dad and Emerson got roped into quizzing me. Mom hired a coach to teach me how to picture words in my head and another to train me in staying calm during competition.

The stereotype of parents with kids who do stuff like that, kids who study the dictionary every day in order to *win*, is that they're pushy stage moms, trying to derive their own life satisfaction by wringing everything they can out of their kids' performances. That's never been my parents. The spelling thing—that was all me. They just gave me what I needed to make my own dream come true. They told me over and over again that I could quit at any time if I wanted to and they would love me every bit as much. If on any given night I said I didn't want to practice, we didn't practice. They told me that there were no winners or losers and that just by getting up on that stage I was already a champion. I did not ever agree with them.

I didn't know what Turn Them Toward the Sun would have to say about Dad making me go to school when I so clearly did not want to, and I was going to tell him as much, but then Emerson said, "Oh, God, look at this."

She slid her phone across the counter, and on it I saw a new post about me. This one was on the front page of Reddit, which was impressive in a horrifying way, because it's very competitive to get on the front page of Reddit. Mackler had tried to achieve this a number of times, but the closest he ever got was when he painted Abraham Lincoln's face on his stomach and we made a video of him reciting the Gettysburg Address at the supermarket until he got thrown out. Even *that* didn't make it to Reddit's front page.

This post was the apology note that I'd written on Thursday, old news, except some genius had gone through and added reaction GIFs after pretty much every sentence. Some of them were of people silently screaming, some were of children shaking their heads disdainfully. One of the GIFs showed a woman repeatedly stabbing herself in the chest. Apparently this was easier to upvote than Mackler pretending that his stomach was president of the United States.

"I just want to say that every time I read about Winter

Halperin, I feel so much delight," one comment read. "Thanks for entertaining me as I'm stuck at work."

"Some of the comments are nice," Emerson told me. "Like this one." She read aloud over my shoulder. " 'You guys are disgusting. I'm sure most of you have said or thought things just as bad as Winter, and the only difference is that when you said it, no one was paying attention. Stop ruining the poor girl's life.' See?"

"Not really." Because what I immediately saw was the first response to that comment: "I may have made jokes about race, but they've never been as tone-deaf as Winter's. You have to be a truly shameless, soulless person to think something like that. Sorry if I don't feel guilty about 'ruining' the life of such an individual. I only have so much compassion and empathy, and I'd much rather give it to people who actually have done nothing wrong. Let's get this straight: the middle-class, overeducated white girl is not the victim here."

This commenter sounded so certain that I believed him. I believed that only truly shameless and soulless people would do as I had done.

But it wasn't my fault that I was middle-class, overeducated, white, or a girl. All of that was just an accident of my birth. Did it mean that I wasn't qualified to be a victim? I understood that I'd offended people. But my *entire life* was being systematically torn to shreds. Was what I had said—who I *was*—so irredeemable that I could never again deserve sympathy?

"You can't listen to what other people say about you," Dad told us. He held up the robot figurine as if it were proof. "Especially not if it's bad, but even if it's good. You need to have your own sense of self-worth, unrelated to what anybody tells you your worth is. *Capisce?*"

The prototype robot's head fell off.

"Crap," Dad said, going down on hands and knees to retrieve it.

I had a sense of how much my self was worth. I had a crystal-clear sense. *Nothing.*

I stopped scrolling through the Reddit comments when I came to a username I recognized. It was Jason's.

"I'm one of Winter's black 'best friends,'" he'd written. "Though I'd say *best* friend is a stretch. It's really weird and uncomfortable for her to use me as some kind of an excuse for that post. I don't enjoy being used. And even if I trusted her before, I definitely don't anymore."

Nearly a thousand people had liked that.

I let the phone drop onto the counter, and I cradled my head in my arms. I thought that if I'd been smart, I should have been prepared for this. After all, in our years of friendship, I'd seen Jason break up with dozens of girls.

I had just never imagined that he'd break up with *me*.

7

My morning classes went by relatively normally—even *pleasantly*, compared to the maelstrom of the internet. (*Maelstrom.* Dutch origin, obviously. If a single word alone could make you want to go to the Netherlands, it's that one.) None of my classmates came up to me and told me that I should do them all a favor and go play in traffic or that I was the perfect example of everything wrong with America. I guess those things are hard to say directly to someone's face, especially when it's someone you've known most of your life. People whispered behind my back, but I knew they would have done the same if I'd gotten sloppy drunk at a party or broken up with the wrong person—if I'd done a normal sort of bad thing instead of a life-destroying sort of bad thing.

Still, almost nobody actually talked to me about what had happened. Like if they didn't bring it up, it wasn't real. Maybe they just didn't know what to say. I mean, what *do* you say?

The one notable exception was Claudette Cruz. I'm not friends with Claudette. I'm far too lame to be Claudette's friend. Claudette has long, voluminous hair that's shaved on one side, and she's in a band and smokes cigarettes in the school parking lot and somehow never gets in trouble for it. Claudette and I have very little to discuss. But surprisingly she was the only one who came right up to me at the beginning of science class and said, as I was sitting at my desk and staring down at my notebook, "What's happening to you is wrong. Hold your head up, girl. They don't know you."

I almost burst into tears. What she was saying to me was no different from anything Emerson had said—but Emerson was my sister, and this was *Claudette Cruz*. She owed me no kindness. And yet, here she was.

I tightened my face and kept staring at my notebook, and stared and stared, and I stopped my tears before they began to fall. By the time I had composed myself enough to say *thank you*, Claudette had walked away and class was beginning—subdued, quiet, with everyone studiously ignoring me.

At lunchtime I sat in the cafeteria with Mackler and Corey, but it felt off-kilter because we were missing Jason. "Where is he?" Corey asked, gesturing toward the seat at our table that was farthest from the trash can and therefore always reserved for Jason. Jason had some neurosis about being too close to garbage. Like he thought it was going to lunge out of the barrel and jump him.

"Where's who?" Mackler asked vaguely.

"Uh, our other friend. You know? The one all the girls go crazy for."

"You mean me?" Mackler asked.

I rolled my eyes and took a bite of turkey sandwich.

"Do you think he's finally breaking up with Caroline?" Corey asked.

Poor Caroline. I had to pity her, as I pitied all of them. "I really think she's the one," Jason had told us when they started going out.

"I thought Kylie was the one?" Mackler had said.

"No, Sierra," I'd said. "*Sierra* was the one. Remember Sierra?"

"I don't," Mackler had said. "I don't remember Sierra. Was she the short brunette?"

"No, that's Gaby," I reminded him. "Gaby was the shortest. Claire was second-shortest. Sierra's normal height."

"Will you guys stop?" Jason had groaned. "Caroline is different."

"Oh, so she's like *Rowena*," Corey had exclaimed. "Rowena was different, too."

That conversation went down at the beginning of May. By my calculations, we should have at least a week left in Caroline's reign before things went south.

Emerson has this theory that people in relationships are like houses. "Some people look like crummy little apartments from the outside," she says, "but once you get inside, you realize this place actually has everything you could want in a home. Some people are real fixer-uppers. Cracked ceilings, water damage. But if you're willing to do the work and show them love, they can flourish."

If Emerson's allegory was right, then Jason was like a show home: totally gorgeous, and it was only once you'd been there a few weeks that you realized totally gorgeous didn't make up for the fact that you had no heat or running water.

"Oh, Jason," Mackler said in a high-pitched voice, twirling a lock of his curly hair and batting his eyes. "It's *so* not *fair* how you didn't come to my game last week!"

"Now, Caroline," Corey said in a comically deep drawl. "You know I love you."

"Oh, Jason, I love you, too!" Mackler puckered his lips and leaned in toward Corey, and Corey went along with it—until he couldn't handle it anymore and ducked his head, leaving Mackler's tongue to make out with the air over Corey's head.

"Ew," said Corey, batting Mackler with his hands. "Ew, ew, ew, you were actually going to kiss me!"

"Totally," Mackler said. "I was really getting into character."

"You don't look much like Caroline," Corey pointed out, running his eyes over Mackler's six-foot-three-inch frame.

"Yeah, and you're about thirty pounds of muscle away from looking like Jason, so suck it." Mackler grabbed Corey's bicep and squeezed. Corey squealed. "Hey, how much would you pay to see me and Corey make out right now?" Mackler asked me.

"A hundred bucks," I said.

"Oh, wow," Mackler said, loosening his grip on Corey's arm. "That's legit money. I could use a hundo."

"No fair," Corey said. "It'd be fifty for you and fifty for me."

"It was my idea, though," Mackler said.

"Yeah, but it's my lips!"

"And it's *my* hundo," I reminded them both.

"How do you spell *hundo*?" Corey asked me snarkily.

"J-A-C-K-A-S-S," I told him.

"Wow," he said, "you really earned that trophy, didn't you?"

"Damn straight."

Being with my friends was already making me feel better, almost normal. Maybe I could get through this. Those people online—they were far off, they weren't real.

But Jason was. And now I saw him across the cafeteria. He didn't come over to our table. His eyes skittered away from us, and then he grabbed a soda and vanished into the crowd.

"What's his deal?" Corey wondered, watching Jason go.

"It's like he does not even take Lunchtime Madness seriously," Mackler said with a sniff.

Lunchtime Madness was one of the many long-term video projects that my friends and I were working on. We'd started this one the first day of the school year, and I actually thought it had even been Jason's idea, though I couldn't remember now: as with all of our videos it had come, over time, to belong to all of us. As far as our concepts went, Lunchtime Madness was one of the simpler ones. Every day, we video-recorded our food, and then at the end of the year we were going to edit it into one long smorgasbord of square cafeteria pizza and off-brand soda cans. We had a lot of ideas for what was to become of the final project. Jason thought we should show it to the school council to really put the fear of God into them about how they were poisoning innocent adolescents. Corey thought we should set it to automatically get sent to ourselves in fifteen years' time, for nostalgic purposes.

Making movies together was the original foundation of our friend group. It started freshman year. I had recently come home from some horrible overnight wilderness retreat that was supposed to promote teamwork but actually was just a thirty-six-hour reminder of who did and did not already have friends in high school. I was one of the did-nots, since I'd come over from the small Jewish day school where I'd been since second grade, and I had no idea how to find my place in this enormous new high school. I stayed in a bunk with thirteen other girls who were all, at least to my eyes, skinnier than I was, and I remember sleeping in my clothes rather than change in front of them.

The last time I'd been on a big group trip like this had been for the National Spelling Bee. I'd had friends from all over the country from the previous two years that I'd made it to nationals, so now we were at the top of the heap, shrieking as we were re-united and running all over the hotel, while the new kids, the ones who were younger or had never made it this far before, hovered nervously with their parents. The previous year I'd finished in tenth place, but I'd studied my butt off since then, and I had this cool, confident sense that *I could rule this place*. Which I guess is how Emerson feels most of the time.

It was the opposite of how I felt a year and a half later as an anonymous, too-chubby, and too-smart freshman stuffed into a retreat center bursting with people who did not care about me. I remember wishing that all of life could be like the National Spell-ing Bee, and feeling even sadder when I realized that in fact *none* of life could ever be like that again. I was too old for the Bee now; I could never go back. The part of my life where I fit in was over.

The wilderness retreat was a total bust, and I came home convinced that I was going to be alone for the rest of my days.

Emerson told me not to be dramatic (which was rich, coming from her) and that I should join a club at school so I could meet people who shared my interests. She offered to introduce me around at the drama club, the singing group, the school leadership board, and the cheerleading squad, which sent me on a concerted hunt for any club at all that my sister had not already claimed for her own. And what I found was FILMMAKERS.

The idea of this club was that its members would make films—shorts, documentaries, animations, you name it—and screen them in front of large audiences, maybe at the local indie cinema even, and send them in for juried film prizes, or at the very least post them online and become YouTube celebrities. They were looking for "camera people, directors, screenwriters, best boys, first grips, postproduction editors, AND MORE," which seemed like stuff I didn't know how to do but could imagine myself learning. All of this was made clear through a handwritten flyer I saw hanging on a locker.

I showed up to the first FILMMAKERS lunchtime meeting, in a science classroom in the old wing of the school, the part that was supposed to get renovated over the summer but hadn't been. I had some sense from Emerson of what high school club meetings were supposed to look like, and FILMMAKERS was not it. There were only three other people in there, for one thing, and none of them was a faculty advisor. There was a boisterous, heavyset guy; a scrawny boy, seemingly too young for high school, who was clutching an instrument case; and a guy who wasn't yet as hot as he is today, but who definitely seemed to belong in a different room from the rest of us.

I sat down at a desk and pulled out a book so I could remain in quiet anonymity until this meeting actually kicked off, but the big guy was having none of it. He bounded over to me with the delight of a golden retriever whose owners have just returned from vacation and introduced himself as Mackler.

"That's a cool name," said the small kid in an envious way.

"It's my last name," Mackler explained.

"What's your first name?" I asked.

"It doesn't matter," he told me.

He was right. It didn't matter.

"So do you like making films?" Mackler asked me.

"I've never done it," I admitted. "Other than recording stuff on my phone sometimes, obviously. But I like watching films. And I like stories."

"Yes," Mackler said, like this was a huge insight. "Filmmaking is totally a storytelling medium!"

"I've never really made movies, either," volunteered the small guy—Corey. "But I had this idea to start this project? Where I make, like, a video diary of my freshman year in high school? And then no matter where I go in life or how much things change, I'll always have this picture of what I was like when I was fourteen. Because, like, I wish I had that from when I was in fifth grade, but I don't, and I don't want to keep going through life forgetting things."

"That," Mackler said, "is rad." To the other guy, he asked, "What's your deal?"

"I'm Jason Shaw," he replied. "I do video editing stuff. You guys want to see?" And he pulled out his phone and showed us this music video he'd made using short clips from 1980s infomercials he'd found online.

"That's *really* good!" Corey exclaimed once we'd finished watching it.

"I am impressed, my dude," Mackler agreed. "You must teach us your ways."

"Sure," Jason said, looking a little embarrassed but definitely pleased to be attracting so much positive feedback.

"Hey, do you guys have any idea where our faculty advisor is?" I asked, checking the time.

"Who says we're supposed to have a faculty advisor?" Mackler asked with alarm.

"Um, my sister?"

"Ah." He sighed. "Well, the jig is up. FILMMAKERS does not have a faculty advisor because . . . we're not actually a club."

"We're not?" Corey asked.

"Not technically, no. I just wanted to make movies with people. So I put up a flyer. And here we are."

"What does it take to become an actual club?" I asked.

"You have to fill out some form or something. I don't really know. It sounded like a lot of work."

I started to laugh. I should have just let my sister sign me up for refilling the cheerleaders' water bottles.

"So does that mean we have to leave?" Jason asked.

"If you want to," Mackler replied.

"Well, *I* don't want to," Corey said. "I want Jason to show me how he made that music video."

"Me too," I agreed.

"Yeah, okay. Prepare to have your minds blown," Jason joked.

"Oh, I *do* like the sound of that," said Mackler.

That was the first and last official meeting of FILMMAKERS. But in a way, every day since then had been part of one never-ending FILMMAKERS project. We'd been a group, a team, the four of us. I was the only girl, but that didn't matter, it was never weird. For all of us, I was just one of the guys.

But today, in the cafeteria four days after The Incident, none of us were in the mood to film anything, especially as it became clear that Jason was definitely not going to join us.

"He hates me," I said, poking at my food.

"I heard that a *lot* of people are hating you these days, Wint," Mackler commented. Corey chuckled weakly, looking at me out of the corner of his eye, clearly not sure whether Mackler had gone too far with that line. Mackler did that occasionally, went too far. But somehow his over-the-top humor never destroyed *his* life. Somehow when he said or did the wrong thing, people were scandalized, but laughing at the same time, like, "Oh, that's just Mackler for you!" Maybe it was because he's a guy. Maybe he had a better sense of humor than I did. Or maybe he had so far just been lucky.

"Yeah, a lot of people hate me, Mack," I agreed, "but apart from Jason, most of them weren't supposed to be my friends."

"That's because people who know you well enough," Corey said, "*we* know you didn't mean anything by it. *We* know you're not some crazy racist. It doesn't make any sense!" He tucked his legs up under himself so he was kneeling, like a little kid. It seemed like now that we were finally talking about what had happened to me, he couldn't wait to really get into it.

"Do you want to go public and tell everybody that?" I suggested. I needed supporters. I needed someone on Team Winter. Someone who wasn't an insane white supremacist group.

"No one's going to listen to me," Corey said. "Who cares what your friends have to say in your defense?"

"Maybe people would take it seriously," Mackler told him, "if it came from you. Because, you know."

"What," Corey said, rolling his eyes at Mackler, "I'm supposed to be, like, the *official spokesman* for black folk everywhere? Nooo thank you. I'm sure this is going to blow over soon, anyway. Anyone who's ever met Winter for a *minute* would know that she didn't mean anything by it."

"Except Jason," I reminded him.

"Yeah, well, *Jason.*"

"You probably shouldn't have posted it online, though," Mackler said offhandedly, popping a French fry into his mouth.

Corey and I both gaped at him.

"What?" Mackler asked, looking wounded.

"*What?*" Corey repeated. "You're the one who just last week told one of the most offensive fat jokes I've ever heard in my life. What was it, like, 'After I banged Therese Marcos, she rolled over, rolled over again, and she was *still* on top of me'?"

"Offensive, and also false," I threw in. "You've never been within twelve inches of Therese Marcos. In your dreams, Mackler."

"That's different," Mackler protested.

"Oh really?" I asked.

"Yeah, because for one thing, I *am* fat."

Corey and I didn't say anything. That's not the sort of statement you can agree or disagree with.

"If I had Jason's bod and I was making that joke about some fat dude, that'd be straight messed up of me. But I have *this* bod, and I was making fun of *myself*, so it's fair game. No one has permission to tell me I can't make fun of myself and my own bod."

"Ugh, *please* stop saying *bod*," Corey said.

"Plus," Mackler said, "*I* didn't put my joke online. I just said it to you guys. And you already know I'm not a total asshole."

"Do we, though?" Corey asked. "Do we really know that?"

"So what are you saying?" I demanded. "That I can only make jokes about white Jewish girls who are good at spelling? That I'm only allowed to make fun of myself? That I should never share anything I'm thinking with anyone other than my closest friends?" What is the moral of this story? *What is the moral of my story?*

"Jeez," Mackler said, putting up his hands as if to ward off my attack. "Chill out. You know I thought your post was funny. *I* don't care."

I slumped in my chair. If I hadn't felt like a lost cause before, I certainly did now. Now that Mackler had felt the need to reassure me that I was funny. That sort of thing *never* happened.

I knew that Emerson and her girlfriends were constantly complimenting one another. That worked for them, I guess, but it wasn't our style. My friends and I liked one another. Up until this moment, we hadn't felt the need to talk about it.

"Even if you *did* do something wrong," Corey said, "the

punishment does not fit the crime. You didn't, like, recreationally murder a thousand babies."

"Do you think he's right, though?" I asked, spotting Jason again across the room. He was sitting with Caroline and a cluster of her girlfriends. I wondered if they were talking about me, and then I told myself that I was probably being paranoid, and then I thought that I probably wasn't. People *were* talking about me.

I threw the rest of my lunch in the trash can next to me and moved across the table to Jason's empty seat.

"He's not right," Corey said, outraged. "When has Jason ever been right about anything?"

"He thought *Kylie* was 'the one,' remember?" Mackler agreed. "He doesn't know anything about anything, Wint."

"Well, he's right about one thing," I said. "Sitting next to the trash can sucks."

"Winter?" said another voice.

I turned. It was my guidance counselor, Mrs. Vu. I didn't know Mrs. Vu very well, as we tended to interact pretty much only at the start of each semester when she tried to help me figure out how to get out of gym class. She was in her midthirties and she smiled a lot, except when she had to deliver bad news (like that I did actually have to take gym class and the only one that still had space was a semester of touch football with freshmen). Then she got this really pained, sad-eyed expression on her face that made me feel like I should be comforting her rather than the other way around. That was how she looked now. Like a wounded basset hound.

"Would you come to my office for a moment?" Mrs. Vu asked

me quietly, making direct eye contact, as though my friends weren't even there.

Of course, you can't ignore Mackler and Corey when they're nearby. "Why?" Mack asked. "Why does she have to go to your office?"

"Can we come, too?" Corey asked.

"Do you still have that Jelly Belly tub?" Mackler asked. "Can we come and eat Jelly Bellys while you talk to Winter?"

"Oh man," Corey said. "I could eat, like, a thousand cinnamon Jelly Bellys right now."

"You *would* like the cinnamon ones."

"Well, yeah. What's wrong with cinnamon?"

"When I eat cinnamon Jelly Bellys, it's only because I thought they were cherry," Mackler declared. "Cinnamon is wannabe cherry. Cinnamon is a pathetic sack of sugar dressed up in a cherry cloak."

"Winter," Corey appealed to me. "Tiebreaker. Cinnamon or cherry?"

"I don't have any more Jelly Bellys," Mrs. Vu told them. "And only Winter was actually invited to come to my office in the first place."

Mackler groaned. "You're killing us here, Mrs. V."

Mrs. Vu smiled but didn't reply.

"It's okay, guys," I said, standing up. "I'm sure it's fine. I'll see you once we're done."

After all, I figured foolishly, how much worse could my life get?

8

Here is what I won the year I was in seventh grade and was the best speller in the country:

- An engraved trophy.
- Thirty thousand dollars in cash.
- A complete reference library from Merriam-Webster and Encyclopædia Britannica.

The trophy went on a shelf in my bedroom. The cash went into my college fund. The reference books went into a bookcase in the living room, where everyone in my family could access them equally—though it turned out that almost none of us ever actually *did*, because it was easier to look things up on the internet. Emerson felt bad about this, like our family was single-handedly putting the reference book industry out of business. When debates erupted at the dinner table, she insisted on looking up the answers in the physical encyclopedia or atlas just so my research collection would know that it was important. Since Emerson left for college, the books have developed a fine layer of dust.

In short, I didn't use my prizes on an everyday basis, but that didn't mean that I wanted them to be taken away.

"The Scripps National Spelling Bee is stripping you of your title." That's what Mrs. Vu said once we were seated in her office, the door closed.

"What does that mean?" I demanded. I felt my breath coming faster and faster, and Mrs. Vu handed me a paper cup of water, but I didn't drink it.

"Good news," Mrs. Vu said with an attempt at her trademark smile. "You can keep the cash prize and the reference books. Legally they don't have any way to repossess those from you. They would like you to return the trophy, though again, they cannot legally *force* you to do so."

"Good news," I repeated fuzzily.

"But the title is no longer yours," she explained. "You can't include it on your résumé. When you look up the list of all National Spelling Bee champions, your name won't be on it."

"What? Whose name will be there instead?"

Mrs. Vu's forehead creased. "Whoever came in second, I believe."

"Janak Bassi?" I screeched, my breathing growing even more ragged as I remembered him. "But that's not fair. He lost in the twenty-seventh round. He misspelled *pococurante*."

"I understand that, but—"

"I spelled *pococurante* right. I did. I won."

"And you will always know that," Mrs. Vu said. "But Scripps no longer wants your name associated with the Bee."

"Why?" I choked out.

I knew *why*, of course, but there was still some missing explanation here, some connection that I did not understand.

"Because you've offended a lot of people involved in the Bee," Mrs. Vu explained in a gentle tone.

"It was just a stupid joke!"

"And that's something else that *you* know and the people who know you know. But *they* don't know that, and they were hurt by your words. Members of the organizing committee, other families and school systems involved in the Bee, various sponsors of the Bee . . . a lot of people were seriously hurt by your remark."

"I didn't mean to hurt anybody," I whimpered, feeling my torso hunching over, my legs pulling in toward me, my whole body crumpling. "Do you know *who* I offended, exactly? Can I explain it to them? I don't want them to be mad at me. I don't want them to feel hurt. Can I just talk to them . . . and . . . and . . ."

I started to sob. It was as if my whole body had been frozen for five days and now it had defrosted in an instant. The online death threats, the memes, the Surprise I Can Spell website, my mom's frustration, Jason's betrayal—I had hardened myself and borne them all. But I couldn't hold myself together anymore. Snot was pouring out of my nose and eyes and mouth. I was wailing, a desperate, wordless plea for help, like an animal speared in a vast expanse of desert.

"I'm sorry," Mrs. Vu said, her own voice wavering. "I'm so sorry,

Winter. I understand that you're upset. That's a completely valid feeling for you to have right now. I know it's hard to believe, but you *will* get through this. You're a strong young woman. I believe in you."

"I don't want to get *through* this!" I gasped out. "I just want to go *back*."

"I understand that," Mrs. Vu said again. "But you know you can't. We have to figure out a way forward from wherever we are right now."

"I'm *nowhere* right now."

"It might feel that way," she said, "but you still have a lot going for you. Your whole life isn't about being the national spelling champion. There's so much more to you, even without that."

"There isn't," I said. "There isn't anything else."

I fell to the floor. What followed was my first-ever panic attack. The rest of the school day was a wash, as I wound up spending most of it in the nurse's office.

My second panic attack came hot on its heels, when googling my name that evening turned up the news, officially, that Scripps had revoked my title. The Jezebel headline was "Nation Rejoices as White Winter Gets What's Coming to Her." It quoted the Scripps press release as saying, "The Scripps National Spelling Bee is an American institution, and we celebrate the American values of diversity, inclusivity, and acceptance. Every child is welcome to compete in the Bee, regardless of race, ethnicity, gender identity, or background. We do not in any way condone Winter Halperin's remark, and to show how seriously we take this matter, we are stripping her of her title, effective immediately."

"At least we know there is some justice in the world," read one of the comments.

"So proud of Team Internet today!" read another. "This is what we can achieve when we work together to stand up for what's right."

Emerson found me fifteen minutes later on my bedroom floor, my body curled over my trophy as though only I could protect it as the room caved in around us. She held me and I held my trophy and we stayed there until I'd lost all track of time. Mom and Dad told me it didn't matter if anyone else knew that I'd won, because forever *we* would know it. "They can take away your title, but they can't take away your accomplishment," Mom told me, which was such a failed attempt at turning me toward the sun that I started sobbing all over again.

"Please don't do this," I e-mailed the Scripps public relations manager, who five years earlier had kindly helped me navigate the flurry of reporters who wanted to interview me after my victory. She knew me. She'd known me since I was a kid.

But she didn't write me back.

The last month of the school year proceeded to pass by like a monster truck running me over again and again. I tried my best to get back to leading a normal life—even if I couldn't feel normal on the inside, at least I should still act it on the outside. But with my infamy, I had lost all claims on normalcy.

For example, that first Wednesday after losing my spelling bee title, I went to the school library to tutor, as I had every

Wednesday since September. My tutee was a very sweet freshman named Kim who needed help in English class. It was actually her English teacher who had recommended me—I'd been in his class when I was a freshman, so he knew and trusted me.

I sat in the library for the full forty-five minutes, but Kim never showed. I found her later in the hallway and asked, "Where were you today? Is everything all right?"

Kim blushed and the friends she was walking with looked horrified, and eventually she mumbled, so fast that I could hardly make out the words, "My parents said you can't tutor me anymore because you're a bad influence sorry." Then she bolted.

My grades took a sharp nosedive, too, which I told myself didn't matter because I'd already been accepted into college—but it felt like it mattered. As a rule, I did pretty well in school, and this did not feel like me. Simple assignments, like book reports and essays, filled me with anxiety. I erased twice as many words as I wrote for fear that any one of those words, taken out of context, would once again condemn me. I was so, so careful. I needed every sentence, read from any perspective, to be safe. Schoolwork that previously I would have finished by dinnertime now kept me up until three or four in the morning as I tried and failed and tried and failed to make it foolproof. More than once I got it nearly all the way, then panicked at the last minute and couldn't hand it in, because *what if I was wrong?*

When the message arrived from Kenyon, it was the day before graduation, and Emerson was having me try on every dress in her closet so we could decide which one I should wear under my cap and gown. (By *we* I mean *she*—I got final say in what I wore, but also I trusted her taste more than my own.) I had just put on a purple sundress, though I hadn't yet zipped it up all the way, when Mom came in, her face pale, her eyes hollow.

"Don't you knock?" Emerson complained, but then she shut up fast when Mom handed me the letter. And maybe at that point the letter shouldn't have been a shock, but it was.

Dear Winter Halperin,

We regret to inform you that we are rescinding our offer of admission to Kenyon College's incoming freshman class. As you likely recall, your official letter of acceptance from the College stipulated that your admission would be contingent upon your continuing to meet the academic and behavioral standards that we expect of all members of our community. Your recent actions do not show the respect that has always been a cornerstone of Kenyon's identity; as such, we must tell you that we no longer consider you a good fit.

The letter went on from there. I kept reading, but I didn't need to. I got the point. In that moment, I got everything.

"What are you going to do?" Emerson asked. She was weeping, and I felt like I ought to be comforting her, only I didn't know how. I should have been the one crying, but she had processed this news faster than I had. I was still blank. "Can you go back to any of the other schools you applied to? See if they still have space?"

"I applied to Kenyon early," I reminded her. "There were no other schools."

The promise of college in the fall was the only thing that had been getting me through these last few weeks. The knowledge that in a few months I could leave here, leave behind everyone who knew who I was and what I had done. I'd even imagined starting college under an assumed name, maybe telling everyone I went by "Winnie" and starting fresh.

And now that promise was broken. I had nothing more to cling to.

There was no escaping myself.

"Some colleges have rolling admissions," Mom said, her voice shaking. "We could apply to a few of those, maybe still get you started in September, or at least not lose too much time . . ."

"Stop it," I said. "Just *stop*. Stop trying to fix this. It's never going to be fixed. Stop trying to pick up these horrible, broken shards of my life and glue them together into something I still want. If Kenyon doesn't want me anymore, no one else will. Don't you get it? This is it. This is all there is."

I wore a pair of old jeans to my high school graduation, as well as dark glasses to try to hide the tears that I wept as three hundred and eighty of my classmates and I crossed the stage. Corey had a graduation party, but I didn't feel like partying, so I didn't go. Jason had a graduation party, too, but I wasn't invited.

Mrs. Vu was wrong when she told me I would get through this. I didn't. The rest of the world did. Within only a few days, my name had slipped from the most-searched term to the two-thousandth, and it kept diminishing from there. Additions to the Surprise I Can Spell site became less and less frequent. The day that I lost my spelling title, an NFL quarterback described America as "the worst dictatorship in history," so everyone was too busy being offended about that to care about me. Two days later, a college fraternity threw a Holocaust-themed keg party, and obviously that sent the internet into a complete meltdown. The next week, the *New York Times* revealed that the CEO of a Fortune 500 company had lied and claimed to be Hispanic at a young age in order to get into a better school. And on and on and on. The world moved on from me a thousand times over.

But I did not move on.

Mrs. Vu had told me that I still had a lot going for me, but she was wrong about that, too: everything I had had been taken from me.

Weeks passed after graduation, and I became different from the Winter I was before. I rarely left the house. I hated to sleep. I said nothing on the internet. I didn't write, not anything, not at all. At my best, I existed. I did not aspire to anything. I did not care.

It takes such a brief time to destroy someone's life and forget that you ever did it. But rebuilding a life—that's different. That takes forever.

9

One month into summer vacation, I was informed by my mother that we had an appointment. "A man named Rodrigo Ortiz is coming over to meet with us," she said, straightening pillows on the couch around me. "So you might want to get dressed."

Getting dressed was something I'd mostly given up on since school had ended. Sometimes Mackler and Corey had come over to chill and play video games and watch YouTube, and for those occasions I would put on a bra. That was my limit.

"Who is Rodrigo Ortiz?" I asked, not moving. I'd been watching TV, as usual, and was in the middle of a particularly compelling episode of *The Real Cheerleaders*. I did not want to walk away before finding out whether Tiffany or Brittany was going to be the top of the pyramid. I had become deeply invested in *The Real Cheerleaders* over the past month.

"He is, with any luck, our savior. Get dressed."

"I don't want to. I want to finish this episode. Watching *The Real Cheerleaders* is my passion now."

Mom rolled her eyes and turned off the TV.

"This is really not very Turn Them Toward the Sun of you," I grumbled, getting to my feet. "You're supposed to let me pursue my own interests. Remember?"

"Yes," she said with a sigh. "I actually do remember how Turn Them Toward the Sun is supposed to work. But I'm just . . . I'm not so sure right now."

"Not so sure about what?" I asked, genuinely perplexed.

She gave me a half smile and said quietly, "Anything."

I felt my breath catch. For so many years, Mom and I were on the same team, working toward a common goal: the Scripps national championship. But we could never go back to that, or to how we were then. Now I had Mom telling me that maybe Turn Them Toward the Sun didn't work. If it produced someone like me, then what was it good for?

But if Mom couldn't even believe anymore in the parenting philosophy that she herself invented, then we were all screwed.

Breathe, I reminded myself. *Breathe. Breathe. Stop thinking about breathing and just do it.*

"None of this is your fault," I forced out through half-collapsed lungs.

"Thank you," she said.

So I went upstairs and I put on clothes. I didn't shower, though. As I said, I have my limits. Before I went back down, I glanced in the mirror, and for a flash the reflection I saw was that fat, awkward eleven-year-old version of me.

An instant later, my vision shifted and I saw myself just as I was: pale from lack of sun, dark-haired, smudges around my eyes, jean skirt, and a shirt I'd long ago stolen from Emerson and kept promising to return just as soon as I washed it. I told myself that I looked better now than I did in that picture that had been shared across all corners of the internet. But I still didn't want to see myself in the mirror.

Rodrigo Ortiz showed up in a sleek black Lexus. I watched him through the living room window. He was clean-shaven and appeared to be in his late twenties or early thirties, wearing pressed slacks, a tucked-in button-down shirt, and sunglasses. Very Silicon Valley. I didn't know if he looked like a savior or not. I didn't know what a savior would look like at this point.

"I'm Rodrigo. And you must be Winter," he said as Mom let him in and he shook my hand.

I nodded and looked toward my mother for help. "Let's all sit down," she proposed. So we did.

"Do you know why I'm here?" asked Rodrigo once my mother had cleared the dining room table of Dad's glow-in-the-dark bouncy balls and we were seated.

"No."

"I thought it would be best for us to hear your pitch together," Mom told him.

"Makes sense. So, Winter, I work for a startup called Personal History."

It sounded like some sort of genealogy website. If the next words out of Rodrigo's mouth had been, "You're related to Thomas Jefferson!" I wouldn't have been at all surprised.

Well. Thomas Jefferson wasn't Jewish. So maybe I would have been a little surprised.

Instead, Rodrigo said, "The mission statement of Personal History is to keep our clients' internet histories just that: personal.

"The internet is still a new land. Like the Wild West, it's relatively lawless. Anyone can post anything online; they don't need any credentials to do so. And anything that's posted can be taken as fact. It's very hard to get something removed from the internet for being factually inaccurate or threatening or harassment or, well, pretty much anything. All of that is protected under the right to free speech."

No argument here. That's why Mom's lawyer hadn't been able to do anything to help me.

"Because it is a lawless land," Rodrigo went on, "internet users take it upon themselves to invent and enforce their own rules. They decide when another user has committed a moral crime."

I'd never heard that phrase before, *moral crime*. But it made perfect sense. That's what was wrong with me. I was *immoral*.

Rodrigo continued, "They decide how that user will be punished. If it's a real, illegal crime—pirating media, for example—then the real criminal justice system can get involved. The accused will get a fair trial and a sentencing. But if it's a *moral* crime, then there's no judge and no jury—or maybe I should say that we, all together, anyone who cares, form the judge and the jury. It's vigilante justice."

"Vigilante justice," I repeated. "I've seen that in movies. That's like when a mob of townsfolk show up with pitchforks to run the bad guy out of town, right?"

"Right," Rodrigo said. "These days, instead of pitchforks, we have internet shaming. The individual who did the quote-unquote 'bad thing' gets dehumanized by all of society."

"That was one of my words," I volunteered.

"Excuse me?" Rodrigo said with a blank smile.

"Dehumanize," I told him.

"I don't remember that," Mom said. "Was that at your school bee?"

I shook my head. "Regionals." I had spelled so many words across so many rounds in so many spelling bees over so many years. If someone asked me now to list them all, I'd never be able to do it. But I recognized them when they came up. They hit my ear with a certain sort of coziness and warmth, giving me the sense that we belonged to one another, me and my words.

But it had never occurred to me that their *meanings* had anything to do with me. Most of them didn't. They were words like *aquatic* or *windily*, beautifully composed words with definitions unrelated to my daily experience. *Dehumanize*, though. To take someone who is human and make them less so. Because if they're not really human, then who cares how you treat them? It wasn't a cozy word anymore.

"What happens in a case like yours," Rodrigo continued, "is that you get punished over and over again for the same crime. Every time anyone searches for you online, they turn up all these articles about what you did wrong. Right now, this is the first page of your Google results."

He reached into his tote bag and pulled out a sheet of paper. I looked at it unwillingly. That BuzzFeed piece of "20

Perfect Responses to Winter Halperin's Racist Post." Of course Surprise I Can Spell. The Reddit post where Jason had left his friendship-ending comment. The *New York Times*. The *Washington Post*'s op-ed about how even though the playing field of racist discourse had changed over the past couple decades, it hadn't disappeared—using the story of me and my post as their first piece of evidence.

"Please put that away," I said, my voice shaking. "You didn't need to print it out. I know what it says. I look at it every day. What, do you think I've forgotten? I don't forget. I *never* forget."

Mom placed a steadying hand on my back. Rodrigo put the printout back in his bag. "You can't hide your head in the sand like an ostrich. That's what *everyone in the world* sees when they search for you. That's what Kenyon saw and what any other college you apply to in the future will see. Internet searches are how employers decide whether to hire you and people decide whether to go on a date with you. *That*—that piece of paper right there—that's who they think you are."

I wanted to scream. I wanted to go to sleep for a hundred years. I wanted to go back to the couch and *The Real Cheerleaders* for the rest of my life. "*I know.* But what am I supposed to do about it?"

"Reclaim your narrative," Rodrigo told me smoothly. "Tell the world who you *really* are. Think of yourself as a product. A brand. If you were a car company and you were getting destroyed by the media because you'd lied on your emissions testing or put in useless airbags, you wouldn't just curl up in a ball and go out of business, would you? Of course not. You'd create a new story about your brand, a positive story—you're the perfect family vehicle!—and you'd plaster that message over every billboard and TV commercial until that was all people could see or remember."

"I'm not a car company, though," I said, perplexed. "I'm a person."

Rodrigo shrugged this off. "Person, brand, same thing."

"So, what, are you some Google fairy godmother who can wave a magic wand and erase my history?"

"I wish," he said. "That would make my job much easier. Unfortunately, the internet is like an elephant: it doesn't forget."

I made a face. That plus the bit where he'd called me an ostrich made for too many animal analogies for any given conversation.

"But what we *can* do at Personal History is shove all that stuff"—Rodrigo waved at his tote bag—"onto the second or even third page of search results. It's still there, but almost no one will bother to keep clicking to get to it."

"Really?" I asked, leaning forward. Despite his needless animal references, maybe this guy *could* be my savior.

"Really," he said. "That's how celebrities and politicians get away with saying and doing crazy stuff. There's already so much *other* material out there about them. They get into a fistfight in an elevator, and okay, news about that is going to be the first Google hit for a few hours or days. But soon after that it's going to get replaced by all the new stuff they're doing: the charitable works and fashion shows and albums and sailing trips and pregnancies and whatever else celebrities do."

"So I just have to release an album and get pregnant and everyone will forget about the other things I've done?" I asked.

Mom groaned. "She's joking," she explained to Rodrigo. "Sometimes people can't tell when she's joking."

"I'm pretty sure he knows that, Mom," I said. "I'm pretty sure that's why he's here."

"Don't get pregnant," she said to me.

"That's really not an option currently on the table," I reassured her.

Rodrigo laughed. Actually, he said "ha, ha," which is not the same thing as laughing. "Our clients aren't celebrities," he said. "They're just everyday people who don't want their past actions to haunt them for the rest of their lives."

"Who are your other clients?" I asked.

"People who want to change their search results and keep their personal histories personal."

No details. Rodrigo was a true professional, even though his job seemed quasi-made-up. I tried to imagine who else might hire him. Maybe if a nude picture of you had been leaked. Or if you'd been arrested years ago. Or if someone had spread a nasty rumor about you and it wasn't even true.

I wondered if those people would think I was innocent if they knew about me. If they'd feel like we were in the same situation, comrades in arms against a corps of vigilante justice enforcers. Or if they'd just think, *Glad it's her and not me.* Or, *She had it coming.*

"What we do is create new information about our clients. New search results. Just a lot of *noise.*" Here Rodrigo waved his hands in front of his face. "So all anyone can make out is the story that *we* are telling."

"Does that work?" I asked, intrigued.

"Absolutely," he said, folding his hands on the table.

"Kina hora," Mom murmured.

He raised his eyebrows at her, and I considered trying to explain to him how or why my mom sometimes talks like she's straight out of the shtetl. Even though this is the twenty-first century and she is a third-generation American who grew up in the extremely un-shtetl-like city of Cleveland, Ohio. But I decided not to say anything, because really there is no explaining my mother.

"She means 'knock on wood,'" I translated loosely from the Yiddish.

"So what's your proposal for Winter?" Mom asked him.

Rodrigo pulled a glossy packet out of his bag and started going through it with us. It looked like a printout of a PowerPoint presentation. But a really fancy and corporate PowerPoint. Much more impressive than the last one I'd created, which was for science class and was about the life cycle of a butterfly.

"I'm not going to beat around the bush," Rodrigo said. "This is an especially challenging case, because Winter's story exploded *so* much and went *so* far. It's not a small-town scandal that we're trying to contain, a few local newspapers and blogs that we need to push down in the results. It's *big* news sources, and those have really high SEO."

"Essy-what?" Mom asked.

"SEO, Mom," I told her. "It means search-engine optimization."

Rodrigo said "ha, ha" again. "You want to do my job?" he asked me.

I kind of hated Rodrigo. But I also kind of thought he might be a genius. So I kept listening.

"We're trying to beat out a lot of big-name media. So the way we do that is we *flood* the internet with new information about Winter. All positive, clearly. Or not even positive, if we can't get that, but *inoffensive*. Plain. Palatable. Generically *nice*. You know what I mean? So here's a photo of Winter playing with a puppy, here's a news story about Winter doing a good deed, here's a blog of Winter's favorite recipes—that sort of thing."

"Whoa," I said, getting that shaky feeling again. "I'm not going to flood the internet with content. I'm not putting *anything* online after what happened. I don't need to put up a photo of me with a dog just so those trolls have a new opportunity to comment that I'm fat and ugly and no wonder I play with dogs since I basically am one myself."

"I agree with Winter," Mom told Rodrigo. "After all this happened, I advised my daughters to remove their social media presence entirely."

Advised was a gentle way of putting it. If you asked Emerson, she'd say *ordered*. Mom hadn't needed to tell me twice. By the time it even occurred to her that we should delete our social media, I'd already taken down every single thing that I could, eliminated every profile and app that I'd ever had. It meant that now I didn't know when parties were going on, or what everyone was watching on TV, or when my friends were at the movies together. I only found out about things if someone messaged me directly. But it was worth it, and honestly I didn't feel like going to any parties, anyway.

Emerson, on the other hand, had been outraged. "I'm nineteen years old," she said. "You can't tell me what to do."

"I have never told you what to do," Mom had pointed out reasonably.

"Look, I *need* my social media," Emerson tried to explain to Mom.

"You don't *need* it. Your father and I didn't have anything like that when we were your age, and we turned out fine."

"That was a completely different era. People need different things now! And why just *us*, by the way? You're the *master* of putting your life online. Didn't Turn Them Toward the Sun start as a *blog* where you reported on everything we did, for anyone to read whenever they wanted? Shouldn't you have to take that down, too?"

"Emerson, it's not wise for you to be putting yourself out there in this way."

"Just because Winter made a stupid mistake? Why should *I* be punished when *she's* the one who posted the wrong thing? I've never done anything like that, and you have no reason to believe that I would!"

It had made me so, so sad to hear Emerson say that. Even though I knew she was just arguing whatever points she could to get to keep her Twitter and Instagram and Snapchat and everything else she used to remain important and relevant. I knew she didn't mean anything against me, specifically.

But she'd still said it. There was a type of person who was offensive, and there was a type of person who wasn't, and I was the first and she was the second.

Now Rodrigo said to me, "You're smart to get rid of all your social media accounts. It's playing with fire for someone in your shoes. That's where I come in. It's not only that I come up with this strategy. I execute it. I create the new accounts, I post the pictures,

I plant the news stories. I create and manage an entirely new identity for you. Online only, of course."

"But it's not online only," I reminded him. "In real life, I'll still have to play with dogs and cook recipes and stuff."

"Well, if you do that, that's great. Take pictures, send them my way, and we'll use them. Whatever you don't actually do, I'll just invent."

"You can do that?" Mom asked, her eyes wide.

"As I said, anyone can make up anything on the internet."

I squirmed in my chair. "But what if you're posting things about me that I don't like?"

"I'll let you or your mom check over everything before it goes out," he said. "You'll get full veto power. But I'm pretty good at creating content. And to be honest, Winter"—he lowered his voice like this was a secret between us—"I don't know that there's much I could put out there that's worse than what you've already got."

I hated that we lived in a world that could support a business like Personal History. Rodrigo was too slick and smarmy, and his entire job, when I thought about it, existed to exploit strangers' desperation. His entire very, very profitable job. And I knew this not only because of his fancy car or his fancy clothes, but also because on the last page of his glossy presentation, I saw how much my Personal History service was going to cost. And it was . . . astronomical.

"Can we really afford this?" I asked Mom, my mouth hanging open. I didn't know the details of my family's budget. But I knew that Mom didn't make a regular salary; she got paid based on how much work she did—book royalties, speaking honoraria, client consultations, etc.—and I knew that she had been home a lot more this summer than she usually was. And I knew that in a few weeks Emerson would be heading back to her pricey out-of-state university. And I knew that this dollar amount was something you would pay only if you truly had no other options.

"We do what we have to do," Mom said, and pressed her lips together tightly.

"I'm serious. Does Dad know how much this costs? I mean, how could this possibly be worth it?"

"Winter," Mom said, briefly taking my hands in hers. "It's worth it because this is your *entire life*." And she headed upstairs to get her checkbook.

I stared at my hands, unable to speak. I was so full of emotion: anger at myself for getting us into this position, anger at Rodrigo for taking advantage of my need, anger at Mom for calling him in here, anger at the entire world who did this to me, and gratitude—so much gratitude—for the lengths my family would go to try to right my wrongs.

"Do you think I deserve it?" I asked Rodrigo when I looked up.

He'd taken out his cell phone the moment Mom left the room and was typing away, maybe crafting a new inoffensive post on behalf of another screwup. He glanced at me when I spoke, though, and asked, "Deserve what?"

"Do I deserve your services," I said, "after what I did?"

He sighed, leaned back in his chair, and clasped his hands behind his head. He looked briefly, sort of, like a normal person, like one of the younger teachers at my school, maybe, and not a guy who capitalized on other people's misery. "Look," he said, "I'm not the moral police. My services go to whoever can afford them, and it's none of my business whether they deserve it.

"But if I had to say? I think what you did is no worse than what a zillion other people do every day. The only difference is that you got caught. I looked into it. You only had about a hundred followers when you made that post. You made the mistake that so many people make online, of thinking you were just talking to your friends. And if that one lady hadn't reposted you, you would have been right, and today you wouldn't even remember writing that post in the first place and none of us would be here right now."

"What one lady?" I asked, sitting up straighter.

"You know, that influencer, the one who reposted you to her fifteen thousand followers."

"What?" I said.

Rodrigo blinked at me. Now he really looked human. Maybe that had been his problem earlier: he just didn't blink enough. Plus there was the bit where he didn't really know how to laugh. He was missing some key human functions. "How did you think so many people all over the world found out what you'd said?" he asked. "They had to get it from an influencer."

"Who was she?" I asked.

"What does it matter? She was somebody with fifteen thousand followers who wanted to make fun of you for thirty seconds of her life."

"It matters," I said. "It matters to me." Could she be someone who I knew in real life, someone who'd had a vendetta against me? But who had a vendetta against me? And why would anybody with fifteen thousand followers even know who I was?

"She's some reporter, I guess," Rodrigo said. "She's not very fa-mous. I'd never heard of her." He clicked around on his phone and then held it up. "This is her," he said. "Lisa Rushall, at *The Pacific*."

Lisa Rushall.

I remembered her.

"How do you know that?" I whispered.

He furrowed his brow at me, like he couldn't tell if this was me making a joke again. "That's my *job*," he said.

I thought about what my mother had said that first weekend: *Nothing is a secret on the internet if you're looking for it.* Not even the identity of the individual who destroyed my life.

Mom came back downstairs then, and she held out a check to Rodrigo with a number so large that it made me want to throw up.

"Wait," I blurted out. They both looked at me. "I don't want to do this."

"Why not?" Mom asked, with only a small, strained amount of patience in her voice.

"It seems . . . wrong," I tried to explain. "It's lying. And cheat-ing. And it's using money—*your* money, your money that you work so hard for—to buy my way out of this. That's not fair."

"Nothing that's happened to you is fair," Mom reminded me. "This is all such mishegoss."

Mishegoss. Yiddish, of course, because it's my mother. Means *cra-ziness* or *ridiculousness. Mishegoss* was Emerson's friend-group drama, every word that came out of Mel Gibson's mouth, and now this.

"I don't just want to *appear* better, you know?" I tried. "I want to *be* better."

Rodrigo gave me a pitying smile. "That's a great long-term goal, Winter, but you know the two aren't mutually exclusive. You can start by allowing me to help you *appear* better, and you can work on the actual self-improvement from there."

"I don't feel right about it," I insisted. "I'm sorry, Rodrigo. I'm sure you're really good at what you do and you've helped lots of people . . . but we're not that rich, and if I'm just some spoiled kid who lets her parents buy her way out of everything, no matter what it costs them, then that makes me an even *worse* person than I am already. I can't afford to be any worse."

"So what's *your* plan?" Mom asked me.

"I don't have one."

"Exactly. You don't have one. You're moping around and doing nothing, and now that I've found a viable option for fixing this situation, you won't even take it."

"Maybe I should go," Rodrigo suggested, looking uncomfortable, or perhaps impatient. "You have my card. You know how to get in touch with me if you change your mind."

"No," Mom said to him, at the same time that I said, "I don't want to just airbrush over this; I want to *fix* it."

Mom and I glared at each other, and I felt like an asshole, because I was glaring at her for trying to help me. She was doing this so that I wouldn't have to suffer. There was no limit to what she would do so that I wouldn't have to suffer, and for that reason, I was mad at her.

"You don't believe in telling us what to do," I reminded her.

She nodded slightly.

"So don't tell me what to do here. Let me try to figure out some other way."

"Fine," Mom said. "But you have to really try. And if you can't . . ."

"Then Personal History will still be here," Rodrigo inserted. "I'm always ready to help."

Which perhaps was true, depending on your definition of *help*.

We saw him out into the bright sunshine and watched him drive away in his fancy car. "Please just consider it, Winter," Mom said quietly. "Maybe he can make this all go away."

I didn't believe that for a moment, not unless he could make *me* go away. But I would figure something out. I had to. And if nothing else, Rodrigo had, in mentioning Lisa Rushall, given me something invaluable: someone else to be angry at, someone else to blame, and the promise that maybe this wasn't all my fault.

10

I overheard some of Mom and Dad's conversation about Personal History once Dad got home from work that evening. They were in the kitchen, preparing dinner as they talked. I was in the living room, kind of trying not to hear them, and kind of totally trying to hear them.

"I'm proud of her for saying no." I could barely make out Dad's voice, he was speaking so quietly. "You know my thoughts on it."

"He was nice enough," Mom defended herself.

"Of course he was nice. He wanted the job."

"This was an opportunity," she said. "It might not have worked, but at least it was something to try. Now what?"

"Just let it play out," Dad said. "She has to learn to live with the consequences of her actions. We can't teach her that every time she makes a mistake, we'll be here to clean up after her."

"Have you *seen* her? She's clearly depressed. She's so . . ."

The kitchen faucet turned on, and whatever I was "so" got lost in the sounds of running water.

". . . but she's only seventeen" was the next thing I heard Mom say.

"She's not a child, Darlene. She's a high school graduate, and she needs to figure out what's next for her."

"That is precisely *why* I asked for Rodrigo's help."

"It's outrageously expensive, especially for something that might not even work," Dad said.

"Better a problem you can throw money at than one you can't."

"That's only true if you *have* the money."

"Well, fortunately, I do," Mom said.

"Assuming the money keeps coming in," Dad pointed out.

"And why wouldn't it?" Mom asked. I felt distinctly like I should not be hearing this. I should go upstairs. But their voices had grown louder as they grew more frustrated, and I wanted to know where this conversation was going.

"Well," Dad said, "for example, Mountain State asked you not to come after all."

"That's *one* conference," Mom said in a tight voice. "One. And not a particularly good one, either. I hardly think you can draw any conclusions from that."

"Your publisher said book sales are down."

"Nonfiction sales always take a dip in the summer. What are you trying to say?"

"I just want you to consider that times change, and trends

change, and Turn Them Toward the Sun may not always be the most popular parenting strategy," Dad suggested. "It may not always be as profitable as it once was."

I knew what he was trying not to say: *I* was the reason that Turn Them Toward the Sun would make less money now than it used to. Because if Turn Them Toward the Sun resulted in a screwup, then how valuable could it possibly be? After all, no parent would ever want to use a strategy to make her daughter wind up like me.

I bit my lip so hard, I tasted blood.

Mom said, "I'm not worried about my business."

And Dad said, "I think you need to be."

"If it were an experimental medical procedure," Mom countered, "one that could maybe save our daughter's life, would you be talking like this?"

"Of course not," Dad snapped. "But that's different. Her life isn't in danger."

"I disagree."

And after that, I forced my stiff, frozen body to stand and climb the stairs to my room. I'd heard enough.

I closed my door and started a list on my phone.

How to be a better person.

And I was going to write down some items under it, but then I felt exhausted. I clicked over to the internet instead. A quick search turned up Lisa Rushall's website. I stared at her black-and-white headshot. She looked more put-together in this photo than I remembered her being when she came to our house five years ago to interview Mom for *The Pacific*, but she was still nobody's idea of a beauty queen. She didn't look mean, exactly, but she wasn't smiling. She was staring semi-confrontationally at the camera, like, *I'm a serious journalist and you can't fool me.*

I hated Lisa Rushall. She had ruined everything. She had taken away my future and my past and everything that made me feel like myself. I hated her and I relished the feeling because it was so liberating to hate someone other than myself.

I didn't think of myself as a vengeful person, but I wanted her to suffer at least half as much as I was suffering. I wanted her to lose at least half as much as I had lost. I wanted her to know exactly what she had done.

She had made me afraid of my own mind, afraid to go to sleep. I used to love that liminal time between wakefulness and sleep, when thoughts floated through my mind and sometimes turned into dreams or ideas for stories, but now I dreaded it. I would lie in bed and toss and turn and sweat, because anything can happen to you even while you're lying in bed and doing nothing at all. I would wake up throughout the night and my first thought every time, before I even processed whether it was light or dark, was what I had done. And I wanted to know if Lisa Rushall felt the same. Did she think of me every time she woke up? Did she think of me ever? And if she didn't, *what was wrong with her?*

While I was here, staring at this screen, I could write something. I could write about Rodrigo Ortiz's visit, or Lisa Rushall, or my parents' disagreement, and try to work my way through it with words. Or I could forget all of that and write a story about something pleasant and completely unrelated to the ashes of my life, like, I don't know, best-friend unicorns frolicking in an enchanted forest. I could write some *Real Cheerleaders* fan fiction; that would be distracting. I could write anything and nobody would have to read it. No one would even know that it existed, so no one could use it against me.

But I couldn't, really. I couldn't write anything at all. And I hadn't been able to for two months.

I once saw a thread online about how to get over writer's block. "Go for a walk," one user suggested. "Get the blood pumping and stop staring at a blank screen."

"Be patient," said another. "Sometimes you don't have anything to say, and that's okay: it doesn't mean that you'll never have anything to say ever again."

Contrary to that, another suggested, "Just work through it. Write down something, even if it's bad—you can always delete it later. Remember, nobody writes perfect first drafts!"

None of this advice had meant much to me at the time, because I'd never really experienced writer's block. Sure, I'd had trouble writing book reports and history essays, and I'd procrastinated and written cringeworthy sentences to try to hit an assigned page count. But that was different. That had felt like trying to walk forward up a steep hill with stones in my shoes when I just felt like sitting down instead.

This felt like trying to walk forward when both my legs had been chopped off.

I gave up and headed down the hall to Emerson's room. She was blasting the *American Idiot* sound track and singing along while applying her makeup.

"Ugh," she said as I flopped down on her bed. "My face is all red and blotchy. You're lucky to have such pale skin, you know that? It takes me so much work to make my skin even start to look like yours."

This is a whole Emerson game. She and her friends can play it for hours. My line was, "No, your skin is gorgeous; *my* skin makes me look like Dracula, and you have such a golden glow about you, like a ripe fruit in bloom." Or something like that. And then Emerson could say, "Oh my God, are you even serious? The way your eyes stand out against your skin—it's perfect. It's like your color eyes were *invented* for your tone of skin." And then I was supposed to say something like, "But my skin is covered in pimples, so I'd give *anything* to have your complexion."

Unfortunately for Emerson, this was not a game that I had ever been any good at. This was part of why all my friends were guys. Instead, I rolled my eyes and adjusted myself on her pillows and said, "You're right, you're a total monster. I wouldn't even hang out with you if we weren't related. Also, what the hell are you wearing?"

"This?" She patted her stomach. "It's a waist trainer."

"It looks like a corset."

"Well, it's not. It's a waist trainer. It's training my waist."

"Training it to do what, shake and roll over?"

She stuck her tongue out at me in her mirror. "You should come with me to the party tonight," she said.

"What party?"

"Oh, you know, it's a big thing up in the hills." She waved vaguely upward, but I *did* know; everyone knew that the parties occurred in the woods way up in the highest of the Berkeley Hills. We hiked there sometimes, but the closest I'd ever come to attending one of the ragers that happened there was when I encountered some crushed beer cans and a condom wrapper in broad daylight.

"It sounds like it will involve leaving the house," I said.

"Look, Wint." Emerson set down her powder brush and came over to sit next to me. "You can't keep your life on pause forever. Eventually you're going to have to see people and, yes, even leave the house. And if you wait too long to do that, I'll be back at school and you'll be doing it alone. So let's get it out of the way now, while I *am* still here with you." When I didn't respond right away, she added, "I'll even do your hair and makeup. You'll look so hot, no one would dare to mess with you."

I loved when Emerson styled me. It took forever, but it was always worth it. Even when she'd lived at home, she was usually too busy, but on the rare occasions when she'd sit down with her dozens of beauty products and me, I would take a million selfies.

But there was no point to selfies anymore, since I no longer had anyplace to post them. I guessed I could take them and just think to myself about how good I looked. I imagined sending them to my friends. Mackler and Corey would be like, "Uh, why are you sending us photos of your face?" Under other circumstances, Jason might actually appreciate it. Jason was a great appreciator of beauty.

"Okay," I said. "I'll go to your party."

In the old days, I wouldn't have gone. I didn't go to big parties in the woods where there was sure to be drinking and hookups and, if the cops showed up, we could all get in trouble. In the old days, I didn't get in trouble.

"I'm so glad you're coming," Emerson said, bouncing up and down a little. "And I'm sure it'll be fine. It was, like, two months ago. Everyone has moved on."

I knew what Emerson meant, but she was wrong. Because there *was* someone who was still, weeks later, obsessed with what I'd done wrong. She was with me wherever I went, every minute, waking and sleeping. She would never move on.

"Before I can start on your hair, you need to shower," Emerson instructed me. "Use a lot of conditioner, but do not shampoo. And shave your legs."

"I'm already bored," I said.

"Fine. I'll come talk to you while you shower."

"Em," I said once I was in the shower and under the stream of hot water. "Do you remember that journalist who came to interview Mom a few years ago?"

"Which one?"

"The one we met. She wrote that big piece for *The Pacific*. Her name was Lisa Rushall."

"Yeah, sure. Why?"

I worked a gob of conditioner through my hair, frowning as my fingers caught on a snarl. "I found out that she's the one who made my post blow up."

"Really? How'd she do that?"

"She shared it with her fifteen thousand followers, and that was all it took, apparently."

I heard Emerson make a harsh sound in the back of her throat. "She should be ashamed of herself. Want me to punch her in the face?"

"I don't actually think you know how to land a punch," I pointed out.

"For the right person, I could figure it out."

"I don't want to physically injure her," I said slowly, half-heartedly shaving a leg and wondering how precise a hair-removal job Emerson expected from me. "I just want to make her regret what she did. I just want her to understand how it feels. I want to destroy her life even half as much as she's destroyed mine."

"Oh," Emerson said with a little laugh. "*Just* that? Well, great. That sounds super-achievable. Look, you want my advice?"

"Not really."

"Let it go."

I turned off the water and reached out for my towel.

"And turn that water back on," Emerson said. "There is no possible way you've already washed and exfoliated your face. Come on, Winter. I'm not an idiot."

"You're the worst," I said, and I turned the water back on.

"Hey now," she protested, "I could be worse. I could be Lisa Rushall."

And that, I had to agree, was a very good point.

11

"*Damn*, Winter," Mackler said when I approached him and Corey at the party. "Heaven must be missing an angel, because you look, like, better than usual!"

"Wow," I said, waving at the camera he was holding up. "You use that line on all the ladies?"

"No," Mackler said.

"Yes," Corey said. "You're the tenth tonight. Heaven must be a lonely place right now. So many missing angels."

"Seriously, what'd you do to yourself?" Mackler asked me.

"Put on some makeup. Oh, and showered for the first time in a week."

"You look like Emerson."

"Gross," I said unconvincingly.

"Winter, Mackler's being an asshole and won't go on the swing with me. Will you?" Corey asked. He meant the rope swing, which had been fraying for my entire life and had resulted in at least two broken ankles that I, personally, was aware of. Swinging out as far as you could was supposed to give you a great view of the city, but frankly I felt like we had a great view of the city from the ground.

"Sorry, Cor. For some reason even I don't understand, I'd like to live to see eighteen," I said.

"Then you're also an asshole," Corey told me.

"Corey, man, keep the focus," Mackler said.

"What's the focus?"

"S'mores, dumbass," Mackler replied. "I'm gonna make the foie gras of s'mores right now. Watch and learn, children."

He stopped recording and stuck his phone in his pocket. We followed him deeper into the trees, where crowds of our classmates were gathered around a puny little fire, drinking beers and singing along with a guy who was playing an old Dire Straits song on his guitar. I saw Claudette Cruz with her crowd of friends, smoking something that did not appear to be a cigarette. I saw a minimum of two of Jason's exes. My heart was beating fast. I hadn't seen anywhere close to this many people since graduation. And more people meant more unpredictability. Any one of them could do anything, at any time. I could drive myself insane trying to watch out for all of them.

"Winter!" Emerson's best friend, Brianna, squealed and grabbed me in a hug. It could have been that my sister had asked her to be especially welcoming as I returned to society, but maybe not— being welcoming was just Brianna's way. "Oh my gosh, I haven't seen you since Christmas, you! How are you? I love your skirt!"

Now it was my turn to say something back like, "Your lip gloss is amazing!" or, "That purse is adorable!" This was how girls communicated that they were not your enemy.

I liked Brianna, but I didn't know anything about her lip gloss or purse. They both seemed cute to my untrained eye, but she didn't need me to tell her that. "You look really pretty, too," I finally managed, which was true, but it sounded nonspecific and forced, and Brianna smiled at me with a lot of teeth and kept walking.

"You should've learned to play guitar instead of oboe, man," Mackler was advising Corey as he speared one marshmallow after another onto a stick. "Look at that gentleman. Look at the devoted honeys he has attracted with his guitar."

"Girls love oboes, too," Corey said. "At band camp last year oboe was voted the sexiest woodwind."

"Who were you up against?" Mackler asked.

"Clarinets, flutes, and bassoons."

"Well, obviously you beat *bassoons*," Mackler said. "Have you ever even *seen* a bassoon? They are like anti-sex. Bassoons are the abstinence-only education of the woodwind section." He continued loading up his stick with marshmallows.

"Hey, guys," I said, "I need to be a better person."

"Nah," Mackler said. "I think you're okay as you are."

"My mom wants to hire this guy to fix my *image*," I explained. "And I don't want to fix my image . . . I mean, I don't *just* want to fix my image. I want to fix *myself*."

"What?" Mackler said.

"I don't just want to *appear* better," I explained. "I want to *be* better."

"Your mom is so zany sometimes," Mackler commented. "My ma's never hired anybody to fix anything about me."

"I can think of tons of ways to be a better person," Corey volunteered. "You could save somebody's life."

"I'd like to save somebody's life," I agreed. "Do you have anyone in particular in mind?"

Corey thought about it. "My great-aunt had another stroke," he said at last. "She's not doing great. You could save her life."

"I think it might be up to the doctors to save her life," I told him gently.

"Whoa, whoa," Mackler said. "There are no bad ideas in brainstorming. There are only good ideas."

"I'm not saying it's a *bad* idea for me to save Corey's great-aunt's life. Just, you know, an impossible one."

"There are no impossible ideas in brainstorming," Mackler replied wearily, as though he had already explained this so many times and he was exhausted. "Only possibilities."

"Sure, but—"

"ONLY POSSIBILITIES," he repeated.

I pulled up my "how to be a better person" list and jotted down "save somebody's life" as item number one.

"If you want," Mackler said, "you could, like, push me off a cliff and then rescue me at the last minute, and then you'd have saved *my* life."

"Sometimes I want to push you off a cliff," I told him. "So I'll bear it in mind."

"Do you want to adopt an orphan?" Corey suggested.

"I like that idea," I said, writing that down as well. "They could sleep in Emerson's room once she heads back to school."

"John Yancey is adopted," Mackler pointed out, "and I don't think of his parents as being, like, *redeemed* because of that."

"What if Winter adopted *two* orphans?" Corey asked.

Mackler shook his head, unimpressed.

"Fifty orphans?" Corey said.

Mackler nodded. "Now you're talking."

"I don't want to be, like, an *orphan hoarder*," I objected. "Can you just picture those headlines? 'Racist Teen Operating Illicit Orphanage from Sister's Bedroom'?"

"I would read that story so hard," Mackler said. "*That* is front-page Reddit material."

"Maybe I could donate parts of my body to people in need," I said. "My hair and blood and liver and kidneys and . . . What else do people need? My pancreas? What does the pancreas do?"

My friends were both looking at me like I was crazy. Like this was somehow crazier than pushing Mackler off a cliff. "*You* might need those body parts someday," Corey pointed out.

And of course he was right, but there was still something in the idea that appealed to me, of cutting apart my body piece by piece, my skin and my brain and my lips and my tongue, giving it all away until there was nothing left in me for anyone to object to. Until I was just a pathetic collection of fingernails and veins, and everyone would feel guilty for their roles in tearing me to scraps.

"I know this is hard to believe, but you might be asking the wrong people," Mackler said. "The most charitable thing I've ever done was give Therese Marcos a back rub this one time when she was having a rough day."

"You didn't even do that," I pointed out.

"I know," Mackler agreed. "But I thought about it."

Give Therese Marcos a back rub, I wrote down on my list.

"Perfect," Mackler said. "Problem solved."

Then I saw Jason show up on the other side of the bonfire. He was holding hands with a girl a year younger than us, Trina Somebody. When he sat down on a rock, she crawled into his lap, curled herself into his chest, and gave him a lingering kiss on the neck.

So apparently the reign of Caroline was over. Now, it seemed, we were on to Trina. I wondered how long it would take Trina to turn out to be crazy.

"Will you guys *please* make up?" Corey asked, observing my glaring at Jason. "That would make you a better person, I bet: not being in a feud with Jason anymore. I need you to stop fighting by my birthday, because I want us all to road-trip to Disneyland together, and that's going to be terrible if you and Jason aren't speaking. You guys are going to ruin my birthday."

"Your birthday's not until next March," Mackler reminded him.

"So what? At the rate those two are going, they probably won't even make eye contact before March."

"You're going to be at college in March," I reminded him. "You guys are *all* going to be at college in March."

"Well, I'm going to come home for my *birthday*," Corey said, like this was obvious.

I shrugged. Maybe he would, maybe he wouldn't. Emerson hadn't.

"Yo, I'm not trying to take sides, but have you tried apologizing to Jason?" Mackler asked me.

"Yeah," I said, "and he completely threw it in my face."

"You could try again," Corey suggested.

"*He* could try," I pointed out. "I'm not going to beg." I pulled my cardigan around me. "I'm going to go for a walk." Being near Jason just made me feel sick. I tried to cling to anger, but mostly what I felt when I saw him was so much shame, and sadness.

I walked away from the crowds and settled myself in the dark, on a bed of leaves under a tree. I sat there for a long time. I had developed a real skill for being still and doing nothing. Some part of me fantasized about Jason coming after me, explaining, reconciling. But that didn't happen. I waited and waited, and that was never going to happen.

When I finally returned to the bonfire, an hour or more had gone by, and I was weirdly proud of myself for not having noticed the passage of time. The singing had stopped, and the air was now charged with drunken drama. Somehow we'd gone from a hangout to a full-on party and I'd missed the transition. The night had gotten away from me. Corey and Mackler were nowhere to be seen—and thankfully neither were Jason and his new lady friend—but Emerson's friend Jenna grabbed me as soon as she saw me.

"You should talk to your sister," she said, clutching my wrist. "*Something* is going on."

Jenna was a drama queen and a gossipmonger, so I didn't know how seriously to take this. "What happened?" I asked.

She shook her head and widened her eyes. "She won't tell me. She won't talk to anyone. But she's *really* upset."

I didn't blame Emerson for refusing to confide in Jenna. That girl could create drama out of thin air. One time she used a change in the cafeteria menu to spread the rumor that the principal was pregnant out of wedlock. (She wasn't.)

Nonetheless, I was concerned. "Really upset" was not usually in Emerson's repertoire. She'd seemed as chipper as ever when she'd brought me here tonight, and I couldn't imagine what had happened to her since then.

"Where is she?" I asked Jenna.

She led me to a large rock. The ground below it was swarming with Emerson's girlfriends, who were all buzzing among themselves about what had happened to their queen bee. And curled into a ball atop the rock, her golden hair dangling off it, was my sister.

I shoved the older girls aside and scrambled up.

"Go away," Emerson said, her voice muffled. "I said I *do not* want to talk about it."

I could see how this had scared off her minions, but it didn't have the same effect on me. "I couldn't care less what you want," I said. "Scooch over."

"Oh," she said, looking at me with heavy-lidded eyes. "It's you."

She flopped sideways and I sat beside her.

"Ughhhhh," she said. "I hate life."

"You only hate life because you're drunk," I said. She stank of booze. It was an incongruous smell for my sister.

"Or am I drunk because I hate life?" she asked. "Which came first, the chicken or the egg? The drunk or the hatred?"

"The drunk," I responded. "Definitely the drunk."

"That reminds me . . ." Emerson looked around. "Where's my beer? Bri said she was bringing me a beer. *Brianna!*"

"Hush," I said. "I'm pretty sure you finished the beer Bri brought you, and then twenty other beers on top of that. What is going on with you?"

My sister was not a big drinker. She partied, obviously: when you're as popular as my sister is, you're *obligated* to party. Gatherings don't even really *count* as parties until Emerson shows up. But she wasn't usually in it to get drunk.

Or, at least, she hadn't been. Maybe she got wasted every night at college and she just didn't tell me about it.

"Everything is terrible," Emerson said simply.

I was struck by the realization that I had *no idea* what was going on in my sister's life. Ever since the moment she'd gotten home, she had comforted me and babied me and asked for nothing in return. Because surely what had happened to me was more dramatic than whatever was happening to her. But what that meant was that I had no clue what she needed now. Any of her friends down on the ground would probably do a better job than her own sister.

"Can you be more specific," I said, "about what, exactly, counts as 'everything'?"

"What?" Emerson said. She burped.

"Can you give me some examples of what all these terrible things are?"

"I don't want to go back to school," she said.

This was the ridiculous ranting of a drunk-out-of-her-mind person. Emerson's life goal had always been to make it on Broadway. The way to get there, she'd told me from a young age, was to attend a college with a top-tier musical theater program. And that's what the University of Oklahoma was.

Okay, maybe she wasn't loving every minute of it. I knew she had gotten very small roles in their productions this past year, and that would have to be a letdown after starring in every high school production ever. I knew she thought one of her professors played favorites and did not count her among their number. I knew it was a lot of work. I knew she'd had a weird relationship with her assigned first-year roommate, and after the first few weeks at school they'd given up on even trying to talk to each other for the rest of the year. And probably other stuff had gone imperfectly, too, stuff I didn't know about because when someone is leading a whole new life fifteen hundred miles away, there are some things that never come up no matter how many messages you exchange.

So maybe Emerson was thinking about any of those issues as she lay crumpled in a heap. But I also knew that she would gladly suffer through all of that and more if that's what it took to make it on Broadway.

"Why do you think you don't want to go back to college?" I asked.

"Because I like it here," she said simply.

"Here, on this rock? It's pretty great, Em, but it's not exactly *college*."

"I mean *here* here. I miss it here. Look at all my friends down there. They're so amazing. I love them. Look at our city!" She flung her arm out, and I did look, down the hills and over the lights in the valley below. It was beautiful. She went on, "Being home is like: oh, yeah, I forgot, this is *great*. Why do I have to leave here again?"

I wanted to have sympathy for my sister. I really, really wanted to. She was clearly sad, and I hated to see her sad.

But as hard as I tried, my sympathy kept being drowned out by my jealousy. She had the options to go back to college or to stay here or to do something else entirely, and I didn't. I had no options. And I would take a weird roommate and a biased teacher in a heartbeat if it meant that I could go somewhere and do something with my life again.

I didn't want to feel jealous of my sister. I wanted to be on her side, and really find out what her issues at college were, and try to help her through them. How do you make yourself feel something different from what you feel?

Emerson rubbed her eyes. "I need to pee."

"Do you want to go home? I can drive your car."

"You failed your driving test," she reminded me.

"Only technically," I said. I had put off taking driver's ed until after the SATs and after I'd been accepted to Kenyon. When everyone else in my year was working toward getting their licenses, I had been single-mindedly focused on getting into school, and I hadn't had a minute to spare for such pleasure pursuits as driving.

It hadn't occurred to me that by the time I took my driving test, it would be two weeks after The Incident and the officer would take one look at my name and fail me. She'd claimed it was because I hadn't stopped for long enough at a stop sign, and I couldn't prove that she was lying, because I hadn't been timing myself, and anyway, she was the expert.

But she *was* lying, and denying me the driver's license I knew I'd earned was simply the one way that a DMV agent could use her little bit of power to punish me.

Emerson swayed slightly, and I pointed out to her that, license or no, we'd be safer with me behind the wheel than her.

"Wowza." She widened her eyes. "Look at you, Miss Law-breaker. When did you turn into such a little rebel?"

Since I realized that there's no point to trying to stay out of trouble. Since I realized that you can do the right thing and abide by the rules a thousand times, and people will notice only the one time when you don't.

"We're not going to get pulled over," I told her, and then we both said together, *"Kina hora."*

"Okay," Emerson said. "I'll let you drive, but only 'cause I trust you."

"That's your first mistake right there," I told her.

"Wrong," she said, beginning her wobbly descent down to the ground. "I never make mistakes."

12

I steered a stumbling Emerson through the gauntlet of her friends, out to the street, and down the road until we came to her car. After I'd settled her into the passenger seat, I said, "Wait here for a second. I want to say bye to my friends."

"Ooh, you mean *Jason*?" Her head flopped sideways to look at me.

Emerson harbored misplaced fantasies about me and Jason falling in love. These fantasies were not based in fact, which meant it was irrelevant that dating Jason sounded to me like a nightmare wrapped in a fancy bow. All Emerson could really see was that Jason was hot—which was, objectively, true—and she liked the idea of my finding true love with a hot person. "Jason and I aren't speaking," I reminded her.

Tunelessly, she chanted, "First comes not speaking. Then comes marriage. Then comes the baby in the baby carriage."

"Sure," I said. "Don't move. I'll be back in a sec."

I locked her in the car and headed back up the hill. I wanted to tell Corey and Mackler that I was leaving and then get the hell out of there. I didn't know why I'd let Emerson talk me into going out tonight, or how I'd fooled myself into believing that hair and makeup could magically transform me into the sort of person who felt at home here—or anywhere, anymore.

I walked as quietly as I could, hiding in the shadows, so as not to attract the attention of any of Emerson's friends. They would want to know what was going on with her and if she was going to be okay and if there was anything they could do to help or, barring that, any confidential information about her that they could use to make themselves seem important. Emerson's friends exhausted me. I was not here to navigate them: I was here to find *my* friends, and then escape.

I saw a cluster of guys lounging on a felled tree trunk. One of them checked his phone, and his face was briefly illuminated. Jason. Not who I wanted to talk to, but if Jason was in that group, then maybe Mackler and Corey were, too. I sighed to myself and slowly edged closer—but stopped when I heard one of them say my sister's name.

"Did you hear Emerson Halperin was having some kind of breakdown tonight?"

"Such a drama queen," one of the other boys responded. They laughed, and I wanted to stomp forward, kick dirt at them, and tell them that they didn't know my sister, didn't know what she went through or how she felt, they only knew how she presented herself to the public—and that was them, *they* were the public—and how dare they judge her based on that incredibly limited understanding of who she was?

But I did not stomp forward; instead, I pulled back farther into the shadows, because I'm just as bad as everyone else and I wanted to hear what they would say.

"Drama queen or no, breakdown or no, she's still the hottest thing to ever go to our school," someone else said, and the rest murmured their agreement. I almost gagged. Are we seriously still in the twenty-first century referring to human beings as *things*?

This was one of the annoying parts about Jason. Corey, Mackler, and I hung out with one another, and sometimes with other people who were basically like us. But Jason hung out with us sometimes, and with his girlfriend of the month sometimes, and with his aggressively masculine sports bros sometimes. And who Jason was shifted depending on who he was surrounded by. When he was with us, there seemed to be no question that making weird, artsy videos was the best and most important part of his life. But when he was out on the basketball court or in a group of guys like he was now, I felt silly for ever believing that.

It wasn't like Jason changed completely every time. It was more like he just kept getting put through different filters.

"I'm so glad we're out of that place," one of the guys with him now said. "On to college girls!"

"Dude, if you think any college girls will have anything to do with you, you're out of your mind."

"What about you, King? You going to stay with your jailbait girlfriend even once you're at Cal State?"

"I don't know, man. We're going to see how the summer goes. Figure it out then. How hard it is to do the long-distance thing. And anyway, Kate's not *jailbait*."

"Jailkate."

"If that's a joke, I don't even get it."

"Because you're slow."

"Because it's not funny."

"Admit that King's girlfriend is basically a child."

"They grow into themselves, though, don't they? Even if it takes a while. Like Emerson's little sister."

My breath caught in my throat. Yes, I'd been eavesdropping, but I hadn't known I was going to be eavesdropping about *myself*.

"Oh, yeah! Did you see her tonight? When she first showed up and it was kind of dark, I thought she *was* Emerson."

"That's dumb. They don't have the same hair color."

"*You're* dumb. Have you ever heard of hair dye?"

"Yeah, but—"

"No, Chase is right. Their faces and bodies and whatever are, like . . . well, like sisters, yeah."

This was nothing I didn't know. Emerson was like me 2.0. Me, only with clearer skin and shinier hair and a tighter stomach. Me, only eighteen months older and with a hundred percent more effort.

"Jason, you're friends with her, right?"

There was a pause. I dug my fingernails into my palms.

"Not really," Jason said at last. His voice was richer and more confident than the other guys'. Or maybe I just thought that because his voice was so familiar to me.

Not really. If I weren't a frozen girl, I might have cried.

"I don't care if she's as hot as three Emersons put together," someone else put in. "I'd never be into her. She's a racist, you know."

There was another brief pause, then a flurry of nervous laughter.

"I thought we're all acting like that never happened," one of them said.

"We're *acting* like it didn't happen, not *believing* that it didn't happen. It's like when Mrs. Pritchard and Ms. Furman were caught hooking up."

A round of hoots and hollers.

"And you'd talk to Mrs. Pritchard like, 'Oh, sorry, I forgot to bring my math worksheet, can I get an extension?' but the whole time what you're *actually* thinking is, *Everyone in the entire school knows that you're having an affair with the gym teacher!* That's what Winter Halperin is like."

"Winter Halperin had an affair with the gym teacher?"

"*No*, idiot."

"This is how rumors get started!"

"What I mean is that *we* can pretend like we don't know what happened, and *she* can pretend like we don't know what happened, but in fact we *all* know what happened. All of us. And we always will."

"It's funny, 'cause she always acted like such a good little girl. Like, 'Oh, teacher, *I* know the answer! Oh, teacher, *I'll* take attendance!'"

"Guess her sister's not the only actress in the family."

"Who knew that underneath it all she was actually, like, a so-ciopath?"

"I saw it coming."

"You did not."

"Okay, well I wasn't *surprised* when I found out the truth about her, how about that?"

"I wasn't surprised at all."

"Has it ever occurred to you that it doesn't *matter* what you think about Winter?" That was Jason's voice again, and this time he sounded angry. "Who put you in charge of deciding if she's good enough?"

"I thought you weren't really friends with her, Jason. Isn't that what you said?"

"That doesn't mean I want to sit here while you talk shit about her," Jason said.

"It's not shit-talking if it's the truth."

"You're not God," Jason snapped. "You're not the Supreme Court. You're not perfect angels yourselves. You don't get to sit here and judge her."

"We weren't, man. That's not what we're doing."

"Seriously, chill out."

"Overprotective much? What is she, Jason, your *girlfriend*?"

"Screw you, man. I'm not going to listen to this anymore. I'm going to find Trina." Jason stood, brushed off his jeans, and started to walk away. I shrank into the shadows and held my breath until he was gone. And then I ran back to the car.

Emerson was right where I'd left her, asleep with her head rolled back and her breath coming out loudly through her mouth. She woke up when I started the car. "Did you find your friends?" she mumbled.

I'd forgotten that was why I'd headed back to the party in the first place. I didn't answer her, and within a minute, she had fallen asleep again.

I didn't understand Jason. Maybe I never had. He thought I was a bad person, but he wouldn't let anyone else say it. I had lost him, as surely as I'd lost everything, through my foolishness and thoughtlessness and this insurmountable evil inside me. I had lost him, but clearly there was some part of him that still felt loyal to me.

Or maybe he was just a good person. Maybe he didn't care about me at all and he just behaved as any good person would, defending the basic humanity of someone else. What did I even know about goodness?

But there was one thing that I did understand, as I cautiously drove through the dark streets, through trees and brushwood toward home. Those guys were right. Well, they were wrong about girls being "things," but they were right about this:

No matter how hard they pretended or I pretended, no one was fooled. Everyone would always know who I was and what I had done. Rodrigo Ortiz could invent for me an online identity, and Emerson could give me a makeover, but those were like Band-Aids on a concussion. What I really needed was to be an entirely different person.

But how do you do that?

13

You need to get over here right now, Mackler's message to me read.

It was a month after the bonfire, which had been my first and last major social event of the summer. It was now late August. Emerson was heading back to school in two days. Since her drunken breakdown, she hadn't once even mentioned the possibility that she might not go back, so I hadn't brought it up, either. That had just been the alcohol talking. Mackler was heading off to UC Santa Barbara in two days, too. Corey would be here for another week, and then he'd be on his way to Chicago. And I would be here still, of course. I had nowhere else to go and no way to get there. I had applied for a few jobs: cashier at a bookstore, ticket-taker at a cinema, server at a café. None of them called me for an interview. I wasn't that surprised. Any of them would have googled me, and I knew exactly what they would have seen.

When Mackler's message came, I was glad to have something to do. I biked over to his house and was ringing his doorbell half an hour later.

"Dillydally much?" he asked when he answered his door. He was wearing a white bathrobe, shorts, and nothing else, which didn't seem like extremely weird behavior only because he was Mackler.

"What do you think the etymology of *dillydally* is?" I mused. "I assume it has something to do with the word *dally*. But is the *dilly* part, like, a cutesy mispronunciation that eventually became part of the language?"

"You're missing my point," Mackler replied.

"I don't think I am."

"My point is that Corey and I are very hard at work here on a video *masterpiece*, while you have been *dillydallying* your day away."

"Since when do you guys make video masterpieces without me?" I asked.

"Since you stopped hanging out anywhere outside of your living room. Come on."

I followed him down the hallway and into the kitchen, where Corey was waiting for us. Mackler's house was comfortingly familiar: the excessive number of throw rugs all covered in dog hair, the conflicting scents of candles with names like "Island Dream" and "Peppermint Truffle." It made me sad to think I probably wouldn't be back here again until Christmas break. The only unusual thing in Mackler's house today was that his kitchen counter was crowded with a half dozen bottles of Gatorade.

"What's this video?" I asked.

"It's for a contest," Corey explained as Mackler rearranged the bottles. "The winner gets a year's supply of Gatorade."

"So what's that," I said, "like one Gatorade?"

Corey rolled his eyes. "We did the math, and if we win, we're going to need a thousand bottles for the year."

"Minimum," Mackler threw in. "And that's assuming you don't want in on the prize. Do you?"

"All right, fine. I'll take a bottle a month," I said. "Just so I can feel like I'm part of it. What's the contest entry going to be?"

"Well, I'm going to be this total honey master," Mackler explained.

"What's that?" I interrupted. "A beekeeper?"

Mackler sighed with annoyance. "Master of all the honeys."

I thought about this for a second. "So, like, a sex fiend?"

"Fiend has a lot of negative connotations. I'm the *honey master*. That's why I'm wearing this sensual bathrobe. And I'm going to explain to the camera how I get all my honeys. My secret is Gatorade, obviously."

"Obviously," Corey echoed, rolling his eyes.

"Like I've got the yellow Gatorade for the shy honeys, and the blue Gatorade when I'm trying to reel in a honey who's way too good for me."

I raised my eyebrows at Corey. "You're letting him get away with this?"

"You try to stop him," Corey replied.

"Yo, leave the props alone," Mackler ordered, knocking a Gatorade bottle from my hands. "I'm trying to run a professional film studio here, for Chrissakes."

"So we needed you here, obviously," Corey told me.

"You'd be fools to try to do this without me," I agreed.

"I was thinking you could introduce each color of Gatorade—"

"No," I said quickly.

Corey stopped in surprise, and Mackler said, "I agree with Winter. Lame idea. She should be each one of the honeys, but wearing a different disguise each time. Like sunglasses for the green Gatorade and a fake mustache for the purple Gatorade."

"I thought *I* got to play the honeys," Corey objected.

"You can take turns being honeys."

"No," I said, "Corey can do them all. Sorry, guys, but I don't want anything else about me online."

"It's not going to have your name," Corey tried.

"Someone might recognize my face."

"Not if you're wearing a fake mustache," Mackler pointed out.

"It's not like anyone's even going to *watch* this one," Corey said. "We're just submitting it to a contest. Probably some Gatorade employee will look at it for thirty seconds and delete it and that will be that."

"Check that negativity," Mackler told him. "We are going to be champions."

"You never know who's going to watch something you put online," I said.

"Will you at least write the script for it?" Corey asked. "Mackler did a first draft before we called you over, and it's the worst."

When we used scripts—which we didn't usually; usually we improvised everything and then fixed it up in edits—I always wrote them. That was my role, just as Mackler's role was to wear a weird costume whenever that was called for, and Corey's role was to set up the camera angles, and Jason's role was to make sure the edits got done. We knew our jobs and we carried them out with gusto.

But not anymore. I couldn't anymore. "Just film it, okay?" I said. "You don't need a script for this one."

Corey sighed and pulled out his phone. Mackler got into position, which was him sitting on a stool at his counter, his bathrobe adjusted for maximum chest hair visibility, the bottles arranged before him.

"Getting laid is hard work," he said in a somber tone, facing Corey's phone.

Corey immediately cracked up.

"Okay, well, you ruined that take," Mackler said. "Corey, get your shit together. The pursuit of free Gatorade is no laughing matter. Take two."

Corey kept his laughter silent when Mackler started again, but as I watched Mack calmly talk about how this red Gatorade was what gave him the confidence to approach perfect tens, while this pink Gatorade was what gave him the strength to sweep them off their feet, I felt the tempo of my heartbeat growing faster and faster.

Corey was probably right, and no one would bother to watch or care about this video—but what if they did? I could so easily imagine the comments that would get made on this video that did not even exist yet. Comments about Mackler's body. About his voice. About the pile of dirty dishes in the sink behind him.

I'd been kidding when I'd called him a sex fiend because I knew he wasn't: like me and Corey (though not Jason), Mackler was a virgin, and I'd seen him nervously try to ask girls to dance enough times to know that he had no actual idea what he was doing, with or without the aid of electrolyte-enhanced beverages.

But strangers watching this video, they wouldn't know any of that. They would just see a guy bragging about how he attracted so many girls. And if they didn't know him, didn't know this was all a big joke, then wouldn't that sound sexist and predatory and *wrong*?

"You shouldn't make this video," I blurted out.

"Cut," Corey said, unnecessarily.

"What the hell, Winter?" Mackler snapped. "I was almost done. Now we have to take it from the top. Again."

"No," I said. "Don't do this video at all."

"You don't want me to have my year's supply of Gatorade?" he asked in disbelief. "I told you I'd share it with you. Okay, fine, you can have twenty percent, how's that?"

"It's too dangerous, Mack," I said. "Don't you understand? Once something like this is out there, you can't *ever* get it back. It will be part of your life until the day you die or the internet disappears from the face of the Earth. You could be sixty years old and people will still refer back to a stupid video you made when you were eighteen."

"This video is *not* stupid," Mackler said.

I felt desperate tears prickling my eyes. "What if people don't get it?"

"Then they have a lame sense of humor. Their loss."

"That's easy to say now," I told him. "But that's not how it actually plays out. Don't do this to yourself. Don't give them any ammunition. *Please*, Mack."

"Winter, you're freaking out. Take a deep breath. This isn't going to be like what happened to you."

"How do you know?" I demanded.

"Because . . ." Mackler shook his head in frustration.

"Because why? Because unlike me, *you'll* be smart about it?"

"I didn't say that. Jesus, Winter."

I stared at him and wondered if I would ever again in my life feel the confidence and safety that he did.

"Is there another Gatorade video we could make that would be okay?" Corey spoke up. "Maybe you could come up with an idea that wouldn't, you know, 'give them any ammunition'?"

"Yeah," Mackler said, "if you'd just write a script, this wouldn't even be an issue."

I frowned. "Maybe if it was, like . . . your dog drinking Gatorade?" Though immediately my mind went to animal rights activists and the outcry they could have over a poor defenseless canine being force-fed electrolytes. Mackler's face wouldn't be out there, so that was safer. But it still wasn't a foolproof plan. "You don't ever *know* how strangers are going to take something until it's too late."

"So then what are we supposed to do?" Mackler asked, throwing up his arms. "Not make anything at all, just in *case* a person might see it and hate it?"

I felt something shrivel inside of me, like a popped balloon. I'd handed in my own creativity—but did my friends have to do the same? Did *everyone* have to seal their lips to stay safe?

"I guess you could make the video," I said slowly, "but not submit it for the contest."

"So what would we do with it?" Corey asked, perplexed.

"Just, like . . . watch it?"

"Sounds like a lot of work for no payoff," Mackler said flatly. "This is dumb. We only have a couple more days here. This is the last thing we're going to do together before I leave. And not to be all dramatic about it, but you're ruining it, Winter. You're ruining our last thing by being paranoid. Maybe no one else is willing to say this to you, but I'm not one to shy away from hard truths." Corey rolled his eyes, but Mackler was really warming to his topic. "Winter, you can't go on like this. You're not *Hitler*, you know."

"I am aware of that, Mackler, thank you," I snapped. "What's your point?"

"My *point* is that there are some truly villainous people in the world. Murderers and rapists and child molesters. That's not you. Hitler killed millions of people. Last time I checked, you hadn't killed *anybody*. I'm sorry to be the one to break this to you, but you are not even close to as evil as you think you are."

"Oh, and that's all it takes to be a good person?" I said sarcastically. "Not killing people?"

"You do lots of really good stuff," Corey told me.

But for the life of me, I couldn't think of what that good stuff was.

"The difference between you and Hitler," Mackler told me, "is that he set out to destroy people. That was his goal. He was like, 'Hey, you know what I'm so all about right now? Genocide!' You, on the other hand, didn't *mean* to hurt anyone. That's what makes

Hitler one of the most despicable creatures of all time and makes you just unlucky. You've developed some story in your head where you're, like, Satan. But actually? You're just a normal person who made a mistake."

It sounded so simple when Mackler said it like that, so cut-and-dried: a crime was only a crime if that's how you intended it.

But that wasn't how it really went. The world didn't know what I'd intended; they knew only how I had acted. Like that anonymous commenter who had responded to my apology post with, "Why do you think that we care what you were *trying* to say?"

I knew that in the real world, Mackler was right, sort of. Like if you killed someone, you were judged differently if it was in self-defense or if it was premeditated. The question of whether you were *trying* to hurt someone was relevant in a legal trial.

But as Rodrigo had pointed out, the internet wasn't the real world. There was no trial, no judge, and no jury, and nobody except my friends cared one whit about my intentions.

"I know this has been really hard for you," Corey said to me gently.

"Even though it was months ago," Mackler interjected.

"It was months ago," Corey agreed, "but it was hard, we get that. And we're trying to be sympathetic. It's just . . . Well . . ."

Mackler jumped in again. "What Corey's trying to tell you," he said, "is that you're not much fun anymore."

Corey hit his shoulder. "You don't have to be an asshole about it!"

"Seriously, Corey, you call that a punch? You have, like, gummy bear arms. And Winter, I'm not trying to be a dick, but if your best friends can't point out to you that you're so scared and moody and, like, *overflowing* with self-pity that hanging out with you is pretty bleak, then who *is* going to tell you that? I mean, you want to know why we started this movie without you? It's because you're kinda a killjoy."

I just stared at him. I had no words. It wasn't enough that I had to live through this, had to relentlessly stay alive while they all went barreling off to college and their bright new futures, but now I also had to be happy and *fun* about it?

Then the doorbell rang.

"My goodness, I wonder who *that* is!" Mackler said, readjusting his bathrobe and heading for the front door.

"Who is it?" I asked Corey.

Corey looked studiously at the Gatorade bottle in his hands and didn't reply.

"*Corey,*" I said, kicking his sneakered foot.

"I don't know?" he said unconvincingly.

My skin tingled. "Please tell me you didn't—"

"Oh, hey, look who's here, guys!" Mackler said with exaggerated surprise as he reentered the kitchen. "If it isn't Jason Bono Shaw!" The "Bono" was part of Mackler's ongoing campaign to learn Jason's middle name. It wasn't happening. Certainly not today.

"Winter. I didn't know you'd be here." Jason looked past my shoulder, toward the refrigerator.

"I was just on my way out," I said, but Mackler blocked my path to the door.

"Hell no," he said. "You two are both being big babies, and

Corey and I are sick of it. Shake and make up. If not for yourselves, then for us. We feel like the children of divorced parents, don't we, Corey?"

"I actually *am* the child of divorced parents," Corey said, "so I guess—"

"I'm leaving for college in *two days*," Mackler interrupted, looking between me and Jason. "Do you get that? We might never see one another again."

"But we probably will," Corey said.

"*But we might not.* Let's start this new chapter in our lives with a clean slate, and other literary imagery like that. We've been friends for too long for your issues to ruin everything."

I squeezed my eyes shut. *Like an ostrich,* I heard Rodrigo's voice in my head.

Maybe Mackler was right: we'd been friends for too long, and shared too much, to let something like this fight come between us.

"Can you guys please get over this?" Corey asked as Jason and I stood at opposite ends of Mackler's kitchen, a collection of Gatorade bottles between us.

I'd tried that night at Jason's house, but I would try again. If not for the people we were today, then for the debt I owed to the fourteen-year-old versions of ourselves. "I'm sorry," I said. "I shouldn't have posted that joke. I know I shouldn't have. It was insensitive and thoughtless. I understand why you felt hurt. I wish I'd never done it, and I wish I could make it up to you."

Jason nodded. "Thank you for apologizing," he said formally. "I appreciate it."

"Perfect," Corey said. "Now we can be friends again."

"*Not* perfect," I objected. I widened my eyes at Jason. "That's it? That's all you have to say for yourself?"

He blinked at me.

"Jason, come on. Meet me halfway here. You can also say sorry. I get that you're mad about the post, but that should have stayed between us. You didn't also have to make some big public statement about it. 'I'd say *best* friend is a stretch,' " I quoted him. " 'Even if I trusted her before, I definitely don't anymore.' Seriously? At least when I hurt you, it was an *accident*. I didn't *mean* to do it. I know that doesn't make my behavior okay, but still. You, on the other hand, you *set out* to hurt me. What about *that*? How exactly are you planning to take that back? Do you even *want* to?"

"*Damn,*" Mackler whispered. Corey looked back and forth between me and Jason, wide-eyed, as if witnessing a high-stakes tennis match.

Jason at least had the decency to look ashamed. He bit his lip and stuffed his hands in his pockets. "I didn't know you read that," he muttered.

"Is that a good enough excuse? Because in that case, I didn't know you were going to read my post, either! I didn't know that *anybody* was going to read it. And if stupid Lisa stupid Rushall hadn't stepped in, then nobody would have."

"Who's stupid Lisa stupid Rushall?" Corey asked, confused.

"She's the asshole reporter who has it in for me. *She's* the one who reposted my comment to her thousands of followers. *She's* the reason anyone even found out about it in the first place."

"Are you kidding me?" Jason said. He didn't look ashamed anymore. He didn't look formal and detached, either, and he certainly did not look apologetic. He looked mad. "You're *still* not taking responsibility for what you did. You're still acting like this whole situation is somebody else's fault and you're the helpless little victim. *That's* your apology—blaming someone else?"

"What's *your* apology?" I shot back.

He swallowed hard and said in a low voice, "I'm not sorry."

I couldn't speak for a long moment. I was going to start to sob, which I *never* did in front of my friends, because then they would all realize that I wasn't one of the guys, after all. I was a girl, and the worst kind: the kind of girl who believed that she actually mattered to Jason Shaw. The kind of girl we made fun of.

"Maybe this wasn't a good idea," Corey muttered to Mackler.

Then I couldn't hold back my tears any longer. I ran out of the kitchen, out of the house, and away. Jason was an athlete, and of course he would have been able to catch up to me easily if he'd wanted to. But he didn't come after me. So I guess he didn't want to.

And that was the last time I saw my friends before they left for college.

14

I found something that promised to fix me.

I don't even know what convoluted chain of Google searches led me there, but somehow I wound up watching a video about a reputation rehabilitation retreat in Malibu called Revibe.

Of *course* it was called Revibe. If you told me you had a business named Revibe, I'd pretty quickly guess it was either a reputation rehabilitation retreat or a spin-studio-slash-juice-bar.

But as silly as the name was, the place sounded like what I needed. It wasn't like Personal History—instead, Revibe was there to repair "the whole person." The video mostly showed shots of the ocean and, like, kites in the breeze and flowers and stuff, and it was narrated by voice-overs telling their stories.

"I'd been fired from my job for inappropriate sexual conduct."

"I got expelled for threatening a classmate. I was kidding, but my school has a zero-tolerance policy."

"Everyone knew I was a liar."

"Even my fiancée couldn't look me in the eye."

"When I picked up my daughter, I had to park around the corner so no one would see us together and know she was related to me."

"I was afraid to leave the house."

"I was so ashamed."

"Revibe helped me when no one else could."

"I can honestly say Revibe saved my life."

"Valerie and Kevin understood what I was going through in a way that no one else could—not my husband, not my closest friends. They understood, and they didn't judge."

"I'm forty-eight years old, and until I attended Revibe, I never really understood how to apologize."

"Revibe, for me, is more than a retreat, a program, or a series of steps. It's almost a religion."

"After Revibe, I got a new job, in a field that matters to me, and I've never felt more fulfilled."

"I was able to make amends with my fiancée."

"Revibe got my life back on track."

"Revibe made me a better person. Not just better than I'd been since my scandal—better than I'd been ever.*"*

"Thank you, Revibe."

"Valerie and Kevin, thank you for everything you do."

"Thank you from the very bottom of my heart."

And if all of those endorsements sound kind of bullshit to you, don't be so smug. That just means you've got the luxury of never having been truly desperate.

But I didn't suggest it to my parents, at least not right away.

Because I looked at the price tag, and it made Rodrigo's services seem cheap.

How much did it cost?

Well, how much do you think it costs to save your life?

Soon enough it was time for Yom Kippur.

Yom Kippur is the most-observed Jewish holiday of the year. Its English name is the Day of Atonement, meaning it's when you're supposed to apologize for all your misdeeds and indiscretions of the past twelve months and vow to do better going forward. You celebrate it by spending all day praying at temple, and you don't eat or drink anything, including water, for twenty-five hours.

Even on a good year, Yom Kippur is never a "fun" holiday, but at least in the past I'd had Emerson there for company, and other kids from my elementary and middle schools. Now basically everyone I knew was away at college. The Jewish calendar moves around in relation to the solar calendar, which meant that this year Yom Kippur fell on a Wednesday in the middle of the semester. No one was traveling home for that.

Also, every other year, I'd been apologizing for things like "disrespecting my elders" or "making fun of Jason's girlfriends." So on a lot of levels, this was a particularly unpleasant Yom Kippur.

My family's temple is huge. It's like the Jewish equivalent of a megachurch, especially on the High Holidays. Even people who don't show up for services any other time of the year come out of the woodwork on Yom Kippur. You can't find a parking spot within four blocks of the temple, and police are stationed at every intersection to halt traffic so still more worshippers in suits and ties and *kippot* can make it across the street and into the synagogue.

There are not that many Jews in the world. This was something I didn't realize when I was little and went to Jewish day school and assumed the whole world was like my world. In fact, I learned when I was older, only about two percent of the United States is Jewish, and only one-fifth of one percent of the world's population is. So there is something kind of empowering about our being out on the street together, like we are strong in number after all, or at least we are on that one day.

Because so many people turn up for the High Holidays at my temple, they open up the back of the sanctuary and fill it with folding chairs. But my family has reserved seats in the actual pews, twelve rows back from the bimah, on the left side. We angled for those seats for a long time. We'd started out in the folding chairs, and it had taken years of maneuvering before we got moved up, at which point Mom said that she'd achieved her life's work, though I'm fairly sure she was kidding.

I sat between my parents, as I always did, and I stood when everyone stood and sat when everyone sat and read responsively or silently as each prayer called for.

But I had trouble believing any of it.

Every year, Yom Kippur goes like this: all the Jews of the world spend hours and hours praying that the wicked will be vanquished and that evil will evaporate from the Earth. Now, for the first time in my life, I felt bad for the wicked. What if they didn't want to be vanquished, even though that *would* be better for the world? What if they didn't want to evaporate?

Between afternoon and evening services, my parents and I went for a walk around the lagoon. There's not much you can do on Yom Kippur: you can't watch TV or use the computer or your cell phone, you can't eat or do any work. (Not that this stopped me from quickly turning on my phone while in the temple bathroom stall, unable to wait until the holiday was over to check the internet to see if my life had been torn apart yet again.) Basically your Yom Kippur options are praying, napping, and walking. As we walked, my parents argued about whether the new rabbi's sermon was better or worse than the old rabbi's sermons had been, while I looked at the lagoon and tried not to imagine drinking it all down.

Just a week and a half ago, on Rosh Hashanah, the Jewish new year, my parents and I had come out to this very spot for *tashlich*, a tradition where you cast your sins into the sea—or for my family, the lagoon, because it was closer. For *tashlich* you take pieces of bread and assign to each one a bad deed that you've committed over the previous year. Then you throw them out to the water, where the birds swoop in and eat them. The birds of the Bay Area must be filled with sin.

I'd gone through nearly a loaf of bread, throwing out bad deed after bad deed long after my parents were ready to go home. Yet here I was still. Why couldn't my sins stay at sea? Why did they seep back into me every time?

At a break in my parents' conversation, I said, "I have an idea for what I should do," and they both fell silent.

One of the greatest atonements I needed to make this Yom Kippur was to my mother. The summer was gone, and with it was any excuse she might have had for slow work. The school year was back in full swing, and this should have been her busiest time for speaking engagements and consulting gigs, but it wasn't. She didn't say a word about it, never blamed me, never even mentioned there was a problem, but it was plain that, day after day, we were both just sitting at home. And unless somebody did something, maybe we would be forever.

How do you atone for ruining the livelihood of one of the people you love most in all the world? *Can* you even atone for that? Or should you just evaporate?

"That's great, Winter," Mom said carefully. "What's your idea?"

"It's a reputation rehabilitation retreat down in Malibu," I said. "It's called Revibe."

"What does that mean, 'reputation rehabilitation retreat'?" Dad asked. "I've never heard of such a thing."

I nodded. "It's pretty new, and it's one-of-a-kind. The idea is that victims of public shaming go through a five-week program together, with the help of qualified professionals, to overcome their circumstances and forge a path forward." That was word-for-word what their website said. I added, "It's a lot of volunteer work and personal reflection, and it's supposed to really make you become a better person, from the inside out. It's the only thing I've seen that seems like it maybe has a shot of bringing me back some approximation of my old life." I wanted that. My old life. I'd never wanted anything more desperately. "They have a new session starting at the end of November. If you think it's a good idea."

"I think it's a terrific idea," Mom replied immediately, and I could see the relief in her eyes, the hopeful glint, that we were no longer going to take this lying down, we were doing *something*.

"Hold up," Dad said. "We don't know anything about this place. What kind of 'qualified professionals' are we talking about here? What exactly qualifies them? And who are these other 'victims of public shaming' you'd be there with? I'm not sending you off to spend five weeks hobnobbing with criminals and sociopaths."

"Do you think *I'm* a criminal or a sociopath?" I asked quietly.

"Of course not."

"These are people like me, Dad. They're people who made mistakes, and they can't get past them, and they need a second shot."

Dad rubbed his eyes. "This is a hard decision to make on an empty stomach, Winter."

"Sorry."

"How is this any better than that Google results fixer your mother tried to hire?"

Mom gave an aggrieved sniff.

I answered, "Because Revibe cares about the whole person. Their goal isn't just to make you *appear* better; it's to make you *feel* better and *be* better."

"Is it a cult?" Dad asked bluntly.

"Oy gevalt!" Mom exploded. "Why are you so suspicious? Your daughter has found something she's excited to do, and these are people who want to help her. What's the problem?"

"Mom said I had to find a solution," I reminded him. "And I did. This is it."

"I don't understand how it works," Dad insisted. "And I don't understand their motivation. *Why* would they want to help Winter?"

"Why would anyone want to help anyone?" Mom asked rhetorically. "Why do they need a selfish incentive to do a mitzvah?"

"Money," I answered Dad. "They want to help because they get paid for it. Is that enough of an incentive for you?"

Dad harrumphed. "I'm assuming it's expensive. Since it's one-of-a-kind. And in Malibu."

Malibu is down in Southern California, and it's known for being the beach where rich people have second or third homes. Like, anyone you can think of in Hollywood probably has a Malibu house.

"We'll make it work," Mom said quickly. Dad gave her a look, and I knew she was speaking from her feelings, not from practicality; she had no idea what this cost and was confident she could do it anyway. She would go bankrupt trying to save me, if she had to.

"I'm going to pay for it myself," I told them, the words bitter on my tongue.

"How?" Dad asked reasonably.

"I'm going to use my prize money."

"From the spelling bee?" Mom asked. "Oh, honey, you can't do that. That's your college money."

"I'm not going to college," I reminded her.

There was an awkward pause. Then Mom said, "Not right now, no, but you will. You're going to reapply this fall . . ."

"We'll be looking at a different sort of school from where we were looking last year," Dad conceded. "Okay, Kenyon's off the table, but there are literally thousands of other options."

"And what if *none* of them will take me?" I asked.

"You're being defeatist, and you're getting way ahead of yourself," Dad said. "You *will* go to college. It doesn't have to be fancy, or private, or out-of-state, or a four-year program. Frankly, I don't care where you go. But you *will* get a degree, Winter; that's not negotiable."

"Fine," I said, not because I believed him, necessarily, but because I needed to win this immediate battle before fighting a future battle. "But let's not kid ourselves: it's not going to be the sort of college that I need my prize money to afford."

They didn't say anything, as they pictured, perhaps, the places I could now wind up as compared to the places we had for so long imagined.

"I need to go to Revibe," I said. "And I need to pay for it myself. Otherwise I'm never going to get better."

"Okay," Dad said wearily, "we'll consider it." And I got the sense that if he had not been fasting, and there had been any fluid in his body right then, he might have cried. But I didn't look at him. I kept my eyes fixed firmly on the distance, on the birds that were swooping around, always scanning for just one more crumb of sin.

15

Mom drove me the seven hours from home down to Malibu. The last section of the drive was on the Pacific Coast Highway, which is where car commercials are often filmed. You know, the ones where the car is zooming down a windy road, a mountain on one side and the ocean on the other, an endless blue sky overhead, with the words *Trained drivers on a closed course. Do not attempt this at home* on the bottom of the TV screen. It was stunning and looked like an alien planet compared to my home. Northern California and Southern California are in the same state, but they are not the same place.

Dad hadn't come with us, though he'd helped me load my luggage into the car and even printed out physical maps for our drive—an odd gesture considering we all had GPS, but a touching one. If I'd been leaving for college, they both would have come with me. Together they would have gone through parent orientation, and offered opinions on which drawer I should use for shirts and which for socks, and demanded that my roommate come out to lunch with us. I knew this because they had done all of that for Emerson one year prior. But I wasn't leaving for college; I was leaving for rehab, so things were different.

It was weird to think about. I, who had been too much of a good girl to ever try any drugs, or drink any beers, or commit even the pettiest of crimes, *I* needed to be rehabilitated.

"At least it's pretty," Mom offered as the waves crashed against the beach, surfers out in the distance and seagulls circling overhead.

"*Pretty* doesn't even begin to cover it," I said. "Try *breathtaking*."

"*Sumptuous,*" Mom suggested.

"*Resplendent,*" I said.

She screwed up her face, struggling for a moment, before saying, "*Magnificent?*"

"*Pulchritudinous,*" I volunteered.

She nodded with admiration. "Very pulchritudinous."

This turned out to be even more true when we found the retreat center itself, up a private drive flanked by palm trees. The house was cream-colored and massive, which maybe I would have been able to handle calmly, but when I saw the fountain out front, with a marble dolphin spurting water high into the air, I cracked up. "What *is* this place?"

Mom caught my laughter. "It's a good thing your dad didn't come," she managed to say between giggles. "He would have lost his mind."

"Do all rehab centers look like a multimillionaire from the

1980s brought to life a fevered nightmare of a Venetian palace?" I asked.

"That is exactly what it looks like, isn't it?" she marveled. She put the car in park, then took my face in her hands. "You're something else, Winter, you know that?"

"Um. In a good way or a bad way?"

"You're headstrong," she said. "You and your sister both. I raised two headstrong daughters."

That didn't exactly answer the "good or bad" question.

"That's what got me into this trouble in the first place," I pointed out.

"But it's also what's going to get you out of it," she told me. "Look at you, Winter. Look at this place you've found, this thing you're making happen. You could have gone with Personal History when I suggested it, but instead, you found your own way."

I still couldn't tell whether this was a compliment or a critique. Did she think my way was going to be better or worse than her way? "Do you still think I should have done Personal History?" I asked.

"I think you should do whatever is going to work," she said firmly.

"Do you think this is going to work?" I looked again at the dolphin fountain.

"I think you're going to bust your *tuchus* to make it work."

And that was an assignment if ever I'd heard one.

We got my suitcases out of the car and pulled them up the stone drive, past the dolphin, and through the grand entry, where we were greeted at the enormous doorway by a couple with big smiles on their faces. I recognized them from the promotional video, so I smiled back. They both looked to be in their midforties. She was wearing slim-cut jeans, a V-neck black shirt, and strappy wedge sandals, as well as a delicate scarf around her neck, which seemed unnecessary for the weather, but fashionable. He had a reddish-brown beard with some flecks of gray and was dressed in jeans and a polo shirt. They looked very LA, though maybe I just thought that because I already knew where we were.

"Welcome to Revibe, Winter," the woman said warmly, shaking my hand. "I'm Valerie Pigott, and this is my husband, Kevin. We're the founders of Revibe, and we'll be your advisors for the next five weeks."

"So glad to have you." Kevin shook my hand, too. "And you must be Mom."

"Darlene Kaplan," she introduced herself. "Thank you for everything you're doing for Winter."

That's a Turn Them Toward the Sun technique, by the way. Say thank you in advance for what you *want* your kid to do ("Thank you for helping me do the dishes!"), and then they will be motivated to do it. Much more effective, Mom said, than ordering a child to do the dishes (which can get a "You're not the boss of me!") or asking (which can get a "No"). It generally worked, too. Most of Turn Them Toward the Sun did. People who didn't want to hire my mom just because of me were idiots.

"Don't worry, Darlene," Kevin said, "we'll take good care of her."

"I'll show you to your room," Valerie said, and she led me and Mom down a long hallway. Paintings hung on the walls—wherever there were walls and not windows, which was not as often as you

141

might expect. Valerie kept up a running commentary as we went. "We have six other Vibers this session. We gave you one of the downstairs bedrooms—I think you'll like it. It gets amazing sunlight in the mornings. If you turn right here, you'll come to Kevin's and my offices. You'll meet with one of us at least once a day to go over your progress and set new goals.

"This is the Great Room. I love the skylights in here, don't you? We gather in the Great Room for conversations that include everyone, and it's where we eat together, as a family. We have a cook who's just terrific. If you have any food restrictions, let us know and Meghan will work around them. Last session we had a Viber who was allergic to all fruits and vegetables—can you imagine? I'd die!—and she said she'd never even realized just how much she *could* eat until she came here and had Meghan's cooking.

"Here's your room. It's sweet, isn't it? I hope you'll forgive the carpeting. I'm going to leave you here to get settled. You have about an hour to yourself, and then everyone is going to meet up for orientation in the Great Room. If you want fresh air, you can keep going down your hallway and you'll come to the porch. It's lovely there: comfy Adirondack chairs and couches and a gorgeous view of the ocean. I find it very soothing to go out there sometimes just to meditate or watch the sun set. Please don't open the window, though. We don't want the air to get out."

Mom and I agreed with everything Valerie said, or at least we did not *dis*agree, and then she left us alone. My room was smaller than I'd been expecting, considering the grandeur of the building overall, and that was a relief to me. There were no original oil paintings or dolphins or chandeliers in here, just a normal-size bed and a normal-size closet.

I sat down on the normal-size bed and tried to catch my breath. I was nervous, because I was in a new place with new people and new rules, and what if nobody liked me, or what if I did it wrong in some way, or what if Revibe just couldn't fix me at all and then there was nowhere else to turn?

But I also felt excited. I'd spent months getting kicked around, like a stuffed animal in the grip of a manic toddler. And now I was actually *doing* something, rather than just letting other people do things to me. I was acting, rather than just reacting. And even if Revibe didn't work and it couldn't fix me, because I was unfixable, even then I was here because this was my choice, and that was worth something.

And it was worth something to be away from home, which had become so lonely. I heard from Emerson in some way or another every day, but she was my only guaranteed interaction with the real world. I messaged with Mackler and Corey occasionally, but for the most part they were preoccupied with their new friends and adventures. And since I wasn't fun anymore, I didn't want to take up too much of their time.

Mom got busy unpacking my suitcases, organizing things, arranging my toothbrush and toothpaste in a little cup, and telling me where she was hanging my laundry bag. It was annoying (like, this room is not that big, you don't need to tell me where you hung the laundry bag, I will look around for one second and see it with my own eyes). But I didn't protest, because I knew that she was nervous, too, and this was just her way of trying to prove that everything was fine. As long as she could keep my socks in pairs and my washcloths folded, she was still in control.

"Mom," I said, and she looked up from the shirts that she was arranging into rainbow order. "It's going to be okay."

She didn't even pause before replying, *"Kina hora."*

I nodded. *Kina hora,* indeed.

16

After Mom and I said our goodbyes, I made my way to the Great Room for orientation. Valerie and Kevin were seated in armchairs, and the other seven of us joined them in a circle. They started out by giving us some background on where we were and what we were going to do—some of which, of course, I already knew from my research on the program.

Valerie and Kevin had started Revibe three years back. They had both worked in start-ups, and when Valerie's dating app, Lovr, sold to AOL for what sounded like an unfathomable amount of money, they "retired" to Malibu, purchasing this massive beach house that we were now all staying in. Kevin took up surfing and cycling, and Valerie read a book a day—"But we felt unfulfilled," Valerie explained. "We wanted to help people, and here we were, with time and resources and no real direction. What came next for us, we wondered?"

Valerie had observed frequent flare-ups of verbal attacks on her app. She described an instance of a white woman claiming the username "JustAChinaDoll" and getting hassled by other users until she quit. She described a man who said he was looking for "skinny chicks only PLEASE," and the community was so enraged that they figured out his real identity, forwarded his profile to his boss, and managed to get him fired. "I could go on and on giving examples of this sort of thing," Valerie said.

"And of course it wasn't only on Lovr," Kevin added. "We were seeing these sorts of showdowns about what is and is not acceptable behavior on the internet, what's offensive and who should have to pay for it, all over the place. It really hit home one day when I myself was publicly shamed." He made eye contact with each of us, as if to let us know that he wasn't going to hang his head low about this; he wasn't ashamed anymore. "My words were taken out of context in a news story about Silicon Valley. I had intended to communicate that I'd never trusted anyone as much as I trusted my first business partner, but it came out sounding as though I had never trusted anyone else I'd ever worked with, which was understandably offensive to them. And that was it; everyone turned their backs on me.

"It was one of the most devastating experiences of my life. Now obviously, I knew that this sort of thing happened to people. I just always assumed that it could never happen to *me*, because *they* must have done something to deserve it. After this experience, it wasn't a *they* versus *me* thing anymore; it was *us*, all of us, this could happen to any of us."

"But Kevin is strong," Valerie said. "He figured out coping

mechanisms. And they worked. We realized that if they worked for him, they could work for others, too. That's why we started Revibe."

Kevin added, "My dad was a serious alcoholic for most of his life. It wasn't until he was in his late fifties that he joined Alcoholics Anonymous, and it saved him. It saved me, too, and my whole family. I'll be grateful to AA forever. So I definitely relied on some of the principles of AA. Then we added in some techniques from other drug and alcohol rehabilitation facilities, and a solid helping of programming from yoga and wellness retreat centers, as well as our own insider understanding of internet culture. Out of the best of all that, we created the Revibe technique. You might be familiar with some aspects of our program, but as a whole, our approach is completely unique."

This made me immediately dislike Kevin, since modifying *unique* is one of my pet peeves—either something *is* unique or it's *not* unique, but "completely unique" is redundant.

Then again, maybe it wasn't fair to dislike a guy I didn't know who had suffered as I had, and who was trying to help me, just because he didn't know that *unique* was an absolute.

"So that's us," Valerie summed up. "Before we get any more into how Revibe works or what's expected of you, we want you each to introduce yourselves to the group. Specifically, please share with the group why you are here. We want to hear your stories. We *need* to hear your stories. Everyone in this room has experienced a life-changing incident of public shaming. I know that can be very difficult to talk about, so I promise we won't make you do it again. But it is important that we do it once, and at the beginning, so we all can truly understand where everyone else is coming from. This is a safe space. Nothing you say will leave this room. So please, tell us your stories."

Jazmyn was sitting next to Valerie, so she went first. She was a year younger than I was and she was from Austin, Texas. She had pink streaks in her hair and a diamond stud in her nose, which she later said she pierced herself, using nothing but a safety pin and alcohol. (Whether the alcohol went onto the safety pin to sterilize it or into her mouth so she wouldn't feel the pain was unclear.)

She was a musician—and later, after hearing her play her guitar, I would add that she was a very talented one. She'd been in a band called the Duckface Vagabonds with her friends. "But it was barely a band," she informed us. "The rest of them didn't practice. I'd call rehearsals and our drummer just wouldn't show up. I'd pour my heart into writing songs—I wrote all of our songs, since no one else was doing it—and at best my bandmates wouldn't contribute anything, and at worst they'd shoot down everything I'd come up with. They were my friends, but they weren't real musicians."

So when another local band, You but Good in Bed, asked her to audition to be their new rhythm guitarist, she jumped at the chance.

Even I knew this was a big deal. I'd heard of You but Good in Bed. They had one pretty big single that was used in a beer commercial. It hadn't made me want to buy beer, but it had made me look up who sang the song. My friends and I thought their name was hilarious and would say things to one another like, "You know who I'm really into these days? You but Good in Bed." Or, "I could totally go in for You but Good in Bed right now."

You but Good in Bed was a band of guys—good-looking guys, in that soulful rock 'n' roll way—who were a couple years older than me. I was impressed that they'd asked Jazmyn to join them.

"I auditioned," she said, "and I got in. So I told the Duckface Vagabonds I was quitting, and I . . . I wasn't super-nice about it. I wasn't trying to be *mean*. But I wanted them to know how much their laziness had frustrated me and that I didn't have to put up with it anymore."

The immediate problem with You but Good in Bed, however, was that they didn't let Jazmyn play in shows right away. She learned all the parts, she rehearsed with them, but she never got up on stage. They told her she was in a "trial period" until she could prove her "loyalty to the band." Impatiently, she asked how exactly she could do that, and they told her that she could do sexual favors for them.

"So I did," Jazmyn said in a whisper.

Valerie reminded Jazmyn that this was a safe space and asked if she would go into detail about what "sexual favors" encompassed. Jazmyn gave her an *Are you out of your mind?* look and shot back, *"No."* She added, "It's embarrassing enough that I did it. That I honestly believed it would get me an equal part in this band. But I *did* believe that. That's what they told me, and I didn't have any reason to question them. And I needed this band to work out for me."

It didn't work out for her.

She quit once she figured out that she was being used and that, no matter how useful a sex object she was, she was never actually going to get to perform with them. She felt like a fool. She couldn't go back to the Duckface Vagabonds after the dramatic and smug way she had left them. She had no band. She had no self-respect.

"And then people started to look at me funny," she said, "and whisper and giggle about me."

I knew what she meant. The looks, the whispers, the giggles. I knew those all too well, even though the idea of a sexual favor was so far removed from my own life as to be absurd.

"Everyone had heard what I'd done," Jazmyn continued, "but they hadn't heard the right story—or at least they hadn't heard the *full* story. The story they had was that I was such a big fangirl of You but Good in Bed that I'd hooked up with all of them just to get closer to them. The story they had was that it was *my* idea, and the band thought it was kind of weird, but I really forced myself upon them. No one believed that I actually was—or thought I was—a member of the band. The story they had was that I was a starfucker and an attention whore and a desperate slut."

They posted those names online. They wrote them on paper and stuck them in her school bag. They muttered them as she walked by. They never said them to her face.

"Did you explain what actually happened?" Valerie asked.

"I tried to. But nobody believed me."

"Nobody?" Valerie asked.

"I guess some people did. But not enough for it to help."

Jazmyn had tried to kill herself. "I couldn't see any way out of it," she said. "Even if somehow, someday, everyone else moves on, I will never forget how incredibly fucking stupid I was."

But she didn't succeed in dying. She got treated in a psychiatric ward and went on antidepressants, and she wasn't suicidal anymore, but she still didn't like herself. And then her parents found out about Revibe. "So they sent me here," Jazmyn concluded. "They sent their idiot, screwed-up, slut daughter here, because they don't know what to do about me, either. They would never say it, obviously, but they probably wish I'd succeeded in killing myself. Everyone looks better once they're gone. At least then my parents could get some sympathy."

Next up was Marco, a handsome man in his forties or fifties with wavy hair, off-puttingly white teeth, and a lilting Southern accent. It did not surprise me to learn that he was a politician. Specifically, he was the mayor of a city in Georgia.

Or he had been.

"I have a beautiful, supportive wife and a wonderful little daughter. There's nothing wrong with them at all. They're perfect. I'm not."

He'd cheated on his wife once, early on in their relationship, with a man who'd fixed his computer. She found out almost immediately and was furious and hurt, and she almost left him right then, except that he swore up and down it was only that one time and it would never happen again. So she stayed with him, and for ten years, he stayed true to his word.

"Then I came across this app," he said, his face turning red. "Called, uh, Thrust."

It was for men who wanted to hook up with other men. Which described Marco perfectly, even though, he was quick to add, he had not for a second believed he would *act* on that want. "We all want things, all the time, that we don't do," he pointed out. "You want another slice of cake, or you want to yell at that driver who cut you off, or you want to sleep an extra hour and blow off your nine a.m. meeting, but you don't do any of that because those are the wrong things to do. And we're not *animals*. We can and should act in our long-term best interests, even if that's not what we feel like doing in the moment."

He signed up for Thrust with every intention of being a lurker. He looked at other men's profiles but never reached out to any of them. "That seemed safe," he said, "to imagine myself making a connection with these men without actually doing it." Some of the other users messaged him, but they were easy to ignore. Until there was one who wasn't.

"He was smart and witty and compassionate," Marco said. "He didn't put any pressure on the situation. He just seemed to enjoy talking to me, and I enjoyed talking to him, too. We wrote back and forth every day. And still I thought, *Well, this isn't betraying my wife. This isn't hurting anybody. This is just a friendship.*"

Eventually their e-mails turned into phone calls, which turned into video calls, which led to them finally meeting in person. And after their first meeting, Marco *did* start cheating on his wife. "I felt guilty," he said, "but I also felt happier and more full of life and hope than I had in years. And I felt guilty about feeling happy, but, well, there you are.

"I never considered divorce. I know my actions make this statement hard to believe, but I loved my wife. I still do. She loved me. We'd built a good life. Raising our daughter together was important to us. Then there were our extended families, who believe that both homosexuality and divorce are sins. Frankly, I agree. I'm a sinner, and I didn't want everyone to know that about me, and I didn't want to drag my family into this pit of sin with me."

And then, of course, there were his constituents. It didn't take a political genius to intuit that most voters don't like politicians who are cheaters, liars, or sinners.

After a couple months of intense happiness, guilt, and fear, Marco broke things off with the man he was seeing. "I did a lot of soul-searching, and I knew it wasn't right to jeopardize my entire family and career and moral code for this." He thought that was the end of all of it.

But then Thrust got hacked. The e-mail addresses for all the users were posted online for the world to see. And Marco had made a critical mistake: he'd used his government e-mail address to create his account.

It took no time for the local news to notice that their mayor was a Thrust user. The fact that he hadn't logged on in four months meant nothing to them. Gleeful articles were written about this by the left-wing media, who had wanted him out of power in the first place. The right-wing media accused him of being a disgrace to the party. Both sides called him untrustworthy, immoral, and power-drunk. His colleagues immediately distanced themselves from him; the city legislators acted as though he didn't exist, except to release damning statements about him.

His wife stuck by him in public, standing behind him in a conservative dress and pearls as he gave an apology speech. In private, though, she cried and cried. She took their daughter and went to stay at her parents' house in the countryside.

"She'd forgiven me that first time," Marco said, "so I guess on some level I'd thought she'd forgive me this time, too. She didn't. Even someone as tolerant as my wife reaches her limit."

He muddled through his job for another few weeks, but when it became clear that he was going to be brought to trial over misuse of government resources, he resigned. His wife and daughter never moved back home. Eighteen months had passed since then, and he had no new job. He'd tried to establish himself as a consultant, but nobody would hire him. "I spent my whole life immersing myself in public policy and working on campaigns and building connections, all so I could succeed in politics. That and my family were the foundation of my life. Now that's all gone. So what do I do?"

I recognized Kisha on sight. She'd been one of the stars of a Disney show called *Sense That!* about a mystery-solving team of kids with ESP. I'd watched it when I was a kid—okay, I kept watching reruns into high school, even though I'd clearly aged out of its target audience. Kisha's character was named Charisma, and her

154

power was getting flashes of insight into the future. I had never in a million years imagined I'd ever be sitting across from a TV star, yet here we were.

Kisha was twenty-one now, and the past couple years had shown her decline into post-child-star infamy. I didn't follow celebrity gossip, but even I knew some of the high points: speeding tickets, candid photos of her dress riding up her thighs at Hollywood parties, minor shoplifting charges, Twitter feuds.

"I don't know why I did any of it," she said, and I was surprised that she still had the bubbly, precocious voice I remembered from *Sense That!* "I didn't have one good reason, like Jazmyn wanting to get into a band. It's just that when the show stopped shooting, I was fifteen years old and had no idea what to do with myself. I had lots of money and lots of fans and no idea how the real world worked. I'd been a full-time actress since I was a kid, and I had no perspective on anything. I hadn't been to real school in years. My first kiss was with a Swedish model who was six years older than me, and it was on-screen. My parents divorced—in large part because of *my* career and *my* needs—and in the divorce proceedings I actually had to hire my own lawyer because neither one of them was looking out for my best interests.

"I'm not trying to make excuses for what I've done," she added. "I'm not trying to blame my parents or the network or anything. I did it. I made my choices. I just wanted to give a little context, I guess. The rest of the *Sense That!* kids came out of it fine, so it's not like being a child actor necessarily screws you up. I guess they're all just naturally more responsible than I am. Or luckier, maybe. Or both.

"A lot of teenagers do the same dumb stuff I did," she went on. "But when I did that dumb stuff, thousands of strangers *cared*."

At first I wasn't sure I agreed with her. I was a teenager, and *I'd* never accidentally flashed my nipple while eating lunch. But, you know, I was a good girl. Emerson had gotten speeding tickets. I'd seen plenty of embarrassing photos of Brianna over the years. Mackler was not above a heated Twitter debate. I understood Kisha's point.

"Parents wrote to me that I should be ashamed of myself, because I'd been such a role model and now they wouldn't even let their kids watch *Sense That!* anymore. What was even worse was when I got notes from kids themselves, telling me that I'd betrayed them, that Charisma never would do the terrible things I was doing.

"I haven't been able to find work for a year now. Not even voice-overs or commercials or modeling. Nobody wants to be associated with me. The last brand that I did a campaign for was Lucky Brand jeans, and they stopped using me after five thousand people signed an online petition saying they wouldn't buy anything from Lucky as long as I was associated with them.

"And as for serious acting—movies, another TV show—forget it. They won't say *why* they're not offering me parts. Just that I'm 'not a good fit.' Even my agent has basically given up on me. The one time he's called me in the past three months was to recommend that I sign up for Revibe."

Part of the shaming, she went on, was related to her race. "There were essays and posts and letters to me and about me saying that I was making black people everywhere look bad. Here I was, a famous young African American, so I had the opportunity to represent my race well to the entire world. And I blew it. I'd confirmed every stereotype—that we're aggressive, irresponsible, criminal—and I'd single-handedly set back the fight for racial equality by, like, fifty years. That's what they said.

"And that made me feel so guilty, obviously. And I desperately wanted them to be wrong. I don't want my dumb choices to reflect on anyone other than me. But it doesn't work that way, and I got plenty of messages saying, 'This is just the sort of antisocial behavior I'd expect from *you people*.'

"So that's why I'm here. I'm not trying to be all poor-little-rich-girl about it, but I really don't have anywhere else to go."

Zeke was barely sixteen, and I tried to tell myself I shouldn't be physically attracted to someone who was both younger than me and possibly even more screwed up than me, but it was hard, because he oozed a confidence that was undeniably sexy. He sat with his legs splayed and his clearly pricey jeans slung low on his hips. I tried not to look at him because he made me uncomfortable, but I also tried not to let on that I wasn't looking at him, because that would also be uncomfortable.

Zeke the Hottie had grown up in an apartment building in Manhattan. Ms. Candela, the gray-haired woman in the apartment below his, loathed him. By the time he was old enough to understand his surroundings and the fact that there were people in the world other than him, she had already sworn a lifelong vendetta against him. "I used to stomp around and jump up and down," he said, "and bang pots and pans and cry at night and, I don't know, kid stuff. It drove her nuts. She'd come upstairs and *scream* at me. I was six and she was sixty, and she'd scream right in my face. When I had some friends over for my thirteenth birthday party, she literally filed a *noise complaint* with the police. The cops showed up and they just found a dozen kids eating pizza and playing Spin the Bottle in the living room. I'm pretty sure that's not what we have a police force for."

As much as Ms. Candela hated Zeke, she loved her cat, Dante. "Dante got deluxe cat food that stunk up the whole building. Dante went on walks around Central Park on a *leash*. I kid you not. One time Dante bit me and I had to get a tetanus shot."

What had been a standard feud between neighbors blew up a few months ago. "I was leaving the house for soccer practice," Zeke said, "when I saw Dante out in the hallway. He'd gotten out of Ms. Candela's apartment—he did that sometimes, probably because he wanted to escape her, that crazy witch. I could have tried to bring him back to her. I could have even just left him there, I guess. But I was so *mad*, and, I don't really know how to explain it, but it was like this *rage* boiled up inside me, and I grabbed him by the nape of the neck and tossed him down the garbage chute."

Zeke went on to soccer practice. He didn't want to be late. But he had trouble focusing on the exercises. Once the rage subsided, he felt kind of worried about Dante. Or, if not worried about Dante himself, Zeke at least felt *guilty*. He got through all of practice, telling himself that cats always landed on their feet and everything was fine. He even went out to the diner with his friends after practice to prove to himself just how fine it was. But he wasn't hungry and wasn't listening to the conversation, and soon he made his excuses and jogged home to look for Dante.

Zeke found Dante in the basement, bloodied and broken, barely conscious. So Zeke picked him up, tucked him in his gym bag, and brought him up to Mrs. Candela's floor. He set the cat down on Mrs. Candela's welcome mat, rang the doorbell, and bolted.

"I thought everything would be fine," he said. "Her dumb cat was alive, and she could take it to the vet and get it fixed. No harm, no foul."

But that was when Zeke's real trouble began. Ms. Candela insisted on reviewing the apartment building's security tapes so she could figure out what had happened to her beloved pet. And the tape clearly showed Zeke picking up the tabby cat, glancing around surreptitiously, and then tossing him.

Ms. Candela didn't know what to do with this tape except be spitting mad, but her nephew was more resourceful: he posted the video online, along with a description about what had happened, how much his aunt loved her cat, and photos of Dante's broken, distorted body lying in Ms. Candela's arms. He started a fund-raising campaign for people who wanted to contribute to Dante's veterinary bills and raised more than ten thousand dollars in less than a day. And he posted Zeke's full name and contact information online, in case anyone wanted to let him know what they thought of him.

As it turned out, hundreds and hundreds of people wanted to let Zeke know what they thought of him. He was a sociopath and a would-be murderer. He was soulless and spoiled rotten. He would grow up to abuse and kill more animals, and, someday soon, people as well. It would be better for the world if he just died now, before he got the chance.

The building management pressured Zeke's family to leave. Zeke's parents owned their apartment and had lived there for twenty years, so at first they refused, but then the management company threatened to sue. Zeke's parents had sent him to Revibe as a last-ditch attempt to keep their home. If he could show that he'd changed, really changed, then maybe they would be able to stay.

"I brought Dante back," Zeke reminded us now. "I could have just left him down there and Ms. Candela never would have found him, but I didn't. I brought him home, and he lived. Why doesn't anyone give me credit for that part?"

I didn't find Zeke that hot anymore. So that was a relief.

"I have a two-and-a-half-year-old daughter, Tabitha, and she's the love of my life," began Richard. "I would do anything for her."

From what I could tell, Richard was in his thirties. His unwrinkled skin and thick hair made him look younger, but his eyes made him look much, much older. "Her mom took off when Tab was a few months old. She had a drug problem. She was clean the whole time she was pregnant, and I guess I thought she'd stay that way for the sake of our baby, but she didn't, or couldn't. That's life, right? Since then, it's just been me and Tab, and I've always told her that no matter what else happens, I'll always be there for her. Daddy's not going anywhere, I told her."

Richard rearranged his work schedule so he could be home

with his daughter as much as possible. He played with her and read to her and took her to the local zoo and playground. He made her baby food from scratch and never let her ride in anyone's car but his own. "I didn't want anyone—least of all her—to think that having just a dad wasn't enough for her. And I wouldn't risk losing her for anything."

One evening Tabitha was playing in the backyard when a tiger loped in from the woods. "I didn't know what it was at the time," he said. "I didn't realize it was a *tiger*, because that didn't make any sense. I heard her scream, so I came running outside—I had only stepped into the house for a minute. And all I saw immediately was this enormous animal—he must have been ten times my daughter's size—and he was coming for my baby."

Richard didn't panic. He swung into action, as though he'd been training for this encounter his entire life. He ran inside, grabbed his shotgun from the gun case, ran back out, and shot the tiger. That was all it took—one shot—and the animal fell down dead. "I'd been doing riflery and hunting since I was a boy," he told us, "and that was hands down the cleanest shot I ever made."

Tabitha, of course, was confused and scared and crying. He bustled her into the house, then called 911 to let them know there was a large animal carcass in his yard. And *that* was when he found out what had happened.

The tiger was named Boxer and had escaped from the nearby zoo—which made sense, as there was no other reason for it to be roaming free. But Boxer wasn't just any tiger (if there is such a thing as "just any tiger"). He was a South China tiger, one of only a couple dozen of his species left in the world. South China tigers were functionally extinct, meaning they lived in zoos, but nowhere in the wild anymore. And now, thanks to Richard, one of these extremely rare and critically endangered beasts was dead.

"The story ran in the local newspaper, and then the animal rights activists came out in force," Richard said. "They called themselves Team Boxer. I don't blame them, exactly. It's true that no one should go around hunting endangered species. But, you know, that's not what I was doing."

The activists threw red paint on his porch, on his car, and even at him on the first day that he tried to return to work. The gun control activists got loudly involved, too. "Why did he own a gun if not to use it?" they demanded. "If he hadn't had the gun in the first place, no one could have gotten shot."

"I own my gun for sport," Richard told us now, "and for self-defense. And that's what this was. I was defending my baby against a wild animal. The critics demanded to know why I didn't grab her and run inside. Why did I shoot the animal instead of shooting a warning shot? I don't know what to tell you except that I wasn't taking any risks with my Tab's life. She needed her daddy to protect her, and that's what I did."

But his protection was short-lived. Team Boxer made the case that he was an unfit parent. He kept guns in a cabinet where they were easily accessible by children. He was violent. He let his daughter play outside in the evening, unsupervised. He was neglectful. His home wasn't safe for a child. If he'd been parenting her the way he should have, he could have just scooped her up and brought her into the house; no tiger should ever have needed to die.

"I know I should have been outside with her," Richard

conceded, shamefaced. "I never stop regretting that I was inside when that animal showed up. But, well, our backyard is really isolated, and it's fenced in, and I could hear everything from inside the house. I figured there was no way anything could happen to my baby without my knowing. And I was only in there for a couple minutes, anyway."

He'd been inside for a couple minutes because he was fixing himself a drink. Yet one more reason, Team Boxer pointed out, why he couldn't be trusted with his daughter.

So social services took Tabitha away. They put her in a foster home after trying and failing to bring home her mother.

"She's been in foster care for the past three months," Richard told us, his eyes welling up. "I can have supervised visits with her, but that's it. She cries every time I have to leave—she doesn't understand.

"So that's why I'm here. I took out a second mortgage on the house and got a loan, and here I am. I need to be rehabilitated. I need to get my daughter back."

The first thing I noticed about Abe was that he used a wheelchair. The second thing I noticed were his eyes, which were wide and crystalline blue. He was a few years older than me and from Westport, Connecticut. "I didn't do anything wrong," he started out, and all of us scoffed, with varying levels of politeness. Because didn't we all *want* to believe that we'd done nothing wrong? Wasn't the point that none of us got to be in charge of deciding whether we had done something wrong?

"I didn't," he insisted. "My father did."

Abe's father, he told us, was Michael Krisch. I recognized that name. Everyone did. Michael Krisch had been a big-deal investment advisor who, it had been revealed a couple years ago, had committed securities fraud and cheated his clients out of billions of dollars. "He'd been running this scheme for my entire life," Abe said, "even before I was born."

Abe had grown up believing his father was one of the greatest businessmen in America, only to learn, at the age of eighteen, that he was a thief of the first order. We all knew that Abe's dad was in jail now. "He's one year into a hundred-year sentence," Abe said bitterly. "I haven't visited him yet, but give me another ninety years and maybe I'll get around to it."

Once the truth about Michael Krisch came out, everyone turned on his family. Abe was deserted by his friends and girlfriend, whose parents had invested (and lost) their life savings with his dad. "My friends' college funds?" Abe said. "Gone. Their parents' retirement savings? Forget it. And that's just the people who I knew personally. My dad handled investments for so many clients and ruined almost all of them. I don't blame anyone for hating him. *I* hate him."

The problem was that they came after Abe, too. Because, while he may not have aided his father, he didn't stop him, either. "I'd been interning for my dad since I was fourteen. He said he wanted me to learn the value of hard work from a young age, which is, in retrospect, a joke. Really what he wanted me to learn was how to get away with cheating people. He had the idea that once I graduated, I'd join him in the family business and we'd become, like, this father-son duo of white-collar criminals. So he hid what he was up to from almost everyone, but he didn't hide it very carefully from me, because in the long run, his plan was to bring me in on all of it. I think on some level he wanted me to appreciate what a mastermind he was."

When the FBI investigation revealed this—that Michael Krisch had been offloading funds into accounts in his son's name, that Abe had known some of the broad strokes of what his father was up to and failed to do anything to stop it—the public attacked him.

"People were angry, and they wanted someone to blame, and I was still there, wandering free and innocent. It just went on and on and on. There's no way to ever escape the legacy my dad left me. So, like Jazmyn, I tried to kill myself. How'd you do it, Jazmyn? You didn't say."

"Pills," Jazmyn replied. "I had to get my stomach pumped."

"I jumped from a sixth-story balcony," Abe said.

They both said it in such a casual way that, for a moment, I couldn't breathe.

"Now I'm paralyzed from the waist down," Abe went on. "I'll never walk again. And some of my old friends feel bad about this— like they shouldn't have pushed me so hard. But people who don't know me? They don't care. I've seen jokes about me online . . . things like, 'Abe Krisch is as bad at offing himself as his father is at making money.'

"This wasn't my crime, but people hate me for it anyway. I'll be paying for it for the rest of my life." Abe gestured to his wheel-chair, as if we might have forgotten. "It's stupid," he concluded.

I told my story last. This wasn't a competition—and if it was, we were all losers—but I was surprised to feel like I wasn't the biggest victim in this group. What I'd gone through was hard, but it wasn't unique. (And it certainly wasn't "completely" unique.) I was even able to make eye contact with each of them as I explained my background as a champion speller, my post, and the fallout. I felt like this was kind of that chance I'd been dreaming of, the chance to speak to an impartial audience and explain why I had done it and what I'd meant. Okay, it wasn't on CNN or NBC. But it was something.

Once I was through, Valerie and Kevin went over some of the key guidelines and principles of Revibe.

"No one is to leave the property without permission," Kevin said. "I promise this isn't as isolating as it might sound: we all leave together every afternoon to do volunteer work, so you will still get to see the outside world! But as a general rule, you need to be focused inward, in a controlled environment with few variables."

"Your phone and e-mail communication will be limited and supervised," Valerie went on. "It's the internet that, in one way or another, landed most of you in trouble in the first place, so you need to take a step away from the internet to solve the problems it's caused."

I didn't disagree—after all, that was why I'd quit all my social media—but the idea that I might not be able to google myself whenever I felt the need made my heart tighten.

"We have signal jammers set up on the property," Valerie explained. "We turn them off for a few hours each evening, and during that time you can make and receive calls and e-mails. But the rest of the time, you simply won't get any reception here. So even if you want to give in to the urge, you won't be able to. If you'd like, you can give us your login credentials so that we can check your e-mail more regularly and let you know right away if something important comes in. I know some of you have children, so it may not always be feasible for you to wait for updates about them."

It was starting to occur to me that I had, perhaps, signed myself up for being a prisoner.

"Even during the internet hours," Kevin added, "you are to use your communication privileges *responsibly*. That means you may not make any statements about your public shaming without first running them past us. Nor may you reveal details of the Revibe technique publicly. Of course, you are *never* to share names or other private information about any other Vibers."

I could do this. Maybe not the bit where I could only google myself once every twenty-four hours—I had no idea how to survive that uncertainty—but the rest of it, I told myself, I could do. I was, after all, a terrific rule follower. And I had promised my mother I'd do everything I could to make this work.

Kevin went on. "There is to be no use of controlled substances of any kind on the property. And it should go without saying that there's to be absolutely no physical involvement with anyone else in the program."

So much for my chances with the handsome animal abuser, then.

"You are all in delicate situations," Kevin continued. "Many of you are emotionally fragile, some of you are underage, you're all away from your homes and families, and your entire focus needs to be on redemption. I assume I don't need to go into any more detail as to why all relationships here are to be strictly collegial."

We shook our heads.

"That's about it for the hard-and-fast rules," Valerie said. "Everything else we just ask you to go into with an open mind and a commitment to getting better.

"The last thing I want to say here is that tonight, telling your stories, is the last time I want to hear any of you explaining why you did what you did, or placing blame on others, or anything else. We've all heard your side of the story now. We all know what you'd like to say in your defense. And now that it's been said, we need to move on from it. If there's one central point for the next five weeks, it's this: *I was wrong*. And the sooner you can say that with conviction, the sooner we will be able to make you right again."

17

It's funny how quickly cliques form in this world. Even at Revibe, where there were only seven of us and we were all screwed up, still some people immediately gravitated toward one another, effectively leaving the rest of us on the outside. I realized this after our meeting. Kevin and Valerie encouraged us to go to bed, saying we had an early and busy day ahead of us tomorrow. Richard, Marco, and Abe all followed their suggestion and headed off to their respective rooms. I went out to the porch to read in the fresh air for a bit, but I found that Kisha, Jazmyn, and Zeke were already out there, huddled in a tight circle that left no room for anyone else to join. Presumably none of them had any preconceived notions about who I was or where I belonged, and I could have marched in there and made myself at home. But also presumably, if they'd wanted my company, they would have invited me to join them in the first place. So I went back inside and to my room, like Valerie and Kevin had said we should.

I did not fall asleep. At this point, I hardly knew how. I pulled out my phone, tried to google myself, and felt a cold sweat seep across my body when, of course, it did not work. I told myself that probably no one had posted anything new about me over the past couple of hours. It was possible, yes. They would have had no good reason to do so, although they didn't *need* a good reason to do so. But, I reminded myself, it was not *probable*. And if anything *had* been posted about me in the past couple hours—if my life had once again been destroyed—well, it would still be there the next time I was able to look, right? If I saw it the instant that it happened, would I really be able to do anything about it? Would that really give me a leg up on stopping it from getting out of control? Okay, yes, maybe, but again, it wasn't *likely* that anything was happening online right now or that I could do anything about it even if it was.

None of this was making me feel better.

I tried to read a book but couldn't focus, tried to write anything but of course drew a blank, tried to watch something on my computer before remembering that that, too, required the internet. There was no way I could do this for the next five weeks. I was going to go crazy.

Once I felt confident that Kisha, Jazmyn, and Zeke would have at last gone to bed themselves, or at least moved indoors, I headed back out to the porch. I was too restless, and this house was too claustrophobic. It was right on the beach, but when you were inside you couldn't hear the surf at all. Every window and door was sealed up tight. All I could hear was the air conditioner.

When I opened the door to the porch, I was surprised and a little annoyed to see a solitary shadowy figure already out there. Whoever it was sat very still, and I considered turning right around and going back to my room again, but then he said "Hey," and I realized that it was Abe, with the wheelchair and the blue eyes. And even though I wanted to be alone, it would be rude to act like I hadn't heard him.

"Hey," I said back, going to sit on the deck chair near him. "What are you doing up?"

"Couldn't sleep," he said. "You?"

"Same."

"Nightmares?" he asked.

I shook my head.

"*I* get nightmares," he volunteered. "Every night. Sometimes I dream that I've let everyone down and I'm running all over, looking for someone I haven't betrayed, but I can't ever find them."

He paused, but I didn't say anything. So he kept going, maybe just to fill the air. "Sometimes I dream about the accident. I dream I'm jumping and then I'm falling, and when I hit the ground, I wake up. And then I can't fall back asleep. So I thought I'd come outside for a bit, try to clear my head."

That was heavy stuff from a person I'd just met, but there was something about the nighttime that made heavy stuff feel natural. I didn't want him to feel like he had to keep talking, keep revealing himself to the air, so I ventured, "I have nightmares, too, sometimes, but mostly my problem is that I'm afraid I'll miss something important if I'm sleeping."

"Do you think anyone here is able to get a good night's sleep?" Abe asked. "Or do you think every one of us is afraid of what might happen when we close our eyes?"

I imagined this, the house full of people who were trapped awake, and alone. "I bet Kevin and Valerie can sleep just fine," I said at last.

He gave a little laugh. "Sure. And maybe Zeke, too. Zeke seems like he might actually be a psychopath."

"You think?"

"I guess that was rude," Abe said. "Zeke could be a really good guy who just happens to like torturing animals."

"Couldn't we *all* be psychopaths?" I asked.

"Maybe. I think Zeke's different, though. He really doesn't seem to think that he did anything wrong."

"Neither do you," I pointed out.

"Oh yeah. That's true. I guess I could be a psychopath, too."

"Nah," I said. "Unlike Zeke, you actually *didn't* do anything wrong."

"Thank you," Abe said. "Because sometimes I wonder. When everyone else tells you that you're guilty, and you're the only one who doesn't agree, you start to ask yourself if you're actually the delusional one."

"I don't think you belong here at all," I told him. "I don't see what you did that you need to repent for. So what if you knew some of what your dad was up to? You were a teenager, and he was one of the most successful investment bankers in the world. And he was your *father*. What were you supposed to do?"

"I could have turned him in," Abe said, sounding disgusted. "I didn't actively do anything wrong. But I didn't do anything right, either."

"You can't be held responsible," I replied.

"You're clearly saying that as someone who didn't lose all her money to Michael Krisch," Abe said, "and that means you're biased. But really, thank you."

"I'm hardly an expert on morality," I said, "so I wouldn't put too much stock in my opinions on guilt and innocence."

The sea breeze lifted my hair, and I tied it back with a hair elastic from my wrist. It was a nice night for sitting outside. It was too late, but it was nice.

"So what were you like before?" Abe asked abruptly.

"Before?" I repeated.

"Yeah. Before your scandal."

"Oh." I pulled my knees into my chest and looked out across the beach, toward where I knew the water was, even though I couldn't see it. In the daytime, I might not have answered him, but in the cloak of night I felt safer. "I was . . . I don't know. How do you sum yourself up? I wrote a lot. I wanted to be a writer when I grew up. Stupid, I know, but I didn't realize that at the time. When I was younger, I won the National Spelling Bee."

"You mentioned that earlier," Abe reminded me.

"Well, it was a pretty defining moment in my life. I went to this small Jewish day school at the time. Then I went to a public high school, which was kind of a shock after spending years with the same twenty-three kids in my entire grade. I was like, *Oh, this is* high school, *like straight out of a movie set.* I graduated in June and was supposed to start at Kenyon in the fall."

"Ah," Abe said knowingly. "The college dream."

"The college dream was my *whole* dream. I don't even know what other dreams look like." I sighed. "Did you make it to college?"

"I went to UConn for two months. Then this happened." He gestured to his legs. "I didn't go back."

"I'm sorry," I said.

He shrugged. "Never mind. Go on. You were telling me your deal."

"Oh, that was about it, I think. In general, I don't know, I was a pretty good girl. I followed the rules, I didn't get in trouble. I guess I wasn't leading an extremely exciting teenage life. I wasn't really popular—not like my older sister—but I wasn't *un*popular, either. I had my group of friends who I hung out with, and that was enough for me. We had fun together. We were always making little movies, or working on some ridiculous scheme that would ultimately go nowhere, or just watching YouTube and playing video games and making fun of things. Normal stuff."

"You had a boyfriend?"

I shook my head.

"Girlfriend?"

"It would have been a boyfriend, but in practice it wasn't anybody."

"Why not?" he asked. "No one in your league?"

I snorted. "Very funny. No, I'm just not the dating type."

"What type of person is 'the dating type'?"

I didn't know how to answer that. People who didn't worry so much about getting into trouble—*those* were the dating type. I thought about how Jason would sometimes sneak home after his curfew. I remembered Emerson's friend Brianna recounting a time when she was shirtless with her girlfriend in the backseat of a car and a cop came up to the window with a flashlight. She laughed when she told that story, but I thought that I'd rather die than get caught half-naked by a police officer, or anyone.

I'd had the chance for my first kiss at the National Spelling Bee, with Janak Bassi, the boy who would years later go on to claim the victory that was rightfully mine. In my everyday middle-school life, no one was jockeying to make out with me, but at the Bee, being one of the best spellers meant that I was also one of the most popular and sought-after people. (The social structures of spelling bees do not translate to the real world.) Janak told me he wanted to kiss me. He told me to sneak out of my hotel room and meet him at the vending machine at eleven o'clock.

Instead, I stayed in bed and chain-locked my door, taking every precaution I could to make sure I did not go to that vending machine. Janak never spoke to me after that, except to let me—and everyone within earshot—know that I made an "ugly face" when I spelled. I'd ultimately had my first kiss a year and a half later at a school dance, where it was not against the rules to kiss someone in the middle of the gym.

It killed me now, how much effort I'd put into always staying out of trouble, always doing the right thing, always making the good choice. You can do that a hundred times, a thousand times, every time but once—and that once is the only time anyone cares about.

I shrugged. "What did *you* used to be like?" I asked Abe. "Before your scandal."

"I was a spoiled brat," he said.

I gave a laugh of surprise. "That's not typically how people describe themselves."

"Well, I'm not going to sugarcoat it. I did a lot of stuff that makes me cringe now, I think because I knew I could get away with it."

"Like what?" I couldn't help asking.

Abe looked like he regretted bringing it up. "You know, like taking out my parents' car at night before I even had my permit, partying too hard on school nights, getting into trouble just so I could get myself out of it . . . that sort of thing."

" 'That sort of thing'?" I repeated with a laugh.

He shrugged. "I wasn't exactly familiar with the word *no*. But I wasn't *all* bad. I used to sing in an a cappella group. I traveled a lot. My mom's family is from France, so I'd go out there every summer to visit them. I liked being outside. I did a lot of hiking, skiing, sailing, rock climbing, skateboarding, whatever . . . I thought I was a daredevil at the time, though I wasn't really. It's easy to be daring when nothing bad has ever happened to you. Once life got hard, it turned out I wasn't so brave after all."

"I think it's brave," I said softly, "to jump." I would never have the guts to climb to the top of a building and throw myself off it. The very thought made me shiver.

He ran his hand over the arm of his wheelchair, as if reminding himself that it was still there. "It's not," he said simply. "Living is brave. Quitting is cowardly."

I rested my head against the back of my chair and looked up at the night sky. I felt almost, if it was possible, like I might fall asleep.

"Did you ever think about it?" Abe asked.

"Quitting?"

"Yeah."

I rolled my head away from the stars to look at him. "You know, usually people don't ask me if I've thought about killing myself until we've known each other for at least a week."

"These aren't usual times, Winter," he said, "and we are no longer usual people."

I sighed. "Of course I've thought about it. I'm not made of stone. You can't receive a message telling you the world would be better off without you without wondering if that's true, and I haven't gotten *one* e-mail like that; I've gotten hundreds.

"Everything I've worked for in my life has been taken away from me. I'm a burden on my family. I have no idea what I'm going to do from here—how I could ever get into college, or get a job, or make a new friend, how I can move on with my life. I don't know who I *am* anymore. I can't escape from the awareness that everything we do is like an incredibly delicate glass sculpture that can be knocked over by the slightest breeze and can never be pieced back together—and you have no way of predicting when that breeze will come. Of *course* I've thought about it."

I would never in a million years say that to my friends or family. They would panic. The only thing that could make my mom more stressed out about me would be if she also thought she was responsible for keeping me alive. I wasn't telling Abe because I trusted him more than anyone at home, or because I liked him more. I didn't even know him. I was telling him just because he knew what I meant.

"But you didn't do it," he said.

"No."

"Because you didn't want to end up like me?"

"Because I didn't want them all to be right. Think about it: if I died, that would be the end of my story. I'd always be remembered as the preternaturally good speller who turned out to be a racist bitch, the end."

"If I'd died," Abe said, "I'd always be the spoiled brat who helped his dad steal billions."

"Then it's a good thing you didn't die," I commented.

"That's the nicest thing anyone has said to me in a while," Abe observed.

"Well," I reminded him, "I do have a way with words."

18

The next morning began our first full day at Revibe, but it turned out to be essentially the same as the day after it and the day after that. Revibe, I quickly learned, was relentlessly the same. "Structure," Valerie told us on day one, "is the key to staying on the right course." The idea, as I understood it, was that we were all by nature people who made terrible choices. But if we were given a safe schedule from which we did not deviate, with every choice already made for us, then we would have far less room for error.

Our structure was based around "the Three Res"—pronounced *rees*, so as to rhyme with *three*. The Res were, in daily chronological order, Rehabilitation, Redemption, and Repentance. Together, they formed the backbone of Revibe.

Every morning started with Rehabilitation, which meant a seven a.m. yoga class. To be clear, this required waking up *before* seven. Every morning. Even though I had trouble falling asleep much before three.

Our yoga instructor was a sprightly young woman who referred to the body's "core" every other sentence and refused to breathe silently or even quietly. "Your breath is your gift to the world!" she hollered at us. "Use it! Use your breath! Fill your lungs with *air*!" She had more different ways of expressing the sentiment "breathe" than I'd ever known was possible. As a word person, I was impressed, but as a non–morning person, I wanted to hit her.

I felt awkward in yoga at first, especially compared to Jazmyn and Kisha, who were both skinny and flexible and casually sporting performance-grade workout clothes. Eventually I figured out that no one was watching me, but considering how bad I was at keeping the different warrior poses straight, they probably should have been.

Abe was thrilled to announce that he was physically incapable of doing yoga and looked murderous when the teacher told him that she could easily modify the poses so that he could participate from his wheelchair. "You can breathe, can't you?" she said matter-of-factly. "As long as you can focus on your breath, you can do yoga."

Abe seemed to want to argue with that but, short of holding his breath, couldn't find a way.

After yoga was breakfast time. The kitchen was stocked with more fresh fruit than the seven of us could ever hope to eat—not only strawberries and apples, but also papayas and loquats and other things that had been picked off nearby trees and transported to Revibe by bicycle. "Revibe is a carbon-neutral center," Valerie told us. "If food can't be harvested within biking distance of where we are, we shouldn't be eating it."

Mealtimes were the thing that seemed to really freak out Richard. "Where's the *food*, though?" he kept asking, looking around wild-eyed.

"There's yogurt," Kisha pointed out.

"Yogurt?" he yelped. "Just yogurt?"

"You can put fruit on it," Kisha told him patiently, as if speaking to a child.

"And flaxseed," Valerie added.

"Flaxseed?" he cried.

I wasn't thrilled by the breakfast options, either, but I felt extremely mature about the fact that I wasn't the one having a panic attack about it.

After breakfast, it was time for the next part of Rehabilitation: morning prayer. This seemed to come naturally to Marco, Richard, and Kisha, but it creeped out the rest of us.

"I'm not religious," Zeke whined. "I don't belong to any religion at all, so I can't pray."

Obviously, I had some experience with prayer. But it definitely wasn't something that I, or anyone I knew, did every day. It reminded me of being back at day school.

At Revibe, though, praying was not optional, and that was weird; weirder still was the fact that they really did not seem to care what kind of prayer we were each doing, to what kind of god, if any. There was a wide selection of prayer books from various faiths, and we could each take whichever one we wanted and pray silently to ourselves—or, in the case of Zeke, just sit still and meditate.

This was so far off not only from my religious practices but even from how Judaism was supposed to work that I could not for the life of me understand it. "Why do we have to do this?" I asked Valerie.

"Why do you think?" she asked the group.

Marco replied instantly, "Because putting your faith in God will make you a better person."

"Because people are more likely to forgive you if you show them that you're trying to get forgiveness from God," Jazmyn said dully.

"Both excellent points," Valerie said, sounding pleased with the progress we had already made.

After morning prayer, we went out into the world for Redemption. This was Revibe-speak for charity, basically. Valerie would collect all our phones so we couldn't be tempted by the internet while we were off the premises, and then Kevin would drive us to someplace where we could do good deeds and improve the world, and ourselves. (Kevin's words, not mine.) One day we were sent to a senior center and kept the retirees company for a few hours. This didn't go super-well, as one of the retirees in question had lost her life savings through Abe's father, and when she learned who he was, she spat on him. Literally spat. One day we went to a children's hospital, which went better, since the kids were too young to know who any of us were.

After finishing Redemption for the day, we'd have a dinner of kale and quinoa and other things that Richard didn't believe were real food products, and then we had to do Repentance for a couple of hours before bedtime.

As embarrassing as I found the yoga, and as distasteful as I found the yogurt-based meals, and as weird as I found morning prayer, and as awkward as I found Redemption, Repentance was the hardest, because it was all about writing. We were supposed to write two things every day. One was a journal in which we were to describe all the positive things we were doing to rebuild our lives. Like: "I'm really finding myself through prayer. I'm so much more in touch with my body after doing yoga every day. Today I volunteered at a nursing home and now I understand on a deeper level how much wisdom the elderly have to share."

It all sounded so fake, but, "It's what you *should* be thinking," Valerie told us. "You have to believe your own narrative of your life if you want anyone else to believe it."

The other thing we were supposed to write was apologies. Endless apologies. We were supposed to reach out to every person we had hurt, every person who was in any way angry with us, and tell them that we were sorry.

"Do you really mean *everyone*?" I asked.

"Yes."

"Every single person who posted on the Surprise I Can Spell site? Every one of those thousands of people who posted that I was a disgusting, entitled, elitist, clueless bitch?"

"Every one of them."

"But it's not possible," I said. "There are too many of them. It's a task that will never be done."

"The point isn't to finish it," Valerie said. "The point is to start it."

"Why can't I just write one big apology to everyone?" Zeke

asked. "I can post it online, and anyone who wants to see it will see it, and then I'll be done with it."

"Did any of you try that?" Valerie asked.

Most of us nodded.

"It didn't work, I take it," Kevin said. "If it had worked, you wouldn't be here. So what do you think went wrong?"

"People had already made up their minds about me," I said. "It didn't matter what I wrote in an apology. I was never going to convince them."

Most of the group nodded in agreement. "They needed someone to blame," Abe added. "Something bad had happened to them, and I couldn't convince them not to blame me unless I could give them someone else to hate in my place."

"I don't think that's all it is," Valerie said gently. "I've read your apology, Winter. I've read the apologies that all of you delivered—Marco, I've watched your speech, and Richard, I've seen the interviews you gave.

"Here's why they didn't work: because none of you were really apologizing. Or, I should say, you weren't *just* apologizing. You were also explaining and defending yourselves. You were saying, 'I'm sorry, but I didn't mean to do it, and it's not my fault, and it's not as bad as you think it is.'

"The public doesn't hear that as an apology. They hear it as an *excuse*. The apologies you give need to show that you accept full responsibility. You understand why they're mad at you. You don't think that they're overreacting at all. You're grateful to them for pointing out how flawed you are. You're sorry for hurting them. Signed, sealed, delivered. On to the next one."

"But—" we all said, pretty much at the same time.

"Let me guess," Kevin said. "You *don't* accept full responsibility, do you?"

"Well, no," Jazmyn said. "Because You but Good in Bed actually did—"

"And it wasn't me, it was my dad who—" Abe said.

"And I was trying to save the life of my *child*," Richard said.

Kevin was unimpressed. "None of that matters," he told us. "Maybe it matters to you, and maybe it will matter in your final judgment before God, but to the public, that is always going to sound like you trying to wriggle out of the blame you deserve. The sooner you stop thinking about all those *but*s, the sooner you can start apologizing wholeheartedly, without holding anything back. And it's only then that your apologies will start to work. Trust me; I know this from my own experiences, when I was in your shoes. As Valerie said, that's the starting principle for all of this: *I was wrong*."

"So, what," Abe said, arching his eyebrows, "I'm supposed to write to people who I've never met, whose money my dad stole, and tell them, 'I'm so sorry I did this to you, you're right to hate me, I take full responsibility,' even though actually *it wasn't my fault*?"

"Yes," Valerie said. "That is what you're supposed to do."

"I can't do that," I murmured.

"Well, you don't *have* to," Kevin said. "Nobody's going to force you. If you leave here and you haven't written a single apology, you're not going to get an F in Repentance. You also won't have made any progress. But that is your choice."

I couldn't imagine any of it. I couldn't imagine writing these apologies and not meaning them. I couldn't imagine writing these apologies and believing that they were true. More than anything, I couldn't imagine going home in five weeks and telling my parents that I'd wasted so much of my money coming here, and then I had done nothing and changed nothing.

Was I wrong to have handed myself over to Revibe? Was it so expensive and hard and generally unpleasant that I never should have bothered? Or did all of that mean it was working? And how would I know?

During Repentance, we also had one-on-one coaching sessions with Kevin or Valerie, where they would review our journals and apology letters to make sure we were on-message. Then we got a little snack, a little free time, and after that it was bedtime. We started the whole process again the next day.

The one good thing about Repentance was that this was when they lifted the signal jammer and we could actually get internet access for a couple of hours. We were supposed to use it just to send out our apologies and keep in touch with friends and family, but of course I also used the time to google myself. I searched for the other Vibers, too. I spent hours reading criticisms of them.

"Does this slut legitimately just not understand how the world works?" someone had said about Jazmyn.

"i'd throw *him* down a garbage chute and leave *him* there to die," someone said about Zeke.

"I shudder to imagine what else that poor girl had to go through (sexual abuse???), living alone with a man like that," someone said about Richard and his daughter.

"This is exactly what happens when we let blacks get too famous," someone said about Kisha.

"Tale as old as time here: jews love their money!!" someone said about Abe.

"how can THIS guy be at the center of a sex scandal? i wouldn't fuck him even if i was blindfolded lol," someone said about Marco.

I thought about the broken individuals I had met here and how far off they were from their descriptions online. *These commenters don't know what they're talking about,* I thought.

Once I'd read about the other Vibers' stories, I expanded my search into other people having this experience. The more I looked, the more of us I found. The white filmmaker who had made a racially insensitive movie about American Indians. The schoolteacher who wouldn't let the boys in her class use glitter in their art projects because, she told them, "Glitter is for girls." The comedian who made a rape joke and then, when called out on it, replied by saying, "Looks like I'm the only one with a sense of humor." So many detestable people—or maybe normal people who had done detestable things; who could say? I judged them—but was I one of them? If so, then there were hundreds or thousands of us out there. There were always more.

Surely some of these people really *were* bad people. Maybe none of us here, or nobody I'd read about, but people like the white supremacist group that had come out in support of my post. Such bad guys existed in this world. But when the internet responded to every one of us with the same level of judgment and punishment, then it was impossible to distinguish between who really was or wasn't a true villain. When everything's a ten, then there's no point to having a scale. I felt like I was experiencing outrage fatigue from reading about all these moral criminals.

I knew I should use this time to write my apologies, like I was supposed to do. But whenever I tried, my fingers seized up and my brain bowed out and I couldn't get comfortable in my chair and my laptop was too hot and the screen was reflecting too much glare and I needed a glass of water and I could spend the rest of my life here and never be able to move forward.

That's how Richard found me on the fifth evening, as I sat out on the porch, very clearly not writing a thing. "Glad to see I'm not the only one having trouble with Repentance," he commented.

"It's hard," I agreed.

"I'm no good at writing," he said, sitting down across from me. "I never was. I got a technical degree so I would never have another writing assignment. And now here I am." He laughed with a touch of embarrassment, then added, "I'm not stupid."

"Of course not," I said with surprise, wondering why a grown-up would feel the need to defend himself to me.

"You said you won a national spelling competition. You must be pretty smart."

I shrugged.

"Would you help me with my Repentance letters?" he blurted out. "I have my coaching session with Kevin in half an hour, and I've got nothing to show."

I sat up straighter. "I can try, I guess."

He showed me a piece of paper he'd scribbled on. His handwriting was atrocious—like Jason's, only worse—so I asked, "Can you read it aloud to me?"

"Um. It says, 'I'm sorry about the tiger.'" There was a moment of silence. "I told you, I'm not very good at this sort of thing."

"Who is this going to?" I asked.

"This lady, Robin, who runs Wildlife Watch. It's a nonprofit. She made a YouTube video about Boxer, using footage of him as a cub, and then the photo of him lying dead in my yard . . . She set it to Celine Dion's 'My Heart Will Go On,' and then at the end she came on crying and talking about how her mother used to love visiting the tigers at the zoo, and one of the things she's looking forward to about being a parent is getting to introduce her own kids to the tiger viewing area."

"Wow," I said, "that is dramatic."

"I thought she'd be a good person to apologize to, but I don't know how."

"Why don't you say something like . . . Dear Robin, My heart broke watching your moving tribute to Boxer. I am so sorry that I hurt him—and you, by extension. Both you and your mother sound like such kind and sincere individuals, and hearing your story has taught me so much about kindness. I feel terrible and wish I could erase everything—"

"Hold up," Richard said. "This is really good stuff, but I can't write that fast. What did you say after 'you by extension'?"

"I said, um . . . 'Both you and your mother'—"

"Could you just write it?" he asked, thrusting the pen and paper at me.

I froze momentarily. But this was okay, I told myself. This would be a letter from Richard. Even if it was all terrible and all wrong, at least my name wouldn't be attached to it. At least no one would ever know that I was the one who said it.

So I wrote down the sentences I'd recited to Richard, giving them a few embellishments as I went. I couldn't imagine he believed in it. I didn't think he would want to erase everything he'd done, not if it meant leaving his daughter in harm's way. I didn't believe in it, either. I had no way of knowing if Robin and her mom sounded like kind and sincere individuals or like melodramatic Celine Dion fangirls.

But I didn't have to mean it. After all, nobody knew I had anything to do with it. And if Revibe's method was to be trusted, Richard didn't have to mean it, either. All that mattered was that he send it.

I couldn't make myself do any Repentance of my own. I stumbled through my coaching session that night: I opened up my e-mail account on Kevin's computer, and together we looked at Jason's comment on that Reddit post and talked about what I could say to him and how. But even with all of Kevin's coaching, I couldn't bring myself to write a word, and our session ended the same as always, half an hour later with nothing concrete to show for it.

Still, as I wound down the night with a pre-bed snack of a fig bar and a glass of almond milk, I felt good that I'd written today, even though—or maybe especially because—it had nothing at all to do with me.

19

"I've got something here for you," Kevin said to Richard the next morning as we were all getting into the van to head to Redemption. He handed Richard a printout, and as Richard read it, a wide smile spread across his face. It was, I thought, the first time I'd ever seen him smiling.

"It worked!" Richard exclaimed. "My apology worked." He held up the sheet of paper. "This is an e-mail back from Robin, and . . . she said *thank you* for my apology, and that it could never bring Boxer back to life, but it meant a lot to her to hear that I cared."

"Nice going, buddy," Kevin said, and he gave Richard a high five.

Everyone else murmured with a mix of admiration and skepticism.

"It doesn't exactly *fix* it though, does it?" Abe ventured. "I mean, the tiger is still dead. Tabitha is still in foster care. I don't want to be negative, but this woman isn't exactly in charge of forgiveness, right?"

He made a good point, but Richard refused to let his good mood be dragged down. "Think about it," he argued. "If I can get *her* to forgive me, then I could get other people to forgive me, too. This means that it's not impossible."

And I understood what Richard meant. No, it didn't fix everything. But it counted for something. If you can convince one person that you're not a monster, then maybe you can start to convince yourself, too.

Redemption that day took place at a sanctuary for rescued horses. We were supposed to feed them and muck out their stalls. I'd never been a big horse girl, so this wasn't particularly thrilling for me, but I remembered when my sister had gone through a powerful horse phase and thought that even now, years later, she'd probably be jealous of me.

Or maybe not. It wasn't like we were actually bonding with the horses, as per Emerson's girlhood fantasy. Mostly we were just bonding with piles of their poop.

Someone spoke my name from outside the stall I was shoveling. I brushed a sweaty hair out of my face and turned to see Kisha, looking like she'd spent the past two hours sipping an iced latte on Rodeo Drive.

"Hey, Winter," she said, stepping into my stall. "I love your shirt."

I was wearing an unremarkable striped T-shirt. There was nothing to love about it, and Kisha was a TV star, so I'd have expected her to have better taste. Then I realized that this was one of those *I am not your enemy* lines.

I was surprised that Kisha would even bother to identify herself to me as a not-enemy. She hadn't spoken to me directly since we'd arrived at Revibe—which I did not hold against her, since she was prettier, skinnier, more mature, and more successful than me. (This isn't just me being hard on myself. Those are simply facts. I'm okay with being less than a professional actress in all those fields.) She reserved her socializing for Jazmyn and Zeke. They always sat together at mealtimes and in the van heading to Redemption, and often at night I'd walk past one of their closed bedroom doors and hear the three of them talking and giggling in there.

Also, the reason I was at Revibe was that the public thought I was a racist. And for all I knew, Kisha thought the same.

"Thanks," I said to her, trying to figure out a return compliment to communicate back to her *I am also not your enemy*. "I love your . . . shoes."

Shoes was a bad choice. We'd known we were going to be wading through hay, mud, and shit today, so we'd all worn broken-in sneakers or hiking boots. I am terrible at being a girl.

Still, Kisha said, "Thanks." Then she added, "So, listen. I heard you wrote Richard's apology for him."

I didn't confirm or deny it, but my heart started beating faster. Was that against the rules? Was it *wrong*?

This is why you should never write anything. You will always pay for it.

"I was wondering," Kisha went on, "if you could help write my apologies, too."

I didn't know what to say, and she seemed to take my silence as a cue to compliment me more. "You did such a good job with Richard's," she explained, "and it was so inspiring to hear him talk about how it felt to be forgiven today. I'm sure you're super-busy, but . . ."

"No, it's fine," I said. "I'd be happy to help." I was flattered, in fact, that Kisha would ask me.

"Okay, great." Kisha arranged herself on a bale of hay and pulled out a little notebook. "So, let's do one for this blogger Akilah—"

"Now?" I asked. I was still holding my shovel. "Why not wait until Repentance time tonight?"

"Because I don't want them to know that you're helping me, so we should do it now, while they're busy," she replied. "And anyway, I don't feel like doing any more manual labor."

I didn't, either. I just hadn't realized it was optional. This is the thing about being a good girl. If someone tells you that you're supposed to do something, you do it; it doesn't seem optional. I didn't want to be all prissy and goody-goody about it, so I asked in what I hoped was a casual and not condemning tone, "Don't we have to do Redemption? Like, it's one of the Three Res?"

"The important thing isn't that we *do* it," Kisha explained to me. "*Doing* it doesn't make anyone start to like us any more, except for maybe the horses. The important thing is that we can *say* we did it. And I've done it enough today that I can tell people I cared for rescued horses and therefore I now see how fragile life is."

"Oh," I said. "Okay."

"So anyway, this blogger," Kisha went on, tucking her legs up under her. "She wrote this long essay last year that was picked up everywhere. She said that I was desperate for attention, so when *Sense That!* ended and I wasn't a big deal anymore, I couldn't handle it and was doing everything in my power to get the spotlight back on me. So no one should pay any attention to me, because that would only encourage me. So she was writing this essay and would reply to all the comments on it, but that was the last she was ever going to give me. Because she said I'm not as interesting as I think I am—even though she doesn't have any clue how interesting I think I am, but whatever. Oh, and she also said that I refused to admit that I was black. That I thought I was 'better' than other black girls because I was on TV, and that part of my issue was that I couldn't handle just being treated like any other person of color, because I'd been coddled by Hollywood for too long."

"And you want to *apologize* to her?" I asked in disbelief. "Shouldn't *she* be apologizing to *you*? What do you even have to apologize for?"

Kisha shrugged. "For being myself. For not living my life the way she thinks I should. Whatever. It's not that I want to *apologize* to her. It's that I want her to like me. Or at least not hate me. So, can you help, please? Like you did for Richard?"

I blew out a long breath, kicked aside some hay, and pulled off my work gloves. "Yeah," I said. "I think you should say something that makes her think she's totally right, like she got your psychology *exactly*, even though—"

"Can you just write it?" Kisha asked impatiently, holding out her notebook.

Oh, right, of course. That kind of help.

She sat on the bale of hay, humming to herself, while I scrawled,

Dear Akilah, I'm so sorry for what I've done. I feel terrible about how my poor choices hurt you and others. There's no excuse for my actions, and I wish I could go back in time and change all of them—but since I can't, I'm just trying my hardest to be better from now on. Thank you for helping me see the error in my ways and for hearing my apology.

"Perfect," Kisha declared once she'd read it over. "'I feel terrible about how my poor choices hurt you and others'—that's hilarious. What a self-righteous bitch. I didn't *hurt* her. She is completely fine. Don't get me wrong, I definitely screwed up. I definitely would change all my choices, if I could. But I promise, Akilah what's-her-face is *not* the victim."

"Do you want to delete that line?" I asked.

Kisha gave me a sweet smile. It was so funny, having a one-on-one conversation with this person I used to see on TV. I recognized her smile from years ago, and that was weird. "We don't need to delete anything," she replied. "Like I said, it's perfect."

And nimbly she hopped off the bale of hay and sashayed back out.

I put my gloves back on and, as I returned to shoveling shit, I allowed myself a small smile of my own. First Richard, and now Kisha. There were people who believed that I could write. There were people who thought my writing could actually help them. Of course, they were only two against an infinite chorus of detractors. And probably they were wrong. But it felt good to let myself imagine, if only for a minute, that they might know what they were talking about.

20

I called Emerson that evening during the small window of time when the signal jammers were taken down, because I thought she'd enjoy hearing about the horses. Again, it's not like I'd had some intense *National Velvet* communing-with-animals sort of experience, but I did get to feed a carrot to a horse at the end of the afternoon, and I got to pet his velvety nose, and he huffed warm breath onto my hand, and all of that was basically eleven-year-old Emerson's life dream.

But my sister was in a bad mood when I reached her. Rehearsals for the fall musical were not going well. She had a small role, again, and she couldn't really bring herself to care about the show.

"If you had a better role, would you care about it more?" I asked.

"Maybe," she said.

Emerson had always told me it was critical for *everyone* involved in a show to take it seriously. It didn't matter if you were the lead or if you were in the back row of the chorus, she said; the show belonged equally to everyone, and it was in everyone's power, as a collective, to make it succeed or fall apart. Actors who didn't take a show seriously just because they had a bit part were not *real* actors; Emerson had been clear about that for years.

But, of course, whenever she said that, she had been one of the stars.

"You're still only a sophomore," I pointed out to her. "You're a sophomore at one of the best musical theater programs in the country. The bigger roles always go to upperclassmen, you know that. It's not fair, but that's how it is. It'll be different next year."

"The people in my program are *really* talented," she told me.

"I know," I said. "So are you."

She heaved a huge sigh, like I was missing the point. I didn't say anything for a long minute, and then finally she said, "Maybe I'm not as talented as they are."

"One, I doubt that's true," I said. "Two, even if it *is* true, then you'll just work extra-hard and you'll get even better. If anyone can do it, it's you."

"God, Winter, *stop*. I'm not looking for a pep talk."

"Look, I get that you're in a pissy mood," I said, "but you don't have to take it out on me. I'm not giving you a pep talk because that's what I think you're *looking* for. I'm telling you the truth."

"See, this is the problem!" Emerson all but shouted. "You make this so hard. You all make this so hard."

"Who's 'you all'?" I demanded. "And what do we make so hard?"

"I'm *not* that talented. Okay? Can you just listen to the truth?

I am a very good actress. I was better than anyone at Berkeley High. But Berkeley High is not the world, and in the rest of the world, there are people better than me. Not a million people, but *enough* people. And could I be one of the best if I worked *even harder*? Maybe. I don't know.

"But I do know that I don't *want* to work even harder. I'm tired of working so hard, and it doesn't actually seem worth it anymore. It was worth it when it was easy. If it's going to take this much effort, then I don't think it's worth it to me."

"Since when?" I asked. I had trouble believing that she meant any of this. I'd never known my sister to shy away from a challenge. She wasn't dissuaded from going after things that she wanted just because they were hard to get. If anything, that made her go after them with more energy and focus.

"Since I first started college, basically," she said.

"This is what you were talking about at the bonfire," I realized.

An awkward pause. "I didn't think you'd remember that," she said.

"*I* wasn't drunk. *I* remember it perfectly. I didn't think *you* remembered it. Or meant it."

"I don't a hundred percent remember it," Emerson admitted. "But I did mean it. I don't . . . Look, I don't want to be a professional actress anymore."

It really didn't compute. It all seemed like some terrific gag. "What *do* you want to do, then?" I asked reasonably.

"This is what I'm saying!" she cried. "I don't *know* what I want to do. I have no fucking clue. Just not this anymore. But I can't tell anyone. I can't tell my friends here, because then I'm not one of them anymore, I don't care about what they care about, I'm a traitor, essentially. I can't tell most of the people from home, not my old director because she wanted so badly for me to succeed, and not the other theater kids because they wanted so badly for me to fail. I can't tell Mom and Dad because they did so much for so many years to get me here. I can't even tell *you* because you already have this idea about me and who I'm supposed to be, and it's like you can't even hear me when I tell you that *that's not me anymore.*"

"I'm sorry," I said. "I wasn't trying to judge you. I'm just . . . surprised." But maybe I shouldn't even have been surprised, because wasn't this exactly what she had tried to tell me months ago?

"I'm sorry it sounds like I'm mad at you," she said. "I'm just really frustrated. I don't know what to do. At the end of last year, I honestly thought that I wouldn't come back this year. That was my plan. I spent most of that incredibly long car trip from Oklahoma to California practicing how I was going to tell Mom and Dad thank you for supporting my acting career, but now I need to take a semester or two off while I figure out what I want to do with myself."

And then she had pulled into our driveway and walked inside to a changed family.

"So when I lost *my* college acceptance," I said slowly, "*you* had to go back."

"It wasn't your fault," she said.

"But *one* of us had to keep doing what we were supposed to be doing," I said. "And if it couldn't be me, then it had to be you."

Her silence confirmed it. "Do you think Turn Them Toward the Sun doesn't actually work at all?" I asked.

"Of course it works," she said immediately. Our faith in Mom had always been absolute. But now there were so many cracks in it, I wasn't sure how it could hold itself together.

"I'm just saying, I was supposed to be extraordinary at words. And you were supposed to be extraordinary on stage. Everything was set up for us to be extraordinary. And somehow, it got screwed up. So what does that mean? That Turn Them Toward the Sun doesn't work? Or that *we* don't work?"

"I don't know," Emerson said, "and I have to go. I have to be at rehearsal in ten minutes."

"So what are you going to *do*?" I asked her.

"I'm going to keep doing what I've been doing," she said as though it were obvious, then added, "What else would I do?"

She had a point. It's simplest to just keep being who you are, and who everyone expects you to be. It's when you turn out to be somebody different that everything goes to hell.

21

Richard and Kisha came back to me over the next couple of days, asking me to draft other apologies for them, and it wasn't long before Marco, Zeke, and Jazmyn were requesting my services, too. It turned out I excelled at saying sorry, as long as I wasn't saying it for myself. My Repentance time was jam-packed with consultations with my fellow Vibers. They would tell me their stories about each different person who hated them, and I would come up with the right words to try to make that person change his or her mind.

Sometimes my heart really did go out to their victims. For example, Marco asked me to write an apology to his eight-year-old daughter. He said he felt terrible about what his scandal had put her through, but he didn't know how to tell her that. "I've tried to make it up to her," he told me. "I bought her every Monster High doll, but she still won't forgive me." And it made me feel so sad:

for Marco, who did not understand, and for his daughter, who could get an apology with her father's name signed at the end, but not the apology that he really meant.

And sometimes my heart didn't go out to them at all. Like the woman who told Richard that he was living proof that "dumb southern hicks shouldn't be allowed to procreate." I wrote her an apology with the taste of vinegar on my tongue.

Of course no one told Kevin and Valerie that I was doing the other Vibers' Repentance for them. Because if our advisors had known, I'm sure they would have told me to stop, and everyone else wanted me to keep going. Technically, they had mentioned no rule against it.

Late one night in our second week, after everyone had gone to bed, I was sitting out on the porch again, reflecting upon a news story I'd read during Repentance that evening about a teacher in Missouri who had that very day told one of his students that her parents weren't her "real mom and dad" because they'd adopted her. Now that teacher was being systematically torn to shreds. I wondered if he would get fired for saying that. He probably would. The school had nothing to gain by standing by him, and if they fired him, they could distance themselves from the whole scandal. The teacher hadn't apologized yet, and I'd considered e-mailing him some advice but did not, of course, actually do so.

"I wasn't sure I'd see you out here tonight. I thought you'd be exhausted," I heard Abe say behind me.

I turned and gave him a smile. "What does exhaustion have to do with it?" I asked.

That was something else that had become part of my everyday

routine at Revibe: coming out here late at night and running into Abe. I didn't know that he and I had much in common in our previous lives, since his seemed to have been a riot of off-limits snowboarding, late-night sailing, and DUIs, whereas mine was . . . well, none of that, obviously. In the real world, we probably would have never started talking in the first place. But here at Revibe, somehow he and I kept finding more to talk about. I guess it beat our other option, of sitting in dark rooms and facing our nightmares alone.

"Word is that you've done a lot of Repentance today," Abe said, settling next to me.

"So?" I said. "Do you want me to write your apologies, too?"

"Hardly," Abe said. "I don't want some generic, one-size-fits-all Repentance."

"Hey!" I feigned offense. "I'll have you know every one of my apologies is custom-made."

"I'm sure they are," he said, "but I maintain complete creative control over mine. And not to brag, but they are top-shelf."

I was intrigued by this, because out of all of us, I thought Abe had the least to apologize for. The rest of us had made choices of varying degrees of unwiseness, but he hadn't chosen to be born to a master criminal. "Can I read one?" I asked.

"Sure." He took out his phone, pulled up an e-mail, then passed it to me.

Dear Helen, it read, *Thank you for taking the time to list all the ways that I'm letting down the human race. I want you to know that I agree with you wholeheartedly. I am spoiled and exploitative and not that bright. Without you, I might not have realized these things about myself—or might have realized them, but never bothered to try to address them. Your list galvanized me into action. I am now trying to be a better person by praying every day, doing charity work (I've been volunteering at a hospital and it's opened my eyes to those less fortunate than me), and even doing yoga in my wheelchair each morning. I understand that none of this can ever make up for the destruction I've wreaked—and whatever I do, it will always be too little, too late—but I want you to know that I'm devoting the rest of my life to trying to make amends to you and everyone else I've hurt. With infinite regret, Abe Krisch.*

I looked up from his phone to see him grinning at me. "Jealous?" he asked.

"A little, yeah. You don't think you're laying it on just a tiny bit too thick, though?" I said.

"Hey, you should have read my earlier draft. It was, like, three levels beyond this. Valerie told me I should rein it in or else no one would believe me."

I handed the phone back to him. "Well, I've got to give it to you, that is an impassioned apology."

"I told you I was good at it."

"So how come Kisha and Richard aren't asking *you* to do their Repentance for them?" I asked.

"Because they don't *know* that I'm good at it. You led with all the stuff about how you're an award-winning speller and you were going to be a writer and all that. I didn't breathe a word about my e-mail-writing talents."

"Strategic," I acknowledged.

"I try."

"But you don't . . ." I bit my lip. "You don't actually mean any of that stuff you wrote, do you?"

He raised his eyebrows. "Are you telling me I *don't* do yoga in my wheelchair every morning?"

"No, you do, and you're *so* great at it, too. You really use your breath. It's all, like, in your core . . ."

"Hah." He shoved my shoulder lightly.

"But you don't actually believe that this is your fault, do you? Because it's not. It's your father's fault. Don't you know that?"

Abe looked at me like I was a little bit crazy. "Of *course* I know that. That's the first thing I said when I met you all, remember?"

"So why are you admitting to something, and apologizing for something, that you didn't do?"

"Because I have to," he said simply. "Look, I don't care whether a billion Helens out there know the truth about me. I could devote the entire rest of my life to trying to convince them that I'm innocent, and they wouldn't ever be convinced.

"But you know what? I've come to terms with that. I don't need every Helen to think that I'm innocent. *I* know that I'm innocent, and that's enough. I just need every Helen not to *hate* me. I need to be able to go back to college someday and make friends there, and get a job without the boss throwing my résumé straight into the garbage, and visit nursing homes without getting fucking *spat* on."

Me too, I thought. That was exactly what I needed, too.

"If all I need to do for that to happen is take responsibility?" he went on. "Hell, I'll take responsibility for anything they tell me. I'll tell them I personally was stealing their dollar bills out of their piggy banks and eating them for breakfast, if that's what it takes. And do you want my advice, Winter?"

I didn't reply. I suspected I was going to get his advice whether I wanted it or not.

"You should do the same. Admit to yourself that you'll never convince them you were 'just kidding,' you'll never convince them you're not a racist, you'll never convince them of anything. Say what they want you to say and move on. You're smart, and talented, and funny, and pretty, and you don't have to let this dominate your entire life."

I stared at him, shocked by all of it. By the idea that this didn't have to dominate my life indefinitely. The idea that I could never convince them of *anything*, no matter how hard I tried or how true it was. The idea that I was talented and pretty. Could I accept any of that? And what did Abe know, anyway—about me, about anyone?

He gave a nervous little cough and added, "That's my opinion, anyway. But obviously you should do whatever feels right to you."

I nodded and still didn't speak.

"Okay." Abe cleared his throat again. "I'm going to go. Sorry for telling you what to do. It's none of my business."

"It's okay," I said, finally finding my voice. "Thank you."

He nodded, lifted the parking brake on his wheelchair, and drove into the house.

I continued to sit out on the porch for a while longer, thinking. I got what Abe was saying. I got why it was a good strategy and why it worked for him.

But there was one big difference between Abe and me. And it was that, as he said, he knew he was innocent, and for him that was enough.

I *didn't* know that I was innocent.

So for me, that could never be enough.

22

"I'm concerned," Kevin said in my coaching session a couple days later, "that you've been here for two weeks and you still haven't written a single apology. Is that right?"

I nodded, although technically, that *wasn't* right. I had written dozens of apologies at this point, signed with almost everyone's names except my own. But of course Kevin didn't know that.

"Do you want to explain why that is?" Kevin asked.

He knew this by now, but he didn't like the answer. I gave it again. "I don't want to put any words into the world again. The last time people heard the words I had to say, it destroyed my life. I can't believe that it would go any differently this time around."

"But this time, Valerie and I would vet your words first," Kevin said. "That's why we're here."

"You can't know everything, though. You can't predict the future. You could tell me my words are safe, but there could always be someone out there who disagrees with you." I tried to give him a smile. "I don't doubt that you guys know what you're doing."

"Good," Kevin said, "because remember, Winter, I have been exactly where you are now."

"Right," I said. It was helpful, I told myself, that Kevin had been "one of us." That he knew this shame and paralysis firsthand. But at the same time, it made him into a bit of an annoying know-it-all: he wouldn't even consider that maybe what worked for him *wouldn't* work for me. I said, "I can't afford even one more mistake."

"People aren't going to get mad at you for a simple apology," Kevin said, his frustration leaking through his soothing coach voice. "Look at the satisfaction the rest of the group is deriving from their apologies. Look how much lighter they feel. Don't you want that?"

"People can get mad at you for anything," I argued. "I was just reading about an Olympic athlete who didn't put her hand on her heart for the national anthem, and she got bashed online. She didn't do anything wrong! You don't even *have* to put your hand on your heart for the national anthem! And people posted that she was unpatriotic. Can you imagine? She literally brought home a medal for her nation, and somehow she still winds up being *un-patriotic*. You can't always predict what will set people off. So you're right that people *shouldn't* get mad at me for a simple apology, but that doesn't mean they *won't*."

"Who even is this athlete?" Kevin said, sounding tired. "Why were you even reading this? We don't give you internet privileges so you can read this sort of junk. We give you internet privileges so *you can apologize*."

I was silent. It was true that I'd continued to spend my Repentance time digging into case after case of public shaming, reading the articles and the victims' statements and the disparaging comment threads filled with infighting. The names and crimes changed, but in essence it was always the same. I knew that wasn't what I was supposed to be doing, but, well, that's what I was doing.

"Just write an apology," Kevin told me. "It doesn't have to be complicated. I know you take pride in all your big words, and that's great, but you don't need to set such high standards for this. 'Dear so-and-so, I'm sorry I hurt you. I was wrong, please forgive me. Sincerely, Winter Halperin.'"

I refrained from rolling my eyes. The apologies I had written for the other Vibers were far more poetic than that. I felt almost like I ought to give Kevin some tips.

"I can't," I said. "I'm sorry."

"So then how do you intend to do Repentance?" he asked.

"I don't know. I *am* repentant, though. I feel repentant."

"You feel *guilty*," Kevin told me. "It's not the same. You don't feel repentant until you've done acts of Repentance." He sighed deeply and pressed his fingertips together, as though trying to center himself. "Okay, look, let's try this. Let's set aside Sintra Gabel and your friend Jason and your parents and all of them for today. They're complicated; I get it. You have a lot tied up in whether they accept your apologies. The stakes there are too high for you to dive right in. So instead, just give me the name of someone you're *angry* at as a result of your situation. Anyone. Throw it on out here."

"Lisa Rushall," I snapped.

He googled her name and pulled up her website. "Is this her?" he asked.

I scowled at her messy hair, her closed-mouth smile. How many times had I looked at this photo and been filled with a directionless rage? "The very one."

"Okay," he said. "Let's just practice. Let's *pretend* like you're writing an apology to Lisa Rushall. What do you say?"

"I say . . . Why did you have to repost me in the first place? What were you *possibly* hoping to get out of it? Did you ever stop to think—"

"That's not an apology," Kevin interrupted. "You know it's not. And you know people aren't going to forgive you until you start to apologize. Remember: *I was wrong.* Try again."

I blew out a long breath and tried to imagine that this wasn't my life. If this were an apology for Kisha, or Marco, or anyone other than me, I'd have nothing invested in it and I'd know how to do it.

I replied, "I'd say: Lisa, I'm so sorry that I'm such an immoral person. I have a horrible, offensive sense of humor and an overinflated sense of how interesting my opinions are. Thank you for pointing that out to me. Because of you, I'm really getting my act together. I've started taking better care of myself by doing yoga every morning, and taking care of my spiritual health by praying frequently and giving back to the community. I know none of this behavior can make up for my earlier crimes, and I must live with that guilt until the day I die, but I wanted to let you know that I am trying to turn my life around from that dark place of ignorance and judgment, and it is *all thanks to you*! Most sincerely, Winter Halperin."

"See?" Kevin said. He'd been typing the whole time I was talking, and now he turned his computer screen so I could read the words I'd dictated. He'd put it all into the contact form on Lisa Rushall's website. He'd misspelled "ignorance" with an "e" instead of an "a," but otherwise it was what I'd said. He smiled. "That wasn't so hard, was it?"

"Sure," I said dubiously. "I guess spitting out a bunch of lines that you want to hear, even if I don't mean them, isn't that hard."

"We've been over this," Kevin reminded me. "*It doesn't matter what you mean.* You need to get that idea right out of your head. It matters what you *do*. In life, that is always true. You didn't *mean* to be offensive online, but you did an offensive thing; no one cares about your intentions. You don't *mean* your apology here, but you give it anyway; no one knows what's going on inside your head. Actions matter. Intentions don't."

"I just don't feel comfortable with it," I said slowly. "This whole program is founded on, well, *lying*, basically."

"Revibe is *not* founded on lying," Kevin replied. His cheeks turned a little pink, and I realized I'd insulted him—or at least insulted the company that he had invented. "Revibe is founded on what works," he went on. "And it doesn't feel like lying for everybody. Some of your fellow Vibers mean every word of their apologies."

I doubted that, since I'd written most of their apologies for them, but I supposed it was possible. Maybe some of them really had reached that point where they didn't feel the desperate need to explain themselves, to make the world understand that it wasn't supposed to happen this way, that they'd never meant it to turn out like this.

"You took a positive step tonight," Kevin told me. "Thanks for working with me. Now, if you could, go grab Abe on your way out—his counseling session is next." And then Kevin did something on his computer.

"What was that?" I asked.

"Hmm?"

"You just did something. With the Lisa apology. What did you do?"

"I sent it," Kevin said.

I stared at him. "To her?" I squeaked out.

"To Lisa."

"How?"

"I hit 'submit' on the contact form," he answered slowly, sounding like I did whenever I tried to explain the internet to my mother.

"Oh my God." I felt my breathing grow shallow. "Why—why did you do that?"

"Because you have to get past this hang-up you have, Winter," Kevin said, his voice calm and rational. "You identified a person you're in conflict with. You wrote a solid apology to her. But there's something in you that's stopping you from connecting those two things. If you keep holding back, you'll never be able to move on."

"What," I wheezed out. I couldn't get enough air into my lungs. I was breathing so fast, but it was all out. No breath was coming in.

He had put *my words* in print. He had sent them to a person who might *read them*. Not just any person. A person who I *already knew* delighted in ruining my life.

Think about what she had done with my last words.

What was she going to do with these?

"You'll thank me tomorrow," Kevin told me. "I know you might feel a little unmoored at first, but trust me, the more of these you do, the freer and lighter you'll start to feel. You just need to shake the first one out of your system."

"Unmoored?" I barked out. I dug my fingernails into my wrist and doubled over.

"Winter," Kevin said, his voice growing a tiny bit apprehensive. "Take a deep breath. Calm yourself down. Nothing bad has happened. You've been here two weeks and you haven't really been trying. You just needed a little kick in the pants."

My life was completely out of my control. Even here, even now, as I was supposed to be learning how to take my life back, I could find my words stolen right out from under me again, twisted up and spat back out in their ugliest form. I should have learned my lesson, *I should know by now*: never say anything, never write it down, they will always use it against you, your words are dangerous, your thoughts are dangerous, *you are dangerous*. You are dangerous and evil and radioactive. I knew this and yet here I was again: How damaged and stupid was I that I would just keep on making the same mistakes? What was wrong with me, that I could never learn? *Why don't you just shut up? JUST. SHUT. UP.*

I heard noises, far off in the distance, and it occurred to me that I was on the floor, and it further occurred to me that I might die here. I was going to asphyxiate and die. And at the moment, I welcomed that fate. I hoped only that it would come quickly. As I'd said to Abe, I was not brave enough to jump off a roof. But perhaps I was brave enough to stay here, suffocating on the floor, until everything just stopped.

Maybe it was only because I was thinking about Abe, but I thought I heard his voice. I tried to breathe a little quieter for a moment so I could hear if he really was there.

"She's having a panic attack," a voice said, and yes, I did think it was Abe's voice.

"It's really okay, Winter." Kevin's voice. "You just need to calm down and stop overreacting . . ."

Abe's voice was closer now, drowning out Kevin's. "Winter? Can you hear me?"

I nodded.

"Can you open your eyes and look at me?" he asked.

I cracked one eye open. Abe was sitting beside me, leaning over me. He was beautiful. I was a fucking wreck. This really wasn't how I would want him to see me, but there was nothing I could do about it.

"I want you to try to breathe with me," Abe went on, never breaking eye contact. "Can you do that?"

I shook my head.

"Okay," he said. "That's okay. I'm going to breathe, okay? And you can join me if you want to. I'm breathing in . . . and out . . . and in . . . and out . . ."

He kept going like that, and eventually my breathing fell into rhythm with his. I managed to open my other eye to look at him.

We breathed in together. We breathed out together. We kept breathing.

"I'm proud of you," Abe said in between breaths. "You're doing a good job. You're doing really well, Winter. That's right. Just *use* your breath."

I laughed, a wheezy but not quite hysterical laugh, at his impression of our yoga instructor.

"See?" Kevin said from behind his desk, responding to my laughter. "Everything is fine."

My face twisted. Abe must have noticed, because he shot Kevin a sharp look. "I'm going to accompany Winter back to her room," he said. "I think she should lie down. Winter, do you want to go?"

I was more or less already lying down, but yes, I did want to go. I wanted to get away from Kevin and his computer. I wanted to fall into a black hole, or a parallel universe. I tried to stand, but I didn't quite have the energy. I felt like a foal we'd seen at the horse farm the other day: unsteady on my legs, unsure how to move forward. I collapsed back down to the floor and looked up at Abe, helpless. Surely there was an easy way out of here. I simply did not have the strength to figure out what it was.

"If you want to sit on my lap," Abe said hesitantly, "I can drive you back to your room."

"I can take her," Kevin offered. "I don't want you to hurt yourself, Abe."

"She wouldn't hurt me," Abe said, annoyed. "If she would hurt me, I wouldn't have offered."

I didn't want to spend another minute with Kevin. I pulled myself up and sort of flopped onto Abe's lap, like a fish out of water.

It couldn't have been comfortable for him. But Abe just wheeled us around and out the door.

"I'm sorry," I told Abe once we were a ways down the hall, away from Kevin.

"You don't have to be sorry," he told me. "Not your fault."

"You have to be sorry for lots of things that aren't your fault," I reminded him.

"Not this one. And seriously, it's fine. These things happen. My mother used to get panic attacks, though now she has meds that usually stop them before they get too severe. I was starting to get out of practice at taking care of someone going through it, so think about it that way. You're really doing me a favor."

I laughed again. With more air this time. I could probably walk at this point. But I didn't say that, because I didn't really want to. Abe's body felt warm and firm and safe against mine. And it was nice to feel safe now and again, if only for a minute.

We reached the door to my room. "We made it," Abe said unnecessarily.

I got off his lap. "Thanks for being my knight in shining armor."

"It's not exactly *armor*," he replied, tapping his chair, "but it is pretty shiny."

"Oh—no—that's not what I meant . . ." I stuttered.

"Relax, Winter. I'm joking."

"Oh." I bit my lip. "I know it's hard to tell, but I used to have a pretty good sense of humor."

"It's not that hard to tell," he told me. "Do you want to tell me what that was all about? You don't have to. But I'll listen if you want to talk about it."

I briefly explained who Lisa Rushall was and what Kevin had just done. "I hate her," I said. "I want to ruin her life the way she's ruined mine."

Unlike Emerson, Abe did not tell me to let it go. Instead, he said, "I want that, too. So now she has this fake apology from you. What are you going to do about it?"

I shook my head helplessly. "Do you think I could recall the message somehow? Maybe she hasn't read it yet?"

Abe's forehead wrinkled. "I don't see how you could, since he sent it through the contact form on her site."

"Shit."

"Yeah." He seemed to think about it for a moment, then said, "You could try calling her. I bet you could find the general phone number for *The Pacific* and call as soon as the workday starts tomorrow."

"And ask her to just delete the e-mail," I said. "Sure. It's worth a shot." Then I remembered. "Except for how we don't have cell reception."

"Right." He frowned. "There's a landline in Valerie's office."

"But there's also a *Valerie* in Valerie's office," I reminded him. Either she was there with the door open, ready for us to come in and consult with her, or she was elsewhere and the door was locked.

"If I can get her out of there for a few minutes tomorrow morning," Abe said, "would you be able to run in and use her phone to call Lisa?"

"I think so," I said, my stomach tightening at the thought of it. "But how would you even be able to lure Valerie out of her office?"

"I don't know," Abe admitted, "but I'm going to try to figure it out."

"Thank you," I said. "You don't have to help me."

He looked surprised. "I wasn't doing it because I have to."

I unlocked my door.

"You going to be okay?" Abe asked me. I shrugged. Probably not. "Do you want me to keep you company?" he offered.

"Won't you get in trouble if you don't go to your coaching session now?" I asked feebly.

He rolled his eyes. "Like I care." And he followed me into my room.

My heart rate spiked again when he moved to close the door behind him. Not that I thought anything was going to, like, *happen* between us. But with the two of us in here, alone together, anyone could *think* that something might be happening between us. I didn't have a lot of experience with boys in my room. When Mackler, Corey, and Jason came over, we usually hung out downstairs, because that's where the TV and food were. Sometimes we'd go up to my room, but then it would usually be *all* of us. And anyway, it was different. They were my friends. Abe was something else.

"Please leave the door open while you're in here," I blurted out, knotting my fingers together.

"Sure." He did so, then looked at me. "You seem a little panicky still."

"I guess I am."

"You should get some rest," he suggested.

"But if I do that, then who will stay up all night worrying about the nefarious Lisa Rushall?" I asked.

"Hey, I didn't say you need to fall asleep. But you should at least get into bed. When I was a kid, my au pair used to tell me that I never had to fall asleep if I didn't want to; I just had to lie in bed with the lights off and my eyes closed."

"You had an au pair?" I asked.

"Yeah. It's the person who raises you when your parents are busy," he explained.

"I know what it is," I said. "From the French, obviously."

"Obviously." Abe smiled. "Mine was named Leyda. She's from Brazil. She's the best." He added, "I told you I was a spoiled brat."

"I'm not going to hold it against you. My mom is a professional parenting expert," I said, "so I don't know that either of us was raised in such a normal way."

"Seriously?" he said. "That must have been a ton of pressure on you."

"I don't know," I said. "It always seemed normal to me."

"And Leyda seemed normal to me. Now come on. Into bed with you."

First I went to the bathroom to brush my teeth, wash my face, and change into my pajamas. Abe was still in my room when I got back, and I quickly got under the covers on my bed so I wouldn't be parading around in my sleep shorts and T-shirt, which was sure to make us both uncomfortable. Yes, I'd been in my pajamas around him before—but it was dark out on the porch and hard to see what I looked like. He came over to me, and I wondered,

What is he doing?—then he gave my sheets a sharp tug and tucked them tightly under my mattress.

It was so unexpected, I started to giggle. "Did you just . . . tuck me in?"

"Um, yeah." He blushed. "Just something else Leyda used to do when she put me to bed. Now that you've pointed it out, that was weird of me. Never mind."

"No," I said, "it was nice." And it *was* nice, to feel so cozy and secure, as if no one could touch me here, not with my sheets forming a protective cocoon around me. "Any other Leyda bedtime rituals I should know about?"

"Not much," he said. "She used to sing me to sleep, but . . ."

"Yeah!" I said. "Do it! Sing to me."

"No way."

"Didn't you say you used to be in an a cappella group?"

"Yeah, but I'm way out of practice."

"Oh, please," I said. "Like I'd be able to tell the difference."

"Ugh. I don't know. What do you even want me to sing?"

"My sister usually sings songs from modern Broadway musicals. So . . . anything but that."

"All right, fine," he said, which was not nearly enough protesting to make me believe that he actually didn't want to sing. "You promise you won't make fun of me, though?"

"You're talking to the person who just needed help to make it from one end of the hallway to the other."

"Yeah, okay." He cleared his throat. "So, this used to be my solo, back when I was doing a cappella. It's called 'I'll Be,' by Edwin McCain. It's super-cheesy. Don't hold it against me; I didn't write it *or* decide that we should sing it. Oh, and pretend there's a chorus of twenty other guys behind me."

And he started to sing.

He was good. Maybe not *great*, certainly not Emerson level, not Broadway-bound. But his voice was soulful and impassioned. It made me shiver under my covers. It tugged at my heart. And the song *was* cheesy, that was true, but only because it was so earnestly romantic. It was ridiculous to think that anyone could mean what this song said. I knew that it was ridiculous, but for that moment, as he sang for me, it felt believable.

Abe finished the song and gave a little bow with his head. I pulled my arms out from under the sheets to applaud quietly. "That was really good," I said.

"It was okay."

"You should have stayed in that a cappella group," I told him.

"I should have done a lot of things," he said.

It always came back to that: the parts of ourselves we had lost, that could never be reclaimed.

"You ought to go," I said. "It's getting late, and I don't want anyone getting the wrong idea about what we're doing in here. Because of the rules. You know."

I blushed, but Abe just nodded. "All right. Sleep tight, Winter." And he wheeled himself out of the room, at last shutting the door behind him.

Of course I didn't sleep tight. I didn't sleep much at all. But it was sweet of him to suggest it.

23

After Rehabilitation but before we left for Redemption the next morning, Abe put his plan into action. Valerie was in her office, and the other Vibers were brushing their teeth and making their beds before the van came for us at eleven o'clock. With every minute that passed, it became more and more likely that Lisa had read my e-mail and posted it somewhere, that it had been picked up by everyone on the Surprise I Can Spell website, everyone on Reddit, everyone everywhere, that my life was falling to pieces again at this very moment as I was here, unaware of any of it and therefore unable to nip it in the bud.

"We're going to make it look like I fell out of my wheelchair," Abe explained in a low voice, as we were around the corner from Valerie's office.

"Seriously?"

"Absolutely. But I need your help."

"What can I do?"

"Just don't watch me."

I blinked at him. "Is that helpful?"

"Well, I'm not going to pretend to fall out of my chair with you staring at me," he said.

It occurred to me that, somehow, I'd never seen Abe get in or out of his wheelchair. He was always the first one in the van to go to Rehabilitation, so by the time I got out there, he was buckled in and Kevin was storing his chair in the trunk. And when we arrived wherever we were going, Abe was always the last one out. I figured I must have seen him transfer out of his chair at some point since we got here, but now that I was focusing on it, I couldn't think of when exactly that might have been.

"Keep your back to me," he said, "and keep an eye out to make sure no one's coming."

I turned around and listened to the sounds of Abe shifting in his wheelchair, a few thumps on the floor, a bang, and then he said, "Okay, you can look at me again." I did. He was sitting calmly on the floor, his legs in front of him, grinning up at me.

"I don't think Valerie's going to buy that you're in great need," I told him.

"I'm going to make it more dramatic, don't worry. Now can you lay my wheelchair on its side, like it fell over completely and it would be impossible for me to right it by myself?"

I laughed softly and did so. It was lighter than I'd expected it would be.

"Maybe have it lying partially on top of me?" Abe suggested. "Maybe we can convince her not only that I fell and can't get back up but that I'm, like, *trapped* down here."

"You're really enjoying this, aren't you?" I said.

"I feel like I'm using my power for good," he said.

As I was trying to arrange his wheelchair on the ground so that it looked believably impossible for him to get back into without help, Jazmyn rounded the corner.

"Oh!" she said, taking in the scene.

"It's fine!" I chirped, lest she call for help right now, before we were ready. "He's totally fine."

"You were supposed to be our lookout," Abe reminded me.

I rolled my eyes at him. "I was a little busy, okay?"

"What are you guys doing?" Jazmyn asked.

Abe and I looked at each other, not sure how much we could trust her.

"We're trying to get Valerie out of her office," I explained.

"Okay." Jazmyn seemed fine with that. I waited for her to leave so we could get on with it, but she stayed right there, as if waiting to see how this all would play out.

Abe and I exchanged another look. We didn't have much time before we had to leave for Redemption. Either we went through with this now and hoped Jazmyn didn't blab to Valerie or we gave up.

"Okay," Abe said, "let's do this. Go."

He crumbled from his seated position into a prone sprawl on the floor, partially pinned down by his wheelchair, and as I darted away, he howled, *"Valerie! Help!"*

Instantly, Valerie came flying out of her office. Seconds later, I ran in there myself. I grabbed the telephone on her desk, my heart racing. I was doing this. I was about to call Lisa Rushall. My nemesis, my life-destroyer, Lisa Rushall.

And if this went wrong, both Abe and I would be in really serious trouble.

What the hell was I doing?

I found *The Pacific*'s phone number on Valerie's computer and dialed it with fingers so frantic that I got it wrong on the first try. "Come on, come on," I muttered to myself, hanging up and then redialing. This time, a recorded voice answered. "You've reached the offices of *The Pacific*. If you know your party's extension, you may dial it at any time." I paced around the small room, phone pressed to my ear. "For a company directory, press one."

I pressed the number one. Then I was told to press the number five, which I did, followed by the numbers eight-two-zero, and right around the point when I was becoming convinced that Valerie was going to come back and find me in her office before I even managed to speak to an actual human being, a voice answered the phone.

"This is Lisa," it said.

I somehow had not prepared for this.

"Lisa Rushall?" I said stupidly.

"Yes. Who is this?"

"This is Winter Halperin," I said.

Lisa didn't immediately say anything.

"You received an e-mail from me last night," I went on, "and I wanted to ask you to please, please delete it. Please just act like you never received it."

"Oh, here it is," she said in a moment. "I hadn't gotten through all my e-mail yet."

That stunned me for a moment. The whole past fourteen hours, there had been no question in my mind that she was plotting something horrible against me—maybe even something she had already begun to execute. And now it turned out that, all along, she hadn't even noticed that she got an e-mail from me. It made me wonder for a second what the hell I was doing here, sneaking into Valerie's office.

But, I reminded myself, sooner or later, Lisa *would* have read my e-mail, and then she *would* have plotted something horrible. *Again*.

"Just delete it," I told her. "You don't have to read it."

"Oh, *Winter Halperin*!" she said. "Of course. I blanked on your name for a moment."

"You . . . what?" I asked, stupefied. "You 'blanked on my name'? Are you kidding me?"

"What?" she said.

I raised my voice. "You ruined my life, and five months later you can't even remember who I *am*?"

This was not how I'd imagined this conversation going. I'd prepared myself to talk her out of destroying me yet again. I had not prepared for reminding her of my existence.

"Excuse me?" she said. "I haven't ruined anybody's life, as far as I'm aware, though maybe my editor would tell you differently." She said this last bit as though it were a joke.

I wasn't laughing.

"Yes, *you*, Lisa Rushall. You ruined everything. And now how dare you act like you don't even know who I am or what you did? Thanks to you, I'm at a crazy reputation rehabilitation retreat right now, having to write stupid apologies, which is the only reason you got that ridiculous e-mail from me yesterday. I didn't mean it. I mean, I *am* sorry. I'm constantly sorry. I'm sorry I'm alive, I'm sorry anyone has to know me, I'm sorry I ruin everything I touch. But I'm not sorry to *you*. *You* don't deserve my apologies. *You* should be apologizing to *me*."

"What is a reputation rehabilitation retreat?" Lisa asked, like that was the most interesting part of my statement.

"Exactly what it sounds like. Did you hear me? *You should apologize*."

"What's it called?" she asked. "Your retreat, I mean."

"Revibe. Can you—"

"Is it in Malibu?" she asked, sounding excited.

"Yes."

"And you're there right now? That's fantastic!"

"It doesn't feel fantastic to me," I told her.

"I've heard whispers about this place for the past year or so, but it's almost impossible to get any concrete information about it. I've reached out to the owners, but they refuse to talk. Listen, Winter, I'm so glad you called. Could I interview you about Revibe?"

"No," I said immediately.

She paused for only a second. "Then will you connect me to any of the other people who are there with you?"

"No. Are you nuts? Why would I help you?"

"I'd really like to speak with someone about it," she tried. "I think it's fascinating. There's a story about Revibe that's just waiting to be told. What can I do to convince you to trust me?"

"Hmm, let's see . . . Oh, I've got it: you could go back in time to May and *leave me alone.*"

"Anything else?" she asked.

"Delete my e-mail from last night," I said. "Never quote it, or photograph it, or post it where anyone could ever see it."

"Done," she said. "What else do you need?"

I paused. Because maybe there *was* something she could do.

Somehow, and completely without my expecting it, I had something that Lisa wanted. So now the question that occurred to me was: What did *I* want from *her*?

"If you get to ask me about Revibe," I said, "it's only fair that I get to ask you some questions first."

Repentance didn't work for me. The idea that I was supposed to apologize to Lisa Rushall and that would fix me . . . I could not accept that.

But if I could get Lisa to apologize to *me*, if I could get her to actually see what she had done to me and regret it—well, that was the sort of repentance I could really get behind.

"Sure," Lisa agreed. "I'm ready now. Ask away."

This was a gift. This was what I had dreamed of for so long. This was finally my chance to understand *why*. After months of going around in circles, trying to figure out why hundreds of thousands of strangers would band together to hurt me, I could now simply *ask* for the explanation.

Just then, I heard a motion at the door to Valerie's office. I froze, but it was only Jazmyn. And Jazmyn, it turned out, was on our side. *"She's coming,"* she whispered at me, then ran.

"I'm going to need to call you back," I said into the phone before hanging up. And then I ran, too.

24

"So did it work?" Abe asked me quietly as we sat in the back of the van on our way to Redemption.

I glanced up front, to make sure Kevin wasn't paying attention to us, and nodded. "Thank you for creating a diversion."

"Hey, if everyone's going to assume that I'm helpless, I might as well use it to my advantage."

"Want to do it again this evening?" I suggested. "I need to figure out some way to call her back."

Abe looked surprised. "Did she not agree to delete your e-mail?"

"No, she did. But I want to talk to her more. I want *answers*, Abe. And she has them."

And what's so great about Abe is that he got it. Just like that.

"Okay," he said. "So how are you going to do it? I think that if I fall out of my chair twice in one day, they might get suspicious that I'm faking it."

"It would be so much easier to talk to Lisa if they didn't take away our phones every time we left the house," I complained.

"You know that's precisely *why* they do it," Abe said.

I stuck my tongue out at him.

Redemption that day was at a shelter for pregnant teens and teenage moms. We weren't supposed to interact with the girls directly; we were instead there to sort through donations that had been sent into the shelter and categorize them as usable or not, for the mothers or their children, and, if for children, what age group. But we saw the residents as they passed by the room where we were working. They were girls my age, or even younger than me, with beach-ball stomachs or strollers that they pushed down the hall.

Richard's eyes grew watery, and he clutched a baby sweater in his fists, as if unable to assign it to a pile. "I don't want this to happen to Tabitha," he whispered, though it was unclear whether he meant that he didn't want Tabitha to live in a shelter and rely on donations, or he didn't want her to grow up to be a teen mother, or he didn't want that particular sweater he was holding to ever wind up on her body, or all of the above. And I thought that there are so many ways life as you know it can be torn apart, your plans upended. I had found one way, and the girls here had found another. And I thought that Emerson was crazy. Her life *hadn't* been torn apart. Her plans *hadn't* been upended. Who would ever choose to start from square one when they didn't have to?

I went to the bathroom. As I was washing my hands, a girl came in, pushing a sleeping baby in a stroller. She left him next to the sink while she went into one of the stalls. I dried my hands and inspected him. His long eyelashes fluttered, and his tiny hands clutched the yellow blankie that covered him.

"Your son is beautiful," I told the girl when she came out of the stall.

"He got his daddy's eyes," she told me. I nodded even though I didn't know if this was true, since I didn't know his daddy and, anyway, his eyes were closed. "I haven't seen you before," she went on. "You new here?"

"I—oh, no, I'm not . . . I'm just volunteering."

"Right," she said, a sort of curtain falling across her face. "My mistake." And I realized that now she thought I was better than her, or rather that she thought that *I* thought I was better than her—though of course that was nowhere close to true.

"What's your name?" I asked.

"Jessie."

"Hey, Jessie. I'm Winter. I'm volunteering here because I said the wrong thing and everyone found out about it, and now my friends won't have anything to do with me, and I can't go to college, and I can't get a job, and I've basically put my mom out of work, and I'm here because I'm trying to make amends, but it's not going well."

She looked at me with her mouth hanging open slightly. "Uh . . . okay."

"I know that's a lot to say to someone you just met in a bathroom," I went on. "But I didn't want you to think that, like, because you're here and I'm just visiting, that means I'm living this totally dreamy life. Sometimes people look like they're doing fine, and they're really *not* doing fine, you know what I mean?"

Jessie nodded. "I get you."

"So this is weird," I went on, "but do you have a phone I could borrow?"

Again she looked at me like I was nuts. "You don't have a *phone*?" she asked.

"They take it away from me," I explained. "Because of what I did."

I expected she'd refuse, because she didn't know me and had no reason to care, but instead, she pulled a phone out of her bag on the stroller and handed it to me.

"Thank you," I said. "I'll try to be fast."

She shrugged and said, totally deadpan, "Take your time. I love hanging out in bathrooms."

I gave her a weak smile, then called *The Pacific* again. This time, I got through the phone tree with the speed that comes from experience, and within a minute, I was back on the phone with Lisa Rushall.

"Winter!" she exclaimed, like we were old friends. "I'm so glad you called back. We got cut off earlier."

"We didn't get cut off," I told her. "I hung up on you."

"So about Revibe—" she began.

"I'm going to ask my questions first," I interrupted.

"Okay," she said.

"Okay," I said back. "So tell me this: Did you really find my post racist?"

Lisa seemed to consider this for a moment before replying. "I don't remember exactly what you said. Something about how you think African Americans aren't literate and don't deserve to win any contests based on intelligence, wasn't that it?"

"It said, 'We learned many surprising things today. Like that *dehnstufe* is apparently a word, and that a black kid can actually win the Spelling Bee.'"

I glanced across the bathroom toward Jessie to see if she was paying attention, if she was offended and was going to wrench her phone back from me now that she'd heard these words come out of my mouth. But her baby was fussing, and she seemed more focused on him than on anything I was doing.

"Oh, yes, that's right," Lisa confirmed.

"And that sounded racist to you?"

"Do you really want to know?"

"That's why I'm asking," I replied.

"Honestly, Winter, you seem like a smart kid, but yes, it's pretty thoughtless. I don't find it outright *malevolent*, for what that's worth. You look at the blatant racial discrimination that is happening out there—police brutality, voter suppression, the mass incarceration of black men—and what you said doesn't hold a candle to that.

"But what you said absolutely sounds like you've internalized some systemic stereotypes. I don't mean that as a personal attack. As you grow up, you'll find that most people have adopted their societies' stereotypes without even being aware of it."

"So what I said wasn't *good*, but it wasn't the worst thing anyone's ever said, either. Is that what you're telling me?" I asked.

"Sure."

"So then *why*," I asked, my breathing growing fast and ragged, "did you repost it?"

"Because it was such a self-evidently ridiculous thing to say!"

"Do you understand what happened to me because of that post?" I asked her. "Do you have any idea?"

"It got a lot of media attention at the time," she said. "I saw a bunch of headlines about it for a few days there."

"Every major news source ran articles about how I'm a racist. Countless strangers all over the world posted about how much they hated me. People dug up photos of me from when I was a little kid and talked about how fat and ugly and pathetic I was. I got kicked out of college before I even started. I couldn't get a driver's license. I lost one of my best friends. I lost my spelling bee title. I lost *everything*. I . . ."

I couldn't go on. I was shaking too badly. I closed myself inside the bathroom stall so Jessie and her baby couldn't see me.

"That sounds miserable," Lisa said, and her tone was sincere.

I waited for her to take some responsibility. But that was all she said.

"You could apologize," I told her. "I know you can't go back in time and change anything. But you could still say you're sorry now, and that might mean something to me."

She sighed. "I'm sorry you were so vilified. But that's not *my* fault, Winter. *I* didn't send you hate mail, or find old photos of you, or rescind your college acceptance, or tell your friends to stop being your friends, or send you to Revibe . . . I absolutely understand why you're upset that those things happened to you, but *I* didn't make them happen. I don't think I'm the one you really want an apology from."

"But you *did* make them happen," I said desperately.

"How?" she asked. "I'm just a writer. I'm not in charge of the internet. I don't lead a religion or a political party. I didn't tell anyone to do any of that—I *wouldn't* have told anyone to do any of that, and even if I had, they would not have listened to me."

But that couldn't be. This had to be her fault. *This had to be someone's fault.*

"None of them ever would have even *seen* the post if you hadn't put it out there to your fifteen thousand followers," I pointed out. "You know how many followers *I* had? One hundred and sixteen. That was then—now I don't even have an account, let alone, heaven forbid, followers. One hundred and sixteen people, most of whom I knew personally. *They* didn't care what I wrote. *They* knew how I meant it. And if *you* hadn't shared it, it would have gone to those one hundred and sixteen people and then gone away."

Lisa clicked her tongue. "Look, I get that you want to blame me. But *you* are the one who put that post up there. That was your choice. And when you put something online, you have no way of knowing who ultimately is going to see it. That's a hard thing to wrap your head around, especially when you're a kid and you don't have a sense of how big and diverse the world is. But it's the truth.

"I'm sorry you feel hurt by my actions," she said. "But I certainly never intended to hurt you."

I felt like she'd swung a club straight into my chest. Because I understood, finally, why my apology to the internet all those months ago hadn't been enough.

Because I didn't want to hear that she was sorry for how I *felt*.

Because I didn't want an apology with a *but*.

And because it made no difference to anything at all whether she had *intended* to hurt me.

I was no more going to get the apology that I wanted than I'd been able to give it.

"Can't you fix it?" I asked desperately. "Or at least tell *me* how to fix it? You started it. Don't you know how to stop it?"

"I don't," she said.

"You shouldn't start something that you don't know how to stop!" I yelled.

She didn't reply.

No one should start things that they don't know how to stop. And yet we do. We can't help ourselves. And we don't realize how little control we have until it's too late.

"Just tell me why you did it," I pleaded. "You know, I can understand why BuzzFeed or the *Washington Post* would run their stories. I was already newsworthy by then. No one wanted to be the one website or newspaper ignoring this topic that everyone was talking about." I rubbed my eyes. "But why did *you* do it? You could have just as easily *not done it*, and my entire life would be different right now. My entire life would be easier and happier and *better*. So *why?*"

"I don't know," she said.

"That's not an okay answer!" I cried. "Try to figure it out!"

"Why does anybody post *anything?*" she replied, sounding frustrated. "I saw it, it amused me for a moment, I thought it would get a response. I clicked, and it was done. I wasn't sitting around and analyzing my motives at the time. Nor have I given them much thought since then. I don't know what answer you want, Winter, but that's all I've got."

And what answer *did* I want? *Because I'm evil,* I wanted her to say. *Because I am a sociopath and I wanted to destroy you.*

"If you were so offended by my post," I said, "why didn't you message me about it directly? If you'd *told* me you thought it was hurtful, I would have taken it down right away. I swear I would have. Why did you have to shame me? In front of the entire world? Why make it into . . ." I remembered Rodrigo Ortiz's words. "Into vigilante justice?"

I heard Lisa sigh. "Honestly, it never occurred to me to take it up with you privately. I wanted to use your post as an example of a microaggression. I wanted to point out how racist stereotypes persist, even among your supposedly very tolerant and liberal generation.

"I wouldn't have been able to make a point to anyone else if I'd quietly brought it up with you alone. The hope in doing it publicly was that other people could learn from your mistake."

"But it doesn't happen like that," I said, thinking about Emerson's outrage at deleting her social media account, and Mackler's commitment to making his ridiculous Gatorade video. "All those people look at my mistake and think, *Good thing I could never be an idiot like Winter Halperin,* and go on with their lives."

"I'm sorry if that's how you feel," Lisa said.

I'm sorry if. I'm sorry but. These weren't real apologies. These weren't what I needed.

"You know," she went on, "I always thought your mother was pretty much full of shit."

My mouth fell open. Who says that about somebody's *mother*? Especially to a teenager? "What does *that* have to do with anything?" I asked.

"Her whole parenting strategy. The very *idea* that everyone can have a strategy for parenting, that everyone can have the *same* strategy for parenting. It's absurd. She's so smug about it, and she's so wrong."

"She is *not* smug," I shot back. "You don't know her."

"That's true. But I did spend a fair bit of time with her and with her work when I was writing that profile on her, and the whole time, all I could think was, *Easy for her to say.* Not every child can be extraordinary. Not every child *has* to be extraordinary.

"I have a son who's a bit older than you, and he has Down syndrome. He's not starring on Broadway or winning spelling bees or whatever else it is your mother claims every parent can train every child to do if she just really *tries*. Elliot isn't going to be extraordinary by your mother's standards. But he will always be extraordinary to *me*, because he is my son, and isn't that enough?"

"Well, I'm sure it's enough for him," I suggested.

"It should be enough for *every* child, regardless of who they are, or who their mother is. So yes," Lisa continued, "I'll admit that I felt a little thrill when I saw that one of your mother's 'extraordinary' daughters had put her oh-so-special foot into her terribly well-groomed mouth. Yes, I saw the opportunity to be snide, and yes, I was glad for it. So maybe that is also what motivated me to say something publicly.

"I'm not Beyoncé, you know," she went on. "Or Justin Bieber. Or whatever celebrity it is you teenagers are into these days. I don't have tens of millions of followers. I have, as you pointed out, about fifteen thousand. Part of my job is trying to think of things to say that they might find interesting, and might want to share, and might get me more followers. Your post seemed like one of those things."

"And did it work?" I asked.

"I think so," she said softly. "I don't really remember."

So my foolishness had been a tool for her. A means to an end, an end that she may not have even achieved.

"I'm not a bad person, you know," she told me.

And I supposed that nobody wants to think of themself as a bad person. I wondered if even Hitler would have claimed he was simply doing the best he could.

"Why did *you* do it?" Lisa asked me, turning on her reporter voice.

"Because I'm a horrible racist. Obviously."

"No, really," she said. "What made you post it in the first place?"

She waited for my response. I didn't have one ready, because she was the first person who had asked me *why* and seemed to want a real answer.

"I know this sounds stupid now," I began, "but I used to want to be a writer. So I was always making observations—things I thought were clever or poignant or interesting, and then I'd try to phrase them in a way that would make other people think they were clever or poignant or interesting, too."

I stopped.

"I don't find that stupid," Lisa said. "I do the same thing. That's what it means to be a writer."

"Maybe," I said, "except I was *terrible* at it. I was wrong about what was clever, I was wrong about what was interesting. I was wrong about all of it."

"That's part of being a writer, too," Lisa said. "I write all sorts of things wrong. Especially when I was younger and still figuring out my voice . . . yeesh. The biggest difference between me and you is that I have an editor whose job it is to tell me when to shut up."

"Does that help?"

"Most of the time. Even then, there are always people who hate my work. Whatever I write, there will always be at least one reader out there who vocally hates it. Usually a lot more than that. Part of having a perspective means that some people are going to have a different perspective. Stories that don't ruffle a few feathers are playing it so safe that they aren't worth reading *or* writing. You can't be good at this job by caring if people like you."

No wonder I couldn't be a writer. Because I *did* care if people liked me. I wanted so *badly* for people to like me. Getting people to like me was one of the big reasons I wrote in the first place.

More fool I.

"There's a difference between ruffling a few feathers and making the entire world despise you," I pointed out.

"Oh, please. Teenagers really are as dramatic as they say, huh?"

I scowled.

"The entire world does not despise you," Lisa went on. "Most of the entire world does not care about you. Nobody's taking the time to go online to talk about how much they *don't* despise you."

I saw her point. When I'd seen gossip magazine stories about Kisha, laughing at her for going commando on a windy day, I hadn't hated her. But I also hadn't bothered to write my own response in favor of her. I had been neither for nor against Kisha. So yes, there must be people out there who felt that way about me, too.

And I thought about Jazmyn. If I'd read *her* story in the news, I couldn't imagine joining the ranks of people calling her a slut. I would have thought she hadn't done anything wrong and she was being wrongly punished. There must be people out there who felt that way about me, too.

But how was I supposed to trust that they were out there when they were so quiet and the haters were so loud? How was I supposed to believe in them?

Lisa continued, "So if you'll indulge my reporter side for a moment, I'll ask you the same question you asked me. You've told me why you wrote that post. But why did you write it *publicly*? Why not send it to one of your friends, have a chuckle, and call it a day?"

"I guess the same reason as you, sort of," I said. "I wanted attention for it. This is so embarrassing. But I didn't just want to write down things that were clever or poignant or interesting. That wasn't enough. It was never going to be enough. I wanted to write them down . . . and I wanted people to read them. I wanted people to like me for what I wrote. I wanted to be . . . God, this is dumb. This is so dumb. But I wanted to be kind of famous."

"So you got what you wanted," she said.

"Oh yeah," I said bitterly, leaning my head against the beige stall door. "I got it all."

"You know," Lisa said, "based on our conversation, I've changed my mind."

"About what?"

"I'm not going to write an article about Revibe after all. I think this piece would be a lot stronger if it was from the perspective of someone actually experiencing all this—the shaming, the punishment, the redemption. Someone who's really *living* Revibe, if you understand what I'm saying."

"Okay." I wasn't sure I did understand what she was saying.

She clarified. "You should write this article, Winter."

I was blindsided by this suggestion. Oh, in another world, what joy I would have felt to hear it. A professional journalist, telling me that *I* could write a good story—that I could do it so well, I should even do it *instead* of her!

"I'm not writing anymore," I told her. "And I'm definitely not writing about this."

"Suit yourself," Lisa replied. "But if you ever do write it down, send it to me. I want us to have first crack at publishing it before you shop it elsewhere."

"I don't get it," I said. Did she feel guilty about the damage she'd wreaked in my life? Was this her way of trying to make it up to me? "Are you trying to *help* me?"

"No," she said, sounding almost horrified at the suggestion. "I just think you have a story to tell."

"In your dreams," I said, and I hung up.

I flushed the toilet—I hadn't used it; I just wanted to make a loud noise. Then I unlocked the stall door and handed Jessie back her phone. She was holding her son in her arms now, and his eyes were open, a dark, luscious brown—like his daddy's, I assumed.

"Thanks," I said again. "Sorry I was on there for a while and you had to wait around for me. Can I give you some money for the call or anything?"

"It's cool," she said, shifting her son to her other hip. Then she added, "Girl, you are *seriously* messed up."

I leaned against the sink. "Yup." I recalled my dad's suspicions about Revibe, his doubt that anyone would want to help other people just for the sake of it, and I asked Jessie, "Are you sorry you lent me your phone now?"

"Nah," she said. "When I don't know someone's deal, I just try to be nice to them, know what I'm saying?"

I knew exactly what she was saying. I just didn't know why so few people approached it that way, why defaulting to kindness seemed so hard.

"Glad I'm not you, though," Jessie offered, and with that, she and her baby headed out.

25

When I met Abe on the porch late that night as usual, I was finally able to bring him entirely up to speed on my two phone calls with Lisa Rushall. It was a relief to have everyone else in bed so I could let it all out without worrying about who might overhear me.

"So this big-deal reporter wants *you* to write an account of what happened to you," Abe summarized once I finished telling him everything. He was sitting in his usual spot on the porch, near the steps down to the beach, while I paced around in front of him.

"Right."

"And you told her no."

"Right."

"Why?" he asked. "Isn't this your chance to make your side of the story heard?"

"It's too risky. No matter what I say or how I say it, I'm going to offend people. I would just write myself deeper and deeper into this hole. As Kevin and Valerie keep pointing out, no one wants explanations. They only want apologies.

"The best thing I have going for me right now is that enough time has passed that some people have forgotten who I am or why they should care. If I publish an article about it, it'll just remind them to hate me. Would *you* do this, if you had the chance?"

Abe tipped his head back to look up at the sky. "I guess not," he said at last. "But *I'm* not an especially good writer."

"Neither am I."

"Okay," he said, like he didn't quite believe me. "So now that you've spoken to the enemy, do you have any insight into how they work? Why they treat us like this?"

"I do, actually," I said.

"And?"

"And . . . I don't think they're really thinking about *us* at all. Not us as individuals. They're crying out against racial inequality or homophobia or corruption or animal abuse or whatever it is—all stuff that is *bad*, we *all* agree that it's bad—and they're using us as examples of those bad things. Deep down, I don't think most of those people actually want *me* to disappear. They want *racism* to disappear. They want *injustice* to disappear. And then we each get made into, like, these personifications of injustice, and then we each get torn down."

"Really?" Abe said, looking at me.

"Yeah. I mean, I bet there are a few people out there who actually hate *you*, specifically."

"Thanks," he said drily.

"But everyone else?" I went on. "I think they just hate the idea of corrupt rich people lying and stealing from not-rich people, and they've made you into a symbol of that."

"So I shouldn't take it personally," he suggested.

"Sure. If that's even a possibility."

"And since you've talked to this woman, do you have any better idea of how to get revenge on her?" he asked. "How to ruin her life the way she ruined yours and all that?"

I thought about it for a moment. Maybe I should have gotten good ideas from our phone call; maybe she'd revealed information I could use against her. But: "I guess I don't really want to anymore," I said. "It turns out she's not the one cause of my life being destroyed, any more than I'm the one cause of racial inequality." And it felt empty somehow, no longer having Lisa Rushall to blame, but also, in some way I didn't quite understand, it was a relief.

Abe chuckled softly.

"Why is that funny?" I asked.

"It's not," he said. "Just—you're very wise sometimes. I didn't expect to meet anyone like you when I signed up for Revibe. You were a surprise. So that's why I was laughing."

"What sort of people did you expect to be here?" I asked.

"Uh, this is going to make me sound like a jerk, but honestly I didn't think I was going to *like* anyone here. Or really have much in common with them. I thought it was going to be full of criminals and closed-minded brats trying to buy their way out of actually doing the right thing. Not to say that I'm *not* a brat, just that it's not exactly a quality I admire. I thought I was a victim, and then I was going to come here and be grouped in with a bunch of bad guys."

"You weren't wrong," I pointed out.

"Yeah, but then it turned out that basically everyone here is a victim *and* a bad guy. And then it turned out that, unrelated to any of that, I actually get along with someone here."

"You mean me," I said, to make sure.

He laughed again. "Yeah, Winter. I mean you."

I gave him a tiny smile.

"Come over here," he said.

So I did. "What's up?"

"Can you bend down?" he asked, sounding frustrated all of a sudden.

"Why?" I asked.

"Because I want to kiss you."

"Are you kidding me?" I blurted out. I didn't bend down.

Abe stared at me with his crystal-blue eyes. "I swear I used to have some game." He was trying to keep his tone light, but I could hear his voice quaver. "I would have casually moved closer to you. I would have leaned my shoulder against yours. I would have put my arm around you. I would have suggested we lie down together on the beach and look at the stars. I would have worked up to this moment and . . . it would have all been different. But I don't know how to do any of that anymore. It's never casual when I move. It's clumsy and stupid. I don't know what I'm doing anymore. I'm sorry."

"You don't have to be sorry," I told him. Here was a thoughtful, interesting, adorable guy who wanted to kiss *me*—what could he have to be sorry about? "It's just—"

"Let me guess," Abe said, his mouth twisting. "I'm stuck in a wheelchair for life. I know. That's not sexy. Not to mention I'm Michael Krisch's son. That's disgusting."

"That's not it," I said. "I'm just . . . surprised."

He watched me for a moment. I wrapped my arms around myself and looked away.

He sighed. "Look, I get it. You're not the only person to respond to me this way, you know. Maybe that's even how *I* would react if our roles were reversed right now. I just thought . . . I thought you might be different. Because of what you've been through, I hoped maybe you'd be able to see me in a different way. Never mind. I really am sorry. I didn't mean to make you uncomfortable."

"Abe," I said, "that's not what I meant." My head was spinning, and he looked so distraught, and I didn't know what to say or how to explain. "When we're together," I told him, "I'm not thinking about your wheelchair or your father. I just see *you*. And . . . I like what I see." I looked down at my shoes, then back at him, blushing furiously.

"Thank you." He bit his lip. "But to be totally clear . . . you don't want to kiss me."

"I do," I said as I remained standing, out of his reach. Now that I'd admitted it, I wondered when I'd started feeling this way. Was it when he sang to me in bed? When he told me I was pretty? Or had it happened the moment I met him and all along I'd refused to notice? "I want to kiss you." I whispered it as a confession. "But I'm scared."

"Scared of what?"

Oh, God, there were so many things to be scared about. I was scared because I had so little experience with this sort of thing, and most of what I knew about romance came secondhand from the not-great-sharer Jason.

I was scared that I would hurt Abe even more than he'd already been hurt. He was vulnerable, and I was destructive. I imagined thousands of the microscopic pathogens nested inside of me sliding through my saliva and down his throat, infecting him with me.

I was scared because if I kissed Abe now, what would that mean? What would tomorrow look like? And the next day? After all, hadn't I just told Lisa Rushall "you shouldn't start something that you don't know how to stop"? If I kissed Abe, *anything* could happen from that point. And I couldn't handle "anything." I needed to stick with the known, the things I had complete control over, the things I might not screw up.

Kissing someone who I liked, and who thought he liked me in return, was something I was very, very likely to screw up.

I was scared because Abe was a good person and I wasn't. Unlike me, he hadn't done anything wrong. I was scared because I didn't deserve him.

But I didn't say any of that. I didn't even know how to explain it. Instead, I gave him a concrete reason, something that I knew would make sense. "I'm scared of getting in trouble. They said on the first night that any romantic involvement was against the rules."

His eyes were wide and soft, his mouth hanging open slightly. He was hurt, even as I tried not to hurt him. Then he pressed his lips together. "I don't believe you," he said flatly. "You don't want to kiss me because you don't want to kiss me—which is completely fine, and entirely your choice to make—but claiming it's just because you don't want to get in trouble is an insulting excuse."

"It's not an excuse! I *don't* want to get in trouble!" And this was true. On top of everything else—my fear of the future, and of hurting him, and of screwing up him or me or both of us even more than we were already screwed up—on top of all of that, I wanted to do Revibe right.

"Bullshit. If you cared that much about your perfect record, you wouldn't have snuck into Valerie's office this morning. You wouldn't have borrowed a stranger's phone to talk to a reporter about Revibe. You wouldn't have refused to write your apologies in the first place. The truth is, you're perfectly willing to risk getting into trouble when it's worth it to you."

When he put it like that, I wondered if he might have a point. I *thought* of myself as a good girl who always did what she was supposed to. That was who I always had been. But somehow, since the last time I'd bothered to define myself, I had changed.

"What do you want, Winter?" Abe asked in a tired voice.

"I just want everyone to like me," I whispered.

"Well, *I* like you," he said, "but I can't speak for everyone. So I guess that's not enough."

"I'm sorry," I muttered. "I wish I could do whatever I felt like doing, whenever I felt like doing it. I would kiss you right now. But I can't."

"It's okay," he said. "I'm not going to try to convince you."

"It's not my *fault*," I tried to explain.

"No," he said. "It never is, is it?" And he turned and drove inside.

I felt like a rubber band was attached to my heart, and he held the other end of it, and the farther he went, the greater the chance that the band would snap, or that the force of it would wrench my heart out of my chest and drag it along after him. I wanted to run after him and kiss him long and hard. I wanted to do so much more than kiss him. It crashed over me like a wave, this wanting, and it threatened to drown me.

Instead of going after him, I sat down on the floor of the porch and I hugged my knees into my chest, listening to the ocean in the near distance. And I thought, if I weren't scared . . .

. . . what would I do?

26

For three days, Abe barely spoke to me. He was polite enough, but addressed me only when necessary. He made no jokes to me about yoga or over dinner, and he didn't show up on the porch at night no matter how late I stayed out there.

Revibe was lonely without Abe's friendship. I hadn't even realized I'd come to count on it so much until I didn't have it. Jazmyn, Kisha, and Zeke were still friendlier with one another than with anyone else, and Marco and Richard, while perfectly nice, were considerably older than me, and I couldn't think what we might have to talk about other than our crimes. It hadn't bothered me when I was hanging out with Abe, but now I couldn't help but notice that pretty much everyone else only spoke to me when they needed me to do work for them.

Three nights after not kissing Abe, we had a pathetic Thanksgiving dinner with "our whole Revibe family!" as Valerie put it—which is not really the family anyone imagines spending their Thanksgiving with. Later, as I walked past Kisha's closed door, I heard indistinct chattering and giggles, letting me know that Zeke and Jazmyn were with her once again. And I thought, *Screw it.* I wanted to do something spontaneous, something wild, something that didn't feel safe. I knocked on her door.

The room immediately fell silent, and then Kisha edged open the door. "Oh, Winter!" she said. "Hi! Come in. Guys, it's just Winter."

I followed her inside, and she closed the door behind us.

"We were worried you might be Valerie or Kevin," Jazmyn explained.

"Want a beer?" Zeke asked.

They made an odd threesome: Jazmyn, with her dyed hair and piercings; Kisha, who was all LA-chic; and Zeke, who was much younger than Kisha and probably wouldn't have been invited to hang out with her in any world where she had Hollywood guys her own age nearby.

"I thought we weren't allowed to have alcohol here?" I said, realizing this was a stupid comment as soon as the words left my mouth.

They all looked at me kind of funny, and Zeke said, "Uh, yeah, we're not," and took another swig from his beer can.

"Winter, I'm so glad you're hanging out with us," Kisha proclaimed. "You're the best. Isn't Winter the best?"

The other two nodded in affirmation. "You are so good at Repentance," Jazmyn said. "I don't think I would have ever been able to apologize to the guys in the band if you hadn't written it for me. Even the idea of writing to them made me want to die."

"It's bullshit that you had to apologize to them at all," I replied.

Kisha clapped her hands in delight. "See? I love this girl. You think she's so innocent, and then—*bam*—she drops a 'bullshit' into the conversation."

I didn't think it was so remarkable that I'd swear sometimes. Really, how sickeningly good-girl did I seem that it was hard to believe I could use a curse word?

The conversation moved on to other apologies they'd all written and responses they'd gotten. ("I use the ones you wrote for me as a model for every other one," Kisha told me, which made me feel simultaneously proud and ashamed.) Then they discussed Valerie and Kevin's marriage. ("I bet Kevin feels like a wuss since his wife obviously wears the pants in their relationship," Zeke said, and Jazmyn hit him and said, "*How* are you so sexist?")

They deliberated on who the hottest guy at Revibe was. This went on for a while. Apparently Kevin's face was weird-shaped, but he had a pretty good body for an old guy; must've been the surfing. Marco was handsome for his age, "But in a plasticky sort of way," Jazmyn said, which made the rest of us laugh, and she kept insisting, "You know what I mean! He looks like he was built by a machine!" Kisha thought Richard was "hot like a cowboy," and Zeke said that cowboys weren't hot, which led to Kisha hitting him with a pillow until he admitted they could be attractive. Jazmyn posited that Zeke was the best-looking guy here, which Zeke himself agreed with wholeheartedly.

"You didn't mention Abe," I pointed out—not that Abe really

needed his physical appearance dissected by anyone, but still, it seemed like if they were going to be objectifying everyone else, they should be objectifying him, too.

"Oh, right," Zeke said. "You guys are friends."

"He's really nice," Jazmyn offered, even though the relative niceness of the rest of the guys had never come up.

"I bet he'd be hot if he weren't in a wheelchair," Kisha said.

"Are you kidding me?" I said loudly. They all looked surprised: this hadn't been a serious conversation, but somehow, for me, now it was. "What does being in a wheelchair have to do with it?"

"Nothing," Kisha said. "It just means he's not really an *option*, you know?"

"No, I *don't* know," I replied. "Most of these guys aren't really *options*. Marco is married and doesn't seem to be that interested in women, period. Kevin is married and he's our *advisor*. And by the way, we're not actually allowed to get together with *anyone* here, hot or married or wheelchair-using or not."

"That's a good point," Jazmyn conceded.

"Do *you* think Abe's cute?" Kisha asked me.

I thought about how I'd felt three nights ago, when he asked if he could kiss me, and where I might be right now if I'd said yes. If I weren't always so scared of making a mistake or doing something wrong or getting in trouble, if it felt like there was any room in this world for error, if I could possibly believe I could do something without knowing the outcome and trust that it wouldn't ruin everything.

"Yeah," I said, "I think Abe is cute." Though it didn't seem fair that they knew I thought this when Abe himself did not.

"Winter's got a *crush*," Zeke sang.

"No more than Kisha has a crush on Richard," I shot back.

Kisha shrugged languidly. "I mean, I'm not saying I wouldn't."

"Guys!" Jazmyn yelped all of a sudden. "Guys, guys, *guys!*" She was staring at her phone. "They forgot to turn the signal jammer on!"

In a flash, we'd all taken out our phones. Unbelievably, this was true.

"They *never* forget," I marveled.

"Okay, this is amazing," Kisha said, holding aloft her phone, her link to the outside world. "Do you know what this means? We are free to do anything we want!"

We stared at one another, kind of dumbstruck, not totally sure what it was that we wanted to do now that we were free to do it.

"I need to google myself," Jazmyn said, quickly typing on her phone. She blushed. "Sorry. I know it seems like I must be super-self-absorbed—"

"But really you just want to see if anything horrible has happened to you," I finished. She nodded. "It's okay," I said. "I do that, too." Or maybe it *wasn't* okay, but the fact that we both did it made it seem like it was.

"I used to google myself constantly," Kisha said, "but I haven't so much since we got here. Because while we're here, nobody's seeing me, nobody's taking photos of me, so there's not much chance that some horrible new story about me is going to erupt. I'm just doing yoga and sorting canned food for homeless vets. No one's going to bother reporting on that."

The three of us girls looked at Zeke. He was engrossed in his phone. "What?" he asked when he finally noticed us. "I don't go around googling myself all the time."

"How?" I asked, intrigued. I did not have a lot of *respect* for Zeke, but I did have some envy for his ability to simply look away from the train wreck of his life.

"What do you mean, 'how'? I just don't do it."

"You're not even tempted?" I asked.

"Huh? No. If anybody doesn't like me, they're a jackass and an idiot. I don't care what jackasses and idiots think about anything, least of all me."

"Well," I said, "that is a very simple way of looking at the whole thing, isn't it?" While this approach might make Zeke immune to criticism, it didn't exactly seem like one I could adopt for myself.

"Guys, I know what we can do now that we have service," Kisha exclaimed. "We can *leave*."

"And go where?" Zeke asked.

"Literally anywhere! I'm ordering us a car right now." She must have noticed the stricken look on my face, because she clarified, "We'll go drive around for an hour or two. I'm not saying we should leave *forever*, obviously. We'll be back before anyone knows we're gone." She tapped on her phone for a moment, then said, "Okay, done. I told it to pick us up at the end of the drive so Kevin and Valerie won't hear it."

"Rad," Zeke said.

"I wonder if I have time to get changed," Kisha said. We were all wearing our own variations on jean shorts and T-shirts. Even Kisha and Marco, who'd dressed up more in the first few days of the retreat, had basically given up on making themselves look nice, especially when we were at the house. There was no one here to see us, so there wasn't much point. Kisha still put on eye makeup every day, which I assumed was for her own benefit, since there was no one around really to appreciate it—and, with or without makeup, she was far and away the prettiest person here.

"I'm not going to bother changing," Jazmyn said. "We're going to be sitting in a car. It's not like we're stopping by a fashion show along the way."

Kisha nodded reluctantly. "All right, let's just go. It says the driver will be here in five minutes, anyway. Now keep quiet!" She opened the door, and one by one we padded out into the hall. She slid open the door to the porch, and my heart stopped for a moment, thinking Abe might be out there—but he wasn't, of course. He'd be in his room, avoiding me. I felt a little guilty, like I was betraying him somehow by having adventures with people who did not include him.

The three of them crept out of the house, but I paused on the threshold.

"Winter! Are you coming or not?" Zeke whispered.

"What if Valerie and Kevin find out?" I asked, hating how wimpy I sounded.

"So what?" Jazmyn asked. "We're together. What are they going to do to all of us?"

"They could get mad at us," I answered.

The three of them gave me a variety of exasperated and confused looks, all plainly saying, *So?* As though there were worse fates in life than someone being mad at you.

27

We ran down the dark drive, giggling quietly the whole way. There was a thrill and a headiness to it, to staging an escape, even a brief one. To doing something that was against the rules, not knowing if we'd get caught or what might happen if we did—but as Jazmyn had said, what could they do to us, anyway?

We flung ourselves into the car waiting at the end of the driveway and shouted "Go, go, go!" at the driver, as though we were making our getaway from a crime. The driver calmly put on his turn signal and looked both ways before slowly pulling out onto the road. He was obviously not feeling the thrill and the headiness that we were. He was just working.

"Where can I take you?" he asked politely.

"You can just drive," Jazmyn said. "Anywhere is fine."

His speed dropped even lower. "Where are you trying to go, though?" he asked.

"Nowhere," Jazmyn replied.

"I can't drive you if I don't even know where you're trying to go," he pointed out. "Are you trying to go north or south? Can you give me an address to put into the GPS?"

"Oh, for Chrissakes," Zeke muttered.

"You can take us to any open convenience store," Kisha told the driver, her voice honey-sweet.

"There's one at the Shell station that's twenty-four hours," the driver replied thoughtfully. "Is that okay? If not, I think there's one at the Exxon station that might stay open this late, but you might want to give them a call to—"

"The Shell station sounds great," Kisha said impatiently. "Let's please go to the Shell station."

I rolled down my window, letting the breeze of freedom roll through the car in waves. Officially we weren't trapped at Revibe; we left the house every day for Redemption. But now, for the first time since we'd arrived, we were in control of where we were going. We could tell the driver we wanted to go to the Shell station or the Exxon station or even some *other* station if we felt like it. The choice was ours! Our destiny fit into our own hands!

When we reached the promised Shell station, Kisha asked the driver to wait outside for a moment while we picked up a few things.

"You know you have to pay by the minute," the driver told her, his molasses-slow voice sounding concerned for her finances. "Even when you're not in the car, you're still getting charged."

"Yup," Kisha said, her sweetness by now wearing as thin as ribbon candy. "I know. We'll only be a second."

We ran inside, and it was just a crummy, poorly organized gas station convenience store at midnight, but from our excitement, you'd have thought we were on a shopping spree at Bergdorf's. The tile floor was sticky in spots. One of the overhead fluorescent lights kept flickering. The freezer door didn't seal shut, so unnecessary blasts of cold air kept emanating from the back of the store. "I love it here!" Jazmyn cried.

We galloped through every aisle, screeching back and forth about the treasures we found. "Cheetos!" Zeke said. "I am getting a bag of Cheetos! *Look at this bag of Cheetos, everyone!*"

"Make it *two* bags of Cheetos!" Kisha shrieked back.

I grabbed a bottle of Gatorade, in honor of Mackler. "I am going to score all the honeys with this Gatorade!" I yelled. This didn't mean anything to anyone, but I was punchy.

Kisha laughed loudly. "You crazy!"

Jazmyn bought a king-size bag of Peanut M&M's (*"Like a king!"* she informed us), and Zeke bought a disturbing number of Cheetos, and the two of them ran outside to wait with the car. I paid for my Gatorade and then got distracted reading gossip magazine covers while Kisha asked the cashier for a pack of Marlboros.

"Let me see your ID," the cashier said.

Kisha pulled out her license and handed it over. The cashier reviewed it carefully, sucking on her teeth. She seemed to decide that everything was in order, because she turned around and pulled a pack of cigarettes off the wall behind her. She put it on the counter, then nodded toward Kisha's bag and asked, "What's that?"

"What's what?" Kisha asked.

"That shiny thing you got in there."

"This?" Kisha pulled it out. "A pack of gum."

"You get that here?" the cashier asked.

"No, ma'am," Kisha replied.

"'Cause if you got it here, you got to pay for it," the woman told her.

"Yeah, obviously," Kisha said.

"Don't you sass me," the cashier warned. "Now, you gonna look me in the eye and tell me you didn't just take that gum?"

Kisha opened the pack to show her. "I got this weeks ago. See? I already chewed three pieces."

The cashier scoffed, as if to say, *Any thief knows the trick of doing away with three squares of gum in order to make herself seem innocent.*

Kisha put down some bills on the counter to pay for her cigarettes, but the cashier did not immediately take them. She muttered something under her breath, and I couldn't quite make it out, but it sounded like she'd said, *"Oh, I know your type."*

Kisha clearly heard this too, because she replied hotly, "Excuse me? My *type*? What the hell do you mean, *type*?"

The cashier pursed her lips and shook her head. "All I'm saying is, we got security cameras everywhere. So if you took that gum, we gonna know it."

"I didn't take anything from here, you stupid cow!" Kisha snarled.

Everything froze for a moment. Even the fluorescent light seemed to pause in its flickering as we all took in what Kisha had said. Both her face and the cashier's wore matching expressions of horror. What was the cashier going to do?

But then I saw a change in Kisha's eyes. It took her just a moment, but I could practically *see* her going through the Revibe process. And before the cashier could get in another word, Kisha began her Repentance.

"I'm so sorry," she told the woman, her tone once again as sweet as syrup. "That was completely out of line. I shouldn't have said that."

"You shouldn't've," the cashier agreed. "I could—"

"I feel terrible," Kisha plowed on. "I'm a horrible person, and I really regret that you had to suffer because of that. I was wrong, and I'm sorry. And . . ." I saw her throat muscles working as she swallowed, then managed to spit out, "I'd like to give you an extra two dollars to cover the cost of the gum."

She threw down two more one-dollar bills.

"That's a good girl," the cashier said.

And Kisha walked stiffly out of the store.

I ran after her. "What the hell was that about?" I demanded once we were both outside.

"Nothing," she said. "That bitch thought I stole a pack of gum."

"But you *didn't*," I pointed out.

"Yup."

"So why did *you* apologize? *She* should be apologizing to you for being rude and patronizing and—"

"Well, she wasn't going to do that, was she?" Kisha snapped.

"She didn't accuse Zeke or Jazmyn or me of stealing anything."

"I know that," Kisha said. "God. I *hate* that woman."

"Why did—"

"Shut up, Winter," Kisha barked. "Do *you* get questioned about stealing shit? I don't want to talk about this anymore. Get in the goddamn car."

I shut up.

We got in the car. Kisha slammed her door.

Zeke and Jazmyn were still delighting in our daring escape from Revibe and our brief encounter with the real world. As the car pulled away and got back on the road, they were chattering over each other about how badass we were. "And," Zeke said triumphantly, "check out what I grabbed while the lady there wasn't looking." He moved his sweater aside to show off the six-pack of beer nestled inside of it.

We all stared at it. "You just took that," I said, to make sure.

"Hell yeah."

"And the cashier didn't even notice."

"Did not bat one single eyelash," he confirmed, flashing a winning smile of shining white teeth.

"Well," I said, "screw you, Zeke." He looked offended, and Jazmyn gasped, but Kisha gave me a very tiny, very tired smile.

Zeke started protesting, but I tuned him out. I leaned my head against the window, and I thought about Kisha and the way that cashier had treated her—treated *her*, and not the other three of us, because of how she looked.

And I thought about Abe and the way the rest of the group had been talking about him earlier—or not talking about him—because of how *he* looked.

And I thought about the way people went through life like they had a full handle on everyone else's deal. How they could know one side of you and be so convinced that there were no more sides to see. Jason was dangerous, Jazmyn was a slut, Emerson was a bimbo, Mackler was a clown, I was evil incarnate, and that was that. Everyone knew.

That girl Jessie, back at the teen shelter, had said, "When I don't know someone's deal, I just try to be nice to them." How had she managed to figure that out when somehow it seemed to elude the rest of us?

To the majority of the world, you are nobody in particular. They will see the color of your skin, or your weight, or your username, or your GPA, or how much money your parents make, and they will look no further. They will explain you immediately, and they will never forgive you.

I thought about all of this as we drove down the Pacific Coast Highway, along the ocean, and back to Revibe. I thought about all the things we don't say and don't do because we know that some people wouldn't like them.

And I thought: *I don't want to shut up.*

28

During Repentance the next evening, I sat down with a piece of paper and a pen. Lisa Rushall had told me I had something to say. I wanted to see if she was right.

It was hard to start. It was so hard. Even once I'd started, I would take any opportunity to get sidetracked, and then find it hard to keep going. Although I felt like I had a lot to say, it all seemed to go skittering away as soon as I sat down to commit it to paper, as though my ideas were cockroaches running for cover now that I'd turned on the light. And every word I wrote was nearly drowned by the voice in my head that never stopped screaming, *If anyone reads that word you just wrote, they will hate you. They will hate you for that word, and for the next word, too. You are giving them reason after reason to hate you.* I did it anyway.

I started out with an introduction of myself, and a warning:

I am Winter Halperin. I'm the one who went online after the National Spelling Bee and posted, "We learned many surprising things today. Like that dehnstufe *is apparently a word, and that a black kid can actually win the Spelling Bee."*

That's what I wrote. And I put it online for the whole world to see. You can stop reading now, if you want.

I went on from there. I skipped my one-on-one session with Kevin, because I had too much to say and didn't trust myself to stop. I described those terrible and dramatic first few days, as nearly everything and everyone I valued was systematically stripped away from me. I kept getting tripped up there, because I didn't know how to fully explain how devastating it felt. But I tried. I described Surprise I Can Spell and the panic attacks; the look in Kim's eyes when she told me her parents no longer trusted me to tutor her, and in that DMV agent's eyes when she told me I hadn't earned my driver's license; the tears my family cried when we found out I wasn't going to college anymore; the way I wanted to just give up when I read online that my best friend wasn't my friend anymore.

Did I do something wrong? Yes. Unquestionably, yes.

Did I deserve this level of hatred in exchange for what I did? I don't believe I did.

You may think otherwise. You may think I deserve every bit of my punishment, and then some. You are entitled to your opinion.

But I will say that I have spent many months believing I am a bad person. And now I'm finally starting to hope that maybe I'm not. Maybe I'm just like everyone else out there (yes, even you): a generally good person who sometimes does bad things.

But if that's true, then how do I move past the bad things I've done?

I can't say that because I didn't mean them, it's as if I didn't do them.

I can't forget about them or pretend they never happened.

I can try to do good things to outweigh the bad. It might take a lot of good things to even out the scales, but I can keep trying.

I can listen to the people I hurt, really listen, not just to defend myself or to tell myself they're wrong or crazy, but to understand why and how I hurt them so I can understand how to not do it again.

I can apologize to the people I hurt without making excuses.

I can start to forgive myself, maybe.

I can do all of that alone. But for the rest of it, I want to ask for your help.

I need you to believe that people can do something wrong, or even do a lot of things wrong, and not be ruined for life.

Can you do that?

Can any of us do that?

When I was a kid, parents and teachers told me all the time that "everyone makes mistakes" and "no one is perfect." Probably you got told that, too. But then you grow up and you discover that there are some mistakes you can't ever recover from, and some imperfections that are permanent and unforgivable. You thought there was room for experimentation and error, but you were wrong.

I learned that truth when I was still a little girl, competing in spelling bees. I learned that I couldn't afford to ever say one single letter wrong. I learned that life is all or nothing: it doesn't matter how many times you've done something right; all that matters is the one time you do something wrong. And the only champion is the one who is always, always right.

It's too late for me to always do the right thing.

But I would really like if there were other ways to be a champion.

I went on to write about Revibe. I didn't name it, and I didn't name any of the other guests there. Their stories were not mine to tell. But I talked a little about the process, finally writing:

The part I've had trouble with is Repentance. Because there are some people to whom I feel very, very repentant, and I want to apologize to them, and I still don't know how.

And then there are some people to whom I don't feel sorry at all. I know that it would make them feel better, or keep the peace, if I could apologize to them. So maybe I should do that. That's what I've learned to do here. But it doesn't feel right. It seems like it'd be ruining the apologies that I really do *mean if I mix them in with apologies that I'm just saying to try to get people to like me.*

I'm not *sorry to strangers who took to the internet to call me names, or swear at me, or dissect my physical appearance, or describe all the gruesome punishments I deserve, or crow about how great it was that now my opportunities were gone and my dreams were ashes.*

I'm not *sorry to people who preferred to write irate public posts bashing me rather than explaining how they felt.*

I'm not *sorry to anyone who used me as clickbait, who jumped on the train of attacking me because that was the fun news story of the day.*

I want all those people to like me. It would be so great if you all would like me! It would feel so amazing!

But wanting you to like me is not actually the same feeling as being sorry.

Here are some of the apologies I do mean.

I'm sorry to African Americans whom I hurt by implying that they're not as smart as other people. I thought I was being funny, but I wasn't.

I'm sorry to the people whom I brushed off when they actually tried to help me understand what was wrong with what I said. I grouped you in with the people who were being mean to me just for the sake of being mean, and I was wrong.

I'm sorry to Jason McJasonFace Shaw. (Did I guess your middle name yet? Am I close?) Whether you feel the same or not, you're still one of my best friends. When you told me that you felt hurt by my post, I shouldn't have argued with you. I should have simply believed you. I should have tried to understand why. I lost a lot of people over this, and it turns out that some of them I can do without. But I don't like doing without you. My life is worse without you in it, and I want your help to try to make myself worthy of being your friend again.

And I'm sorry to Sintra Gabel. You won the National Spelling Bee fair and square. That's hard, and it's rare, and nobody—including me—should ever undermine that.

I kept going from there. I wrote for a long time, until my hand cramped and the entire side of my pinkie was smeared with dark blue ink. I filled page after page, and I don't know if the words were right or wrong or good or bad, but they were all, all of them, mine.

29

When I finally put down my pen, I looked at the time. It was nearly two in the morning. I had written all through Repentance, all through evening snack and bedtime, and well into the night. I knew that I ought to go to bed at last, to try to get in at least a little sleep before Rehabilitation kicked off yet another early morning.

But that's not what I did. Instead, I walked down the hall and knocked on Abe's door.

"Coming," he called quietly. A long moment passed, and I pictured him on the other side of the door, probably getting out of bed, transferring into his wheelchair, coming across the room to open the door for me.

"Did I wake you up?" I asked when we were facing each other.

"Of course not."

It was wrong that we'd both spent the past three nights awake and alone when we could have spent them awake and together.

"I want to talk to you," I said. "Can I come in?"

"Sure." Abe gave me a tight smile. "Do you want me to leave the door open, so nobody gets the wrong idea about what we're doing in here?"

I blushed as I recalled saying that to him when he'd been in my room. I'd been so worried that someone would think I was doing something illicit, when really that hadn't been the right thing to worry about at all. "I don't care what ideas they get, actually," I replied, and I closed the door behind me.

What was more relevant, actually, was that being behind a closed door with just Abe and a bed was giving *me* ideas. But I wasn't going to go into that.

"So what do you want to talk about that can't wait until the morning?" he asked. Even with his door closed, he kept his voice quiet, and I did as well.

"I wanted to tell you that I'm sorry," I said.

"That's very Revibe of you," he said. "Let's hear the rest of it. You're a terrible person, hardly worthy of being alive; you wish I'd never had to suffer through being exposed to you—"

"None of that," I said. "Screw that. I wanted to explain myself."

"Well, that's *not* very Revibe of you," he said. "Who said you're entitled to explain yourself?" But I could tell he was teasing.

"Me," I replied. "I said I'm entitled to it. The other night, Abe, I panicked, but I swear it had nothing to do with your wheelchair or your dad and everything to do with *you*. I like you. I like you a lot, actually. But I don't like myself very much. And I was scared that I'd ruin you somehow, the way I've ruined so much else. Enough bad stuff has already happened to you. I didn't want *me* to happen to you, too."

"Winter," he said, his clear blue eyes so full of sadness.

"Literally just last night," I went on, "I started to believe that maybe I'm not predestined to destroy everything I touch."

He bit his lip, then said, in a voice even quieter than before, "It would be a pleasure to be destroyed by you."

I felt shaky.

"My sister has this theory," I told him, "that people are like houses. Some are fixer-uppers, some are trophy homes, some are that stifling childhood house that you grew up in. And I want you to know that you are . . ."

"A broken-down hovel made of metal?" he suggested.

I looked at him. Abe's house was like a little doorway that almost everyone walked right past. Maybe it hadn't always been that way, but it was now, since the wheelchair. But if you opened the door and went inside, you'd find a beautiful room, and then another, and then another. And if you stayed there, you'd discover hidden stairways and crawl spaces, enormous attics and basements. The house would expand around you, and no one on the outside would ever think that so much richness could lie behind such a small door.

"You're like a home," I told him. And then I kissed him.

Abe sighed gently against my lips and made a wordless sound in the back of his throat. He kissed me back carefully, slowly, in the way that one might taste a very small and very strong piece of dark chocolate. I rested my forearms on his shoulders and leaned in closer, deeper.

"This can't be comfortable for you," he murmured, opening his eyes a little bit.

"I guess not." I hadn't really been thinking about it before he said it, but I was bending over him, my upper back stooped.

"This might be easier if our mouths were at the same height," he pointed out.

"Okay." I stood up straight. "What do you suggest?"

"You could sit on my lap again," he said bashfully.

"Like when you rescued me?"

"I hardly *rescued* you," he protested.

"You helped." I sat down on his lap. He wrapped his arms around my back and pulled me tightly against him, so I could feel the pounding of his heart. I snuggled my head into his shoulder and kissed his neck, and he smelled so good, so unlike anything else, that it was intoxicating. I could have stayed there for hours, or forever.

And we did stay there for a long time, before I suggested—and I thought about it for a number of minutes before I finally willed myself to open my mouth and say it—"We could move to your bed."

I felt his arms stiffen around me.

"Or not," I added hastily.

He pulled back, and I looked at him. I couldn't parse the expression on his face.

"What's wrong? What are you thinking?"

"I'm thinking a lot of different things," he said, his voice an octave lower than I was accustomed to. "I'm thinking how much I like you." He reached out and played with a strand of my hair that had come loose from my ponytail. "And I'm thinking that I don't want to screw this up."

"You're not screwing it up," I said.

"Winter, I'm a *paraplegic*."

"I know that."

"So there are some things in bed that . . . I can't exactly do. Or I can, but they're more complicated for me. Even just the process of transferring from my chair *into* my bed is complicated. It makes me look pathetic and helpless and weak. I don't want you to see that."

"Look," I said, "we can stay here. We don't have to go to your bed. And even if we do, I don't have to watch you get into it. There's no right or wrong way to do this; we can do whatever we want. But if the only thing holding you back right now is that you're scared I'm going to think you're pathetic and weak and I'm not going to like you anymore, then that's not a good reason." I paused. "Can I ask you to just *trust* that I'm not going to make fun of you or criticize you?"

He gave me a half smile. "I can't trust anyone."

"Me neither," I said. "So I guess that evens the playing field."

"All right." He gave me a little nudge. "On your feet." I stood up, and he wheeled himself over to his bed. "So here's what I do," he said, "and I could be better at it, but whatever. I get my chair right next to my bed. And then I put one hand on my chair and one on the bed. And then I use my arms to push myself on here." Now he was sitting on the edge of the bed. He looked at me, waiting for my reaction. I didn't give him one. "Okay," he went on, "here's the even more embarrassing part. Now I have to use my hands to, like, scoop up my legs and place them on the bed." He did so. "And now I have to scooch myself backward with my arms . . . And *now* I can lie down." He sank against the pillows at the head of his bed and looked at me again, his face red.

"Okay," I said. "So can I join you?"

He gave me a beautiful smile.

I lay down on the bed beside him, and he pulled me close against him. "You are crazy not to think that there's something wrong with me," he whispered into my ear.

"You are crazy not to think that there's something wrong with *me*," I pointed out. "Ask anyone, and they'll tell you how much is wrong with me."

"Like I said, I don't trust anyone." He kissed my forehead and commented, as much to himself as to me, "I can't believe I'm here right now."

"Neither can I," I agreed. This was not the behavior of the girl who once locked herself in her hotel room, lest she unwittingly sneak out and kiss Janak Bassi.

"I want you to know, you're the first girl I've done anything with since I got my chair," he said. "I mean, there's been no one I asked out. No one I kissed. It all just seemed so complicated and impossible. And now it seems . . . possible again."

It was funny, I thought. I wasn't glad for anything that had happened to either of us. I wasn't glad that Abe's father was a thief, or that Abe had tried to end his life, and I wasn't glad that I'd lost my spelling bee title and my chance at going to a top-tier college, or that people all over the world would go on believing I was a racist for as long as they remembered my name.

But if none of that had happened, then we would never have been here together tonight.

So while I wasn't glad for the things that had happened to us, I was glad that they had brought us to this place where I'd never even known I'd wanted to be.

30

I slipped out of Abe's bed and back to my own room shortly before sunrise. I hadn't slept more than an hour or two the whole night, and I felt like hell when I had to go to yoga. But then I caught Abe's eye as I went into Warrior One pose, and he gave me a little smile and I gave him a much bigger smile back, and I thought about how just a couple of hours ago his hands had been on my hips, and his lips had been on my skin, and I just couldn't bring myself to care how tired I felt. *Tired* wasn't even the right word for what I was feeling. I felt buzzy.

Abe and I sat next to each other at breakfast, which probably wasn't a good idea, since all of us sat at the big table and ate together, so there was nothing he and I could say or do that wouldn't be observed by the entire group. After breakfast, he very slowly accompanied me back to my room, and we loitered in front of my door until everyone else had disappeared into their own rooms to make their beds, brush their teeth, and get ready to head out for the day. When we were sure that nobody else was out in the hallway, he stroked my hand with his fingertips and whispered, "I don't know how I'm supposed to pretend that I'm not crazy about you."

I knew exactly what he meant. To me it was so obvious. How could any of the others possibly be fooled?

"Hey," I said, "can I ask you for a favor?" In an even quieter voice, I went on, "I wrote something for *The Pacific* after all."

"You did?" His eyebrows rose.

"Yeah. I mean, maybe. I wrote something. I don't know if it's for *The Pacific* or if I should throw it in the garbage. Would you . . . read it?"

"Yes," he said immediately.

I went into my room, got the papers, and handed them to him. Abe was the first person I'd trusted with my words since The Incident, and I think he understood that, because he just said thank you and wheeled away.

I wondered what in my essay would offend him enough to make him realize that he actually wanted nothing to do with me, because surely there would be something. And then I let myself hope that maybe there wasn't. After all, he knew this much about me, and he didn't hate me yet.

I thought about going after him to let him know, before he had the chance to start reading, that I didn't really *mean* anything I wrote in there. But I held my tongue and I let him go. Because actually, I meant all of it.

Be cool, Halperin, I ordered myself, and I went to brush my teeth.

Shortly thereafter, we all met at the van for Redemption. I thought I was successfully being cool, but apparently I wasn't, because as soon as he saw my face, Abe said, "I haven't even looked at it yet. It's been literally fifteen minutes."

I wrinkled my nose at him.

"Looked at what?" Richard asked as he climbed into the van.

"Winter asked me to weigh in on an apology she's working on," Abe answered smoothly.

"Winter's writing an apology?" Kevin repeated. "That's terrific. You see, I *knew* apologizing to that reporter would grease the wheels for you. The first apology is the hardest. I remember that so clearly. You have to get over the hump, and then with each one you get into more of a rhythm. Like I said, you just needed a little push."

"Hmm," I said, slouching in my seat.

"Do you still do Repentance?" Marco asked Kevin.

"For sure," Kevin acknowledged. "The Three Res are part of my daily routine. They got me out of a dark place, and I'm not ever going back there. Anyway, I believe that you've got to practice what you preach. I can't very well ask you to do the Three Res if I'm not doing them myself."

I was still angry with Kevin for sending that apology to Lisa on my behalf, and for acting so smug about it now. But if I was being charitable about it, he only wanted the things that had worked for him to work for us, too. He'd found a way out, and he wanted to lead us all through it. It just hadn't occurred to him that maybe we didn't all belong on the same path.

Abe returned my essay to me that evening. "I don't know much about writing or journalism or whatever," he said. "I know what I like, but I couldn't tell you *why* I like it. And I don't read *The Pacific* much. So take my opinion with a grain of salt. But . . . I feel like you took everything I don't know how to say and said it for me."

"That seems good," I said cautiously.

"It's probably good," he agreed.

"So you don't think I should burn it," I asked, just to make sure.

"I'd advise against that."

Okay, then.

"So, this Jason guy you wrote about," Abe went on. "He seems pretty special."

"He is," I agreed.

"What's his deal?" Abe asked.

I thought about how to describe Jason. As I said, my friends and I liked one another, but we didn't often talk about it. I said, "He's the perfect straight man in our group of friends. He's funny, but not in a star-of-the-show way. He's, like, quietly droll. We all make movies together, but Jason's the only one who actually bothers to upload the footage and edit it and turn it into something usable. Without him we don't get anything done. He's stupidly vain, but gets embarrassed when he has to speak in front of anyone, even if it's for a little class project. He's good-looking and athletic, so he could be a total jerk if he wanted to, but I don't think the idea's ever occurred to him. He's just a big nerd. I guess what I'm saying is . . . he's complex. He's so many things all at once. And that's what makes him special. He's not someone you can just, like, replace."

"You miss him," Abe said.

"Yeah."

"Are you, like, into him?" he asked. I gave an involuntary laugh, and Abe blushed. "What?"

"No, there's no reason you'd know this, but Jason is a great friend and a *nightmare* boyfriend. Yeah, I thought he was cute when I first met him—he *is* cute—but that's also kind of his downfall. He never commits to anyone, and it never comes back to bite him because he's good-looking enough to always attract someone else."

"Sounds like an interesting guy," Abe observed.

"He is. All my friends are. But I'm not into any of them. Actually . . ." I lowered my voice. "I can't imagine being into anyone but you."

Abe's cheeks turned pink, and he grinned. "I think it's nice that you're fighting for Jason, actually. When my shaming happened, I never tried to win back anyone. Everyone who left me was just gone. I figured if they couldn't see that I was innocent, couldn't give me the benefit of the doubt and stand by me, then they weren't really my friends in the first place. I wasn't going to beg."

"Do you think I'm begging?" I asked, looking doubtfully down at my essay.

"No," Abe said. "I think you're apologizing."

I spent every free minute over the next couple of days typing up my essay. Then I sent it to Lisa Rushall. *I don't know if you were kidding about my writing about Revibe for* The Pacific, I e-mailed her. *But I wrote something. Here it is.*

I was able to read her response during Repentance the next night—though waiting those twenty-four hours was not easy. She wrote, *My edits on your essay are attached. The order of your argument is nonsensical, and you use the words "just" and "really" in almost every sentence. Also, you repeat every idea ten times, in ten different ways. Work on that.*

I opened the attachment to her e-mail and saw my essay covered in margin notes. I almost couldn't see my own words, they were so hidden under Lisa's red marks.

She hated it. It was stupid. It was all wrong.

She hated me. *I* was stupid. *I* was all wrong.

I felt sick to my stomach as I e-mailed her back. *You could have just said you hated it. You didn't have to go into so much detail.* And I closed out of my e-mail.

It was okay, I told myself. I didn't need my work to get published in *The Pacific*. It was safer this way, anyway. I'd written it, and Abe had read it, and that would be enough. Lisa's rejection was protecting me from a much worse response.

But the next time the signal jammer was lifted, I saw that Lisa had replied. *I didn't say I hated it. I said you should revise it.*

That was it.

Fine. I was capable of revising it. It had been a nightmare writing it in the first place, but whatever, sure thing, I could write it again. I gritted my teeth and rolled my neck and started going through Lisa's comments. I deleted the *just*s and the *really*s, except where I *really* needed them. (See what I did there?) I reordered the paragraphs, then deleted the last two lines of almost every one. And gradually, surprisingly, it got better.

My teachers had always told me that I was a good writer. The commenters online had told me that I was a bad writer. And both of these seemed to be immutable truths, something I was or was not. It had never occurred to me that this was an option, too: that I might be an okay writer who could, with help, get better.

I revised and went back through the essay and revised again. Lisa's comments were abrupt and compassionless, just like her. But they weren't wrong.

I worked on my essay for days. To anyone watching me, I must have looked really, really involved in my Repentance. And, in my own way, I was. It was a weird experience, writing something for so long without getting any response to it. Usually I'd write an essay for school in a night, maybe two, and then I'd hand it in. Anything I'd written on my own time, even the longer stories, I'd posted in chunks to critique sites so people could tell me that they liked it as I went. And of course I'd posted a lot of stuff online just as soon as I'd thought it. I could have two likes on something I'd written before I even fully figured out what I meant by it.

So this was different, and difficult. To write and revise, and revise again, without really knowing how anyone would respond to it—except for Lisa, and she didn't have any compliments for me. I sent her multiple drafts, and each time she sent them back with comments all along the margins.

Finally, Lisa asked me to call her. *It's going to have to be between six thirty and nine p.m.*, I replied. *That's the only time I get cell service.*

So she sent me her home number. And during Repentance the next night, I closed myself into my room and gave her a call.

"It's done," she told me.

"What do you mean, 'it's done'?" I asked.

"I mean your essay doesn't have any obvious problems left in it."

"Oh my God," I said. "Do you ever say anything nice? To anyone? It's okay if you don't want to say nice stuff to *me*; I'm just wondering if you even have positive words in your vocabulary."

"This is the problem with your generation," Lisa told me.

"This is?"

"Well, it's *one* of the problems with your generation. You're all so reliant upon A-pluses and smiley faces and gold stars and instant thumbs-ups. If someone doesn't hit 'like' right away, you assume that means 'hate.'"

"I don't think my generation invented the idea of positive reinforcement," I said. "I'm pretty sure everyone enjoys hearing that people like their work."

Lisa made a noise of vague disapproval, or disagreement. "We're going to run this online first thing on Friday," she said, "and then in next week's print edition. All right?"

Panic bubbled up inside my chest. Of course, I had wanted and intended for her to publish my essay. I wanted to come clean, and I wanted people to understand what happened when they attacked a stranger online. None of that would happen if Lisa *didn't* publish it.

But how could I really go through all of this again? Could I knowingly open myself up to the world's criticism and mockery?

"Is my story any *good*?"

"What do you think?" she asked.

"I don't know! That's why I'm asking you. Is it good? Is it terrible? Scale of one to ten?"

She paused. When she replied, her voice was low and direct. "You have to know the answer to that question yourself. Do you believe that you're saying something here that matters? Do you believe that you're saying something true? Do you believe that you're saying something that could, in some way, bring about a positive change?"

I thought maybe those were rhetorical questions, but when she didn't answer them, I realized they were for me. So I thought about it. "Yes," I said at last. "I believe that."

"Okay, then."

"Wait. What if I'm wrong? What if it *doesn't* matter and it *isn't* true, and everybody else thinks it's terrible?"

"If you believe in what you're saying, then some people will, too. And no matter what you believe, or how good it is, some other people will certainly think it's terrible."

"And then what do I do?" I asked.

Lisa laughed at me. "Nothing."

31

I woke up on Friday morning knowing that, if all had gone as it was supposed to, my essay was now out there in the world. I felt like my bloodstream was full of soda bubbles. There were my words, and my thoughts, and my experiences, in a real publication that people anywhere could read and judge. It was both everything I'd dreamed of and everything I feared.

People would be talking about me and my article. I knew they would be. I just didn't know what they would say.

Oh, there's White Winter, throwing herself into the spotlight again.

I can't believe she expects us to feel bad for her.

I don't buy her apologies for a second.

Or maybe the response would be good. That was possible, wasn't it? Maybe the conversation right now was about how people finally understood me. Understood, and heard my Repentance, and could forgive me.

Good or bad, I was desperate to know how people were responding to me.

But the signal jammers were on.

So I couldn't look.

I threw myself into yoga and prayer that morning. We spent Redemption at a soup kitchen, and I focused on making sandwiches as though my life depended on it. I put together more peanut butter and jelly sandwiches in one afternoon than my parents had made for me and Emerson in our entire lives.

When dinner was over and we got our brief period of cell reception, I thought, *This is my chance, this is my chance!*

And then I thought, *I've made it through twelve hours without reading anything about myself. I can make it a little longer.*

It's like Schrödinger's cat, which is this philosophical idea that if there's a cat inside a closed box, you can't tell if that cat is alive or dead until you open the lid. So for as long as the box is closed, the cat is simultaneously both alive *and* dead. Both realities will coexist until you open the box and only one becomes reality.

Googling myself would be opening the box.

So I didn't do it. I didn't read any comments or blog posts or tweets. I did, however, read my essay.

It was different, reading it on *The Pacific*'s website, as if I were seeing it through somebody else's eyes. I knew all the words but felt distanced from them. The headline was RACIST, VICTIM, OR BOTH: WHAT HAPPENS AFTER THE INTERNET TURNS AGAINST YOU. I hadn't known what it was going to be called, hadn't even thought about it, and yet there it was. And there was my name, right below it. I touched the screen with my fingers, and a shiver of pure delight overtook me. I'd always wanted to be a writer. And now I was. It felt good, and magical, and *right*.

When it was time for my counseling session, I left the Great Room and headed to Kevin's office. But he wasn't alone in there. Valerie was with him.

I knew what was going to happen an instant before it began. The joy in my veins crackled a warning.

"*The Pacific,*" Kevin said, his voice shaking with frustration. "You wrote an essay for *The Pacific.*"

"Yes." I looked at them both. Valerie was sitting, head in her hands, but Kevin was on his feet, so I stayed standing, too.

"What the hell were you thinking?" Kevin demanded, slamming his hand down on his desk. I flinched. Valerie didn't show any reaction at all.

"I wanted to share how I felt," I said, with as much confidence as I could muster. "I wanted people to understand my experience so that maybe I could stop it from happening again."

"You can't stop it from happening again!" Kevin yelled. "It will keep happening forever, as long as there are humans and the internet and anonymity. Who do you think you are, that you can write a little personal essay and all of a sudden convince strangers all over the world to just be *nice* and *respectful* to one another?" His voice got high and babyish at the end.

"I—I don't think that," I stammered. "I don't think I'm going to suddenly fix anything. I just . . . When I explained to Lisa Rushall what had happened to me, it seemed to sort of change how she thought about me. So I thought maybe if I could explain it to more people—"

"Who is this Lisa Rushall?" Kevin demanded.

"The journalist at *The Pacific* who helped me with this essay."

"Why were you talking to a journalist about your story in the first place? What is *wrong* with you, Winter?"

I was sick of this. "There is nothing wrong with me, Kevin, and people need to stop trying to convince me that there is. The only reason I started talking to Lisa in the first place was that *you* e-mailed her an apology on my behalf. And I didn't mean the apology, and I didn't want to say it, and if you were going to *force* it out of me, then I needed to explain what was *actually* happening!"

"You needed to—?!" Kevin began to roar, but Valerie cut him off.

"Winter," she said, her voice quieter than Kevin's, almost pleading. "We are here to *help* you. All you needed to do was work with us. You *didn't* need to get in touch with this woman to explain 'what was actually happening.' You could have, and *should* have, simply let her receive your apology. Most likely she would have forgiven you, and then you could have gone on apologizing to everyone else who wanted to hear it, without writing this . . . this . . . *manifesto*."

"I wasn't trying to write a *manifesto* . . . " I began, then trailed off, because maybe that was, in fact, exactly what I'd been trying to do.

"We know what we are talking about," Valerie appealed to me. "We are professionals at this. The Revibe technique is tried and tested, and it *works*. Look at all your co-Vibers. They're doing the work, both internal and external. They're writing their Repentances. They are mending fences, and they are preparing to reenter the world and pick up their regular lives. That's what everyone else is doing, and you could have done it, too, Winter."

"They don't mean their Repentances, though," I said.

I thought about the apology I'd written to Marco's eight-year-old daughter, telling her that I loved her more than anyone in the world and that being her dad was the greatest joy in my life.

I thought about the apology I'd written to the girlfriend of one of the guys in You but Good in Bed, telling her that I was so sorry I'd made her boyfriend cheat on her, but don't worry because he would always love her more than he ever cared about me.

I thought about the apology I'd written to Zeke's downstairs neighbor, telling her that I wept for Dante the cat every night and prayed for him every morning.

"They don't mean a word of it," I told Valerie. "I can't do that. I want to mean what I write. I want to write what I mean. *That's* what makes me a writer."

"That's also what makes people dislike you," Kevin spat out.

I bit my lip.

A tear ran down my cheek.

I mustered all my strength, and I whispered:

"It's okay if some people don't like me."

Valerie picked up the phone. "We're going to need to call your parents."

She turned on the speaker and, after a few rings, I heard my mom's voice. "Hello?"

"Darlene, this is Valerie and Kevin, from Revibe," Valerie said crisply. "We have Winter here with us."

"Hi, Mom," I volunteered.

"Is everything all right?" Mom asked. I heard some shuffling on her end of the line, and then Dad was on there, too, saying, "Hi, kiddo, haven't heard from you in a while."

"We're calling about Winter's essay for *The Pacific*," Valerie explained. "Did you see it?"

"We did!" Mom exclaimed. "Emerson just sent us the link about an hour ago. It's *extraordinary*, honey. One of the best things you've ever written."

"Thank you," I said, trying not to look too smug.

"We're really proud of you," Dad weighed in. "I want to hear about how you got *The Pacific* to publish it."

"I didn't even realize this was part of Revibe's method," Mom said.

"It's not," Kevin said shortly.

A pause. "Excuse me?" Mom said.

"Writing personal essays about how this isn't really your fault and you're not really the bad guy is *not* part of Revibe," Kevin replied. "Winter wrote this herself and got it published behind our backs. She did this instead of participating in healing writing exercises that *are* part of the Revibe technique. She did it in blatant disregard for the customs and values of Revibe, and in so doing she undermined the recuperation process of her fellow Vibers."

"Is this true, Wint?" Dad asked.

Kevin and Valerie watched me, as if daring me to deny it. "I did know it was against the rules," I conceded.

"Why?" Mom asked, her voice cracking. "Winter, why would you break the rules?"

My heart hurt, hearing the pain in her voice. "I couldn't be silent anymore."

"You couldn't have waited until you were home?" Mom asked. "You couldn't be silent for just one more *week*?"

Now Valerie and Kevin were the smug-looking ones.

"I supported you in this," Mom went on, her voice rising with frustration. "When you said no to Personal History, I gave in. When you said you wanted to spend your savings going to Revibe, I agreed with you. I honestly believed that if it was an approach that *you* had chosen, then you would make it work. And now I find out that you're just doing whatever you want down there? You're not even trying? You needed to make this *better*, Winter. We all were counting on you to make this *better*."

"I was trying to make it better," I said, fighting even more tears. "That's why I wrote the essay in the first place." My mother almost never yelled at us. Compared to a lot of mothers, this wasn't even yelling. Maybe it was worse. At least if someone really yelled at you, you could yell back. This was just guilt.

"I'm sorry, Valerie, Kevin," Mom said, modulating her voice. "I shouldn't have gotten so upset."

Parenting experts don't get upset with their children. It doesn't reflect well on them.

I thought about what Lisa had said to me on the phone. *I always thought your mother was pretty much full of shit.* Of course I was always going to take my mom's side against Lisa, or anyone. But her words had stuck with me and made me wonder if she had a point. Not that my mom was completely off base, a charlatan and a liar. But that maybe, sometimes, she could be wrong.

"We're considering sending Winter home," Valerie said.

My head snapped up. "You *are*?"

"It seems clear that you've gotten out of Revibe all you're going to get out of it," Valerie said snootily.

"And we can't have people sticking around here who have no respect for our policies," Kevin added. "We can't trust you."

Everyone broke the rules, was the thing. They drank beers in their rooms and snuck out to gas stations. They got me to write their Repentances. Everyone did things wrong sometimes, but only some of us got caught.

I knew I had only another week, but I didn't want to return to my real life. Because I still didn't know what my real life was going to hold for me.

And anyway, Abe was here.

"Can I say something?" Dad spoke up. "I don't accept that Winter did anything wrong."

"She broke the rules," Kevin replied with exasperation.

"Be that as it may, you read what she wrote, and, well, like her mom and I said at the start of this call, it's pretty darn good. It at least gave me insight into what she's been through, and how to treat people, that I wouldn't have had otherwise. And I know my daughter better than most people. She said what she meant. She clearly put a lot of thought and effort into it. Even if I didn't agree with every word, or I knew other people didn't agree with every word, how could I, as a father, not be proud of that?"

My heart swelled with love for my father. He sounded perfectly reasonable. If I didn't know any better, I might have even thought that he was some kind of parenting expert himself.

"Look," Dad went on, "I'll be honest with you. When Winter said she wanted to go to Revibe, I didn't believe you guys could help her. I thought it was just a clever way to get some money from people who were so desperate, they had nowhere else to go. But I stand corrected. The last time I saw Winter, she wouldn't have been able to write an essay so filled with wisdom and self-awareness. As far as I can tell, it's thanks to Revibe that she's reached this point. She thought you could save her, and I wasn't convinced, but it turns out she was right. You did save her."

Kevin looked confused. Valerie looked flattered. We all stared at the phone in the center of the desk.

"What do *you* want to do, Winter?" Mom asked me.

"I want to stay here," I replied.

"Then we support you in that," Mom said, her voice trembling a little, like she knew her line but had so much stage fright that it was hard to say it.

Kevin sighed. "What's another week?"

They weren't agreeing because they wanted me around, obviously. My dad had talked them into putting up with me for a few more days, not into liking me or respecting me or understanding why I'd done what I had done.

But I could live with that. Like I said, it's okay if some people don't like me.

32

And so I stayed. I steadfastly did not google myself in the evenings that followed, but I did check my e-mail, and I found that you can't avoid people who tell you *directly* that they hate you. The blessing, of course, is that they can't tell the entire world at the same time they tell you: it's a private message of contempt and judgment, and that's easier to handle than a public announcement saying the same thing. And there are many fewer of them. I suppose it takes more effort to write a personal e-mail telling someone that she's a bitch, and the payoff is nowhere near as good.

Still, it hurt so much to read the e-mails that had come in since my piece ran and said things like *ur still a racist u kno* and *do you even know how self-absorbed, closed-minded, and CRAZY you are?* It didn't matter that in my life now I'd seen thousands of messages that said the same thing. I never became immune to it; it never stopped hurting. And I couldn't help but feel like an idiot for bringing this upon myself. Was it worth it?

Then I got another e-mail in response to my essay. And it was different.

Dear Winter,

You don't know me, but my name is Christie. I'm fourteen years old and I play soccer. A couple of my teammates and I figured out that if we each covered up certain letters on our jerseys, we were left with letters that spelled out a not-nice name for Chinese people. (We are not Chinese, by the way: three of us are white, one of us is Latina, and one of us is black.) I'm not going to write the name here because it's not a good word, which we sort of knew, but also we thought it was funny that we could get our jerseys to look like they said that.

So we took a photo and we shared it with the rest of the team because we thought they'd think it was funny, too. Some of them did, but two girls (also white) got offended and went to the coach, and the coach went to the principal, and we got suspended, and somehow the photo wound up online. And hundreds of people made comments about how offensive and horrible we were. I really, really wish we'd never taken that picture. It's not like we dislike

Asian people or wanted to hurt them or anything. We just really weren't thinking.

Anyway, I'm sorry to take up your time—this is way more about me than you need to know! The point is that I felt really awful, like the worst I've ever felt. I was crying all the time and I couldn't eat and I threw up when I tried to go back to school. But then we read your article and it helped us. One of my teammates' moms read it first and showed it to her, and then we all read it.

What you went through is sort of like what we're going through, except yours sounds way, way worse. I found myself relating to so many of the experiences that you wrote about. And it made me feel better to know that someone else has had something like this happen to them and they came out of it okay, and can still do important things like write articles for magazines. I guess I'm trying to say that you're kind of my role model now! I hope that's not weird.

Thanks for everything,
Christie

I reread Christie's e-mail immediately. By the time I finished, I was beaming.

Maybe I had actually done something good.

I had no idea how many people would read or care about my essay, or how many people would hate it. It seemed unlikely to ever go viral. I knew it wouldn't get as high in my search results as that BuzzFeed list or the *New York Times* story back in May. And maybe in my whole life, no matter what I did or wrote in the decades to come, nothing would ever get as high as those. Maybe they would be the first page of my story until the day I die, and forever after.

But they weren't the whole story, not anymore. Because now my essay had been woven into my story, too. And hopefully with time there would be other essays I wrote, or stories or poems or even books. Maybe I'd invent something or discover something or get married or run my own company, and each of those threads would be woven into the fabric of my life so that when I looked at it as a whole, my public shaming would just be one very ugly and painfully threadbare part of it.

I hopped to my feet and headed down the hall for a snack. Let Kevin and Valerie be angry with me for publishing this essay. Let strangers think I was offensive and self-obsessed. I didn't care, because I had helped some girl named Christie. And in return, she had helped me. And wasn't that the entire point of words?

After what seemed like both too long and too short a time, we arrived at our last night of Revibe. Following an abbreviated Repentance, we all met up in the Great Room for closing remarks. Most of the Vibers would be heading to LAX in the morning, while my mom would be coming to pick me up in the afternoon.

We went around and said what we were looking forward to as we prepared to rejoin the real world, and what we were nervous about. "I just can't wait to see Tabitha," Richard said, and I got the sense he would have been weeping if he'd been less of a manly man. "I've never been apart from her for so long. I keep worrying that maybe she's forgotten me, or thinks that I've forgotten about her." He paused. "And real food. I can't wait to eat real food again." He paused once more. "And something to drink. Even a glass of wine would hit the spot by now."

"Though don't you feel so much healthier and more invigorated after five weeks of Meghan's cooking?" Valerie asked him.

"I do," Kisha volunteered.

Richard grimaced.

"I'm not thrilled to be going home to the East Coast in December," Zeke said. "Apparently they already got nine inches of snow there."

"At least you'll have a white Christmas," Jazmyn pointed out. "We never get a white Christmas in Austin."

"I don't care about white Christmases. I'd rather have the beach. I wonder if there's another rehab place around here that I can go to. Like maybe I should develop a drug addiction so I can come back."

Most of the room laughed, except for Abe and me, who caught each other's eyes and shared an *I don't think he's kidding* look.

"Do you feel ready to go back?" Kevin asked Zeke. "Other than the weather, that is. Do you feel emotionally prepared?"

"Yup," Zeke answered immediately. "I Repented to Ms. Candela and her whole family and, like, everyone else in our building."

He hadn't. I had done it for him.

"And I'm going to Repent even more once I see them. They'll never have seen anyone as sorry as I am."

"What about everyone online?" Richard asked. "The ones who accused you of being an animal abuser? Personally, those are the people I'm still worried about."

Zeke shrugged. "Don't care. They don't get any say over whether my parents and I can stay in our apartment. They're assholes."

Abe and I looked at each other once more, rolling our eyes in unison. In a way, Zeke had it the easiest of all of us. He never doubted that he was in the right.

"My wife and I are getting a divorce," Marco said heavily. "I feel like a failure. I failed her. But the good news is that we'll share custody of our daughter. Professionally, I still don't know what the plan is. I'm hoping I can build up my consulting business. Maybe I'm better equipped to do that now than I was before I came here."

I thought about how when we got here, we all just wanted our lives back. Richard wanted his daughter to come home, and Marco wanted to return to politics, and Zeke wanted his parents to be able to keep their apartment. Of course I wanted my old life back, too. Perhaps I would always want that. But it was no longer the *only* thing we wanted. And that, it seemed to me, was progress.

"My friends at school claim that everyone's totally moved on from what happened between me and You but Good in Bed," Jazmyn volunteered. "They said that a teacher was having an affair with one of our classmates, so now that's all everyone's talking about."

"That's so tragic," Valerie murmured.

"I know. But if it makes people forget about me . . ." Jazmyn shrugged. "I don't mean to be heartless here. It's that people seem to always need *something* to be outraged about. And if it has to be something, I'm just glad it's not me anymore."

Kevin said to all of us, "We want to impress upon you that the techniques you've learned here at Revibe are skills you can keep using long after you're gone. The point of a retreat isn't only to give you focused time out of your ordinary lives. It's also to give you tools that you can take home with you and weave into your everyday habits. Continue to practice yoga, connect with a higher power, eat healthy, stay away from intoxicating substances, and take care of your bodies and souls. Continue to do acts of Redemption. We've introduced you to a host of them here. Which ones resonated with you? If you found volunteering at the shelter to be particularly meaningful, then do so on a regular basis at home. If it was working with animals at the ASPCA that helped you, then do that wherever you live."

Kisha said, "That's my plan. I'm going to do lots of really visible charitable work, get it in all the blogs and magazines. You know I don't live too far from here, so I'm going to go back to the children's hospital on a regular basis. I really *like* kids. I liked being on *Sense That!* because I got to be a positive influence on kids' lives, and losing that was one of the saddest things about what happened to me. So volunteering at the hospital, I'm going to be a positive influence on *fewer* kids, but ones who I can actually get to know, and who really need help."

"No more acting?" Valerie asked her.

Kisha gave the TV star smile I knew so well and said, "If I make a good enough name for myself, I bet I'll get offered some jobs."

I bet she would, too. Kisha was not the type to accept defeat.

"That's great that you'll be so focused on Redemption," Kevin told her. "And of course all of you should continue your practice of Repentance. Never stop apologizing. You know how to do it the right way now. The majority of you do, that is."

His eyes flickered past me.

"I know how to apologize," I blurted out. "I've written dozens, maybe even *hundreds*, of apologies over the past five weeks."

"Well, that's funny," Kevin said, "because we never saw any of them."

My fellow Vibers kept their eyes trained on the ground. Only Abe was looking at me. I thought about claiming credit for everyone else's apologies and wiping that smug smirk off Kevin's face. To show him he didn't know me, or any of us, as well as he thought he did.

But did it matter, honestly? My apologies had helped the other Vibers: to varying degrees, they had been forgiven. And my apologies had helped me, too: after weeks of trying on other people's voices and other people's beliefs, I had finally found my own.

Let Kevin and Valerie believe whatever the hell they wanted.

"I know I didn't do the program exactly the way we're supposed to," I told Kevin, "but I want you to know that it helped me anyway. And I'm grateful to you for that."

He looked surprised, but pleased, and I was glad that I could give him at least part of what he wanted; I could give him reassurance that he really was helping people.

"I'm going to apply to college again," I went on. "I'm hoping now that I've been here at Revibe and I can show that I'm working on myself, maybe I'll be a better candidate than I was a few months ago. And I imagine that having an essay published in *The Pacific* could help my case, too."

The group looked uncomfortable at my mention of my *Pacific* article. Everyone knew about it, but officially, they acted as though it didn't exist, because it wasn't supposed to exist.

"I'm going to go back to college, too," Abe offered. "One of the things I got from Revibe is the belief that I *can* live away from home. I can be someplace else, without my mom, and still figure out how to get myself bathed and dressed and fed. Obviously Revibe is a fraction of the size of a college campus, so it's not the *same* thing, but it's made it seem possible. So I'm going to try going back to UConn next semester. But this time I'll be using my mom's last name on all my records. People will be able to figure out who I am no matter what, but at least I won't be leading with that."

I looked at Abe's strong arms and hopeful eyes, his stubby fingernails and lightly freckled skin, and I wished that wherever my new college search took me, it would take me near him. It was a possibility. After all, who knew where the future might take us?

"Are you looking forward to leaving here?" Valerie asked Abe.

"Not really," he said, and looked at me.

"Me neither," I said, and I took his hand.

Everyone saw this. Jazmyn did not look the least bit surprised. Kevin made a strangled sound, as though my continued existence was choking him. Zeke snickered and said to me, "Oh my God, you really can't do *anything* right, can you?"

And I clung to Abe's hand, and I clung to Christie's e-mail, and I said, "Yes, I can."

33

Much later that night, Abe and I met out on the porch, as we had so many nights before.

"Do you remember that first night you tried to kiss me?" I asked him.

He shuddered. "Ugh. Worst. So awkward."

"You said that if you weren't in a wheelchair, you would have suggested that we lie down on the beach and look at the stars together," I reminded him.

"That would have been romantic," he agreed, leaning in to give me a kiss.

"Let's do it now," I said.

He took in the idea, sizing up the five steps that led from the porch down to the sand below. They didn't have a ramp, and I could almost see him calculating it all in his head, figuring out his approach.

"Yeah," he said after a moment. "It is our last night together, after all."

"It is," I agreed, a lump in my throat.

Abe went down the steps backward, fast, holding the railing until his chair thumped onto the sand. He tried to wheel a bit closer to the water, but the sand was thick, and he didn't go far before pulling himself out of his chair and down to the ground.

I lay next to him and rested my head on his chest. The sand was cold and dry, but soft. I could hear the waves lapping against the shore, rhythmic, endless. Abe and I lay there together and watched the stars. We stayed there until the sun rose.

Then he murmured, "I have to go. My car is coming soon."

"Will I see you again?" I asked in a small voice.

I felt his chest rise and fall underneath me. "You'd better," he said. "I'm not going to let you get away that easy."

"Once we have the internet again, we can talk as much as we want," I said.

"You sure? As much as I want is a lot," he warned me.

"I can handle it," I promised.

He sat up so he could look me in the eye. "I hope you'll be in my life for a long time. But I've also learned by now that life doesn't always deliver. I want a hundred nights on a hundred beaches with you. But if I don't get that for whatever reason, I want to make sure you know, while we're both here, just how grateful I am for this night, and this beach."

I had no words. All I could do was nod and kiss him. And kiss him. And kiss him.

And then he got his suitcase, and he left.

In her e-mails to me, my mother had been uncharacteristically vague about what time she was going to pick me up, and I wound up being the last one at Revibe. It was hours after Abe had taken a taxi to LAX, and I was still sitting with my luggage on the front steps, watching the spitting dolphin fountain and replaying our last night in my mind.

I heard a car coming up the driveway and I looked up hopefully, but it wasn't my mom's Prius. It was a dented old blue Honda with loud music seeping out through its windows. This was not the sort of car you generally encountered here in Malibu.

The car stopped in front of me, and Corey climbed out of the backseat. "*What* is *that*?" he asked, pointing at the fountain.

"What?!" I ran down the steps and threw my arms around him, fully distracted from missing Abe. "What are you *doing* here?"

"Picking you up," Mackler answered, getting out of the front passenger seat. "Though, wow, didn't know you were so fancy now. You too good to come with us?"

"Yeah, right," I said, hugging him as well. "Holy *shit*, am I glad to see you guys."

"We're just a passel of poor boys with big dreams," Mackler said. "Maybe they'd let us be chimney sweeps in your Malibu mansion, if we got real lucky."

I didn't reply, because right then the driver of the car emerged. It was Jason.

"Hey," he said, giving me a little wave.

"Hi."

I hadn't seen any of them in person in months, but Mackler and Corey at least I had spoken to. Jason was like a locked box. Aside from a few anecdotes from our friends, I had no idea what he'd been doing, or if his feelings about me had changed whatsoever.

But he was *here*, and surely that meant something.

"Is this your car?" I started out by asking.

Jason nodded. "It was a bargain."

"Incorrect," Mackler said. "A bargain is when you get something valuable for cheap. The Silver Bullet is a piece of shit, and you paid a piece-of-shit price for it."

"Also, Mackler has named it the Silver Bullet," Corey explained to me.

"It's a great car name!" Mackler said.

"It's not silver," I pointed out.

"It probably used to be but then it faded to blue over the years," Mackler said blithely. "That's how things work."

"Okay," I said. "Seriously, though, I'm so glad you guys are here, but *why* are you here? How did this happen? I thought I was waiting for my mom!"

"Well, a couple days ago your sister was chatting with Jason," Corey explained, "and she said that your mom was supposed to pick you up today. And Jason and I were already on Christmas break. So Jason asked your mom if we could come get you instead,

and she said sure, so we drove down this morning and got Mackler from school, and then we kept driving, and now here we are."

I looked at Jason. "That was really nice of you," I told him.

He shuffled his feet a little. "I read your thing in *The Pacific*,"
he said after a moment.

"Oh."

"Yeah. And I read the bit that was about me, and I thought . . .
you know, it takes guts to apologize to anyone as publicly as you
apologized to me there. So I wanted to say thanks."

"You drove seven hours down here in order to say thanks?" I
asked, just to be sure I understood.

"And . . . I'm sorry, too," Jason added. "You were right that I
should have just *talked* to you, rather than bad-mouthing you on
Reddit. I was upset and hurt. But now that it's so many months
later, I feel like . . . I miss having you around. And I wish I hadn't
told the entire internet that I was mad." He shook out his arms.
"Whew. Apologizing is *hard*."

"With some practice, you can get used to it," I told him.

"Who knew Jason had so many feelings, though, am I right?"
Mackler said. He grabbed Jason in a headlock and tried to give
him a noogie, but Jason effortlessly broke away and shoved Mackler up against the car. "Jason Cutiepie Shaw, are you majoring in
wrestling or something?"

"That was not exactly wrestling," Jason told him.

"Thank you," I said to Jason. "Thank you for coming all the
way down here to apologize."

"Your essay made it sound like, I don't know, like you've thought
about it a lot."

I nodded. "A lot" hardly began to cover it. "There was this one night when a bunch of us here went to a convenience store. And the cashier accused one of the girls I was with of being a thief. Just because she was black. No other reason. It was obviously bullshit.

"And I thought that this girl must get treated like that a *lot*, without ever knowing exactly when it's going to happen. And she can't fight it every time or she'd spend her whole life fighting. And I thought that if she saw my post about Sintra Gabel, on top of *everything else*, it could be the last straw. The issue is never one thing. It's that on top of all the other things. Does that make sense?"

"Yeah," Jason said. "I think I tried to tell you that, like, six months ago." But I knew he wasn't too annoyed, because he was smiling.

"I had to get there myself, I guess," I said.

"Well, look," Jason said, "you and I both made some shitty choices, but I guess everyone makes shitty choices sometimes."

"Not me," Mackler butted in. "I never make shitty choices."

"You made one just today, saying we can't go to Disneyland before we go home," Corey contributed.

"Did you say that, Mackler?" I asked. "What a terrible friend."

"Not my choice! My mom's all like, 'Mack, honey, I haven't seen you in months, you need to come home right away so I can feed you those orange blossom cookies you like so much.'"

"She did not say that," Corey argued.

"Swear to God."

"And I have to get home to Mellie," Jason added. "I told her I'd try to see her tonight."

314

"Who even is Mellie?" Mackler asked.

"I have seriously never heard that name before," Corey agreed.

"Mellie's my girlfriend," Jason said.

"Of *course* she is," we cried. "Mellie! Jason's girlfriend! Gosh, it sure will be good to have Mellie in our lives now!"

Still teasing one another, the boys helped me load my bags into the trunk, and then we got in the car.

"Um, guys?" I asked as Jason started the engine. "Why are there so many—"

"Songs about rainbows?" Corey put in eagerly. "I love that song!"

I shook my head. "I was going to say 'bottles of Gatorade in this car.'"

Jason snorted. I kicked some empty bottles out of my footwell and tried to shove the full bottles into the middle seat so that I could sit down properly.

"I can answer that question easily," Mackler said. "We won third place in the Gatorade contest."

"Oh my God," I said, bursting out laughing. "That video? That actually *won*?"

"It didn't *win*," Corey said. "It got third place."

"If first place is a year's supply of Gatorade," I managed to say around my giggles, "then what do you get for third place?"

"We got a seventy-five-dollar Gatorade gift certificate," Mackler told me. "So I have purchased us seventy-five dollars of Gatorade. *For free.* You're welcome, everybody."

"Gatorade is disgusting," I said. "You know that, right?"

"Uh, do I look like I give a shit?" Mackler asked. He tossed a blue bottle back to me. "Drink this one. The honey master loves it. Plus it'll replace your electrolytes so hard-core. You don't even *know* how many electrolytes you can fit inside your bloodstream. It's unreal."

I uncapped it, took a sip, and grimaced. I thought about their Gatorade video filming, and how if I'd had it my way, they never would have done it, and we would have at most three bottles of colored water in this car right now. "Do I still get to share in your riches even though I'm not fun anymore?" I asked.

Corey groaned. "Mack, I *told* you that you never should have said that."

"Winter," Mackler replied, "although there are no such things as stupid questions, I'm going to make an exception here and say that one was pretty stupid. Of *course* you get to share in our riches. Even if you're not fun anymore, you're still our friend."

I rolled my eyes to cover up just how pleased I felt. "And even if you're a total jackass," I replied, "you're still *my* friend."

Mackler nodded and said, with deep satisfaction, "I know I am."

34

The night that I got home from Revibe, I curled up in my pajamas on the living room couch and looked online to see who had been recently publicly shamed.

It felt good to be home, with unchecked internet, toys cluttering the dining room table, and the knowledge that there were food products with refined sugar in the cupboard if I wanted them. But it felt weird, too, to be in charge of my own time and choices, to have no one else's apologies to write, and to hear my parents chatting in the other room, but to know that no matter how late I stayed up, I would not see Abe.

According to my search, the biggest scandal of the day involved a DC journalist named Matt Reedy. Matt was married to a woman, which was relevant because he set up a profile on a gay dating app. And *this* was relevant because he was doing it only to find out who in DC was gay—and, especially, who was a closeted gay politician.

He reached out to anyone whose profile indicated that they worked on Capitol Hill, and if someone responded, Matt invited him out for a drink.

And then he published an article about who they were.

At present, Matt Reedy was the most hated person in the country. His employers had distanced themselves from him. Every other media outlet decried him. I read one journalist's screed that ranted, "How could this man be so dangerously arrogant, so horrifyingly irresponsible, as to out people against their will and without their consent? How could anyone with any humanity do such a lecherous, exploitative thing? And to what end? To get a byline and a higher click-through rate? I am a professional journalist, and that is a debasement of what this industry is."

Those who weren't professional journalists took to their own social media to point out what a despicable act this was. I saw that Emerson's friend Brianna had written her own indictment, and I read that one especially carefully.

"What Matt Reedy and so many entitled aggressors like him don't bother to understand," she wrote, "is that our sexuality is not their business. Reedy goes through life as a straight, white, married, college-educated, cisgender man, which means he's never had to worry about being hated, fired, or attacked just because of who he loves. He's never experienced it and he can't even imagine it. And he can't find in himself one shred of empathy for those of us who know that just holding hands with our partners in public could result in a physical beating. It should be up to me who I come out to and when. There are some people I've known for years who I've never told that I'm gay, and THAT IS MY CHOICE.

To waltz around and out a bunch of men who you know nothing about—you don't know *why* they're closeted, if their families will disown them for being gay, or if they'll lose their jobs—is so SELFISH. AND IGNORANT. AND CRUEL."

She got dozens of likes and comments, and I read those, too. "Matt Reedy has blood on his hands," someone agreed.

"We should post all this same information about his wife and family: their photos, names, sexual interests. See what happens to *them*. Then publish an article about it."

"I quit this site months ago, but I'm rejoining today so I can say how disgusted I am by Matt Reedy and everything he stands for."

"I guess he must want to be the cause of ruining strangers' lives? I guess that must make him feel powerful? I can't think of any other reason whatsoever for doing what Matt Reedy did."

"Plus he's ugly AF."

I agreed with them, up to a point. He shouldn't have done it. No one should ever do anything like that. It was, as they said, arrogant, irresponsible, lecherous, and exploitative. It was selfish, ignorant, and cruel. There were so many big adjectives that had been used for what it was, and I agreed with all of them.

But I also felt for Matt Reedy. Because although he was the most hated person in the country, he was still a person. And unlike that commenter on Brianna's post, I *could* think of other reasons that he might have done it.

Over the past seven months, so many people had shown me such cruelty. But there were also occasions that stuck in my mind when people briefly shone kindness into the darkness that surrounded me. The one that I returned to now was Claudette Cruz, on my first day back to school after The Incident, saying to me in science class, *What's happening to you is wrong. Hold your head up, girl. They don't know you.*

I wondered where Claudette had gone since graduation, if she remembered saying that to me, if she could imagine that it was only thanks to comments and actions like hers that I, too, hadn't jumped from a sixth-story balcony.

It was so easy to hurt a stranger. You could do it without even thinking about it, without even trying. Matt Reedy had done it first, to those innocent closeted gay men who thought they were going on a date with someone they might actually get along with. And now the tables had turned and people were doing it to Matt Reedy in retaliation.

But why couldn't it work the other way? If someone was kind to you, why not pass on that same kindness?

It seemed as good a starting place as any.

I was a writer, after all, and I was done writing apologies under other people's names. Tonight, I wrote a message from myself.

Dear Matt Reedy,

I understand what you're going through. I'm not going to try to offer you any advice, because I don't know you, and I'm not going to offer you any forgiveness, because that's not mine to give.

I only want to tell you that you're not alone. Lots

of us have been where you are. We live through it. And if you live through it, you will come out of it different, but stronger and better than you could ever imagine right now.

That's what I can offer you. Live through it, and we'll see you on the other side.

Sincerely,

Winter Halperin

And writing to that journalist, even though I did not know him and he did not reply, made me feel better. More than any official Rehabilitation exercise ever had, it made me feel like *I can help*. I felt like I had something to say and there were people who would want to listen. So as time went by, I kept going, writing more and more messages of support. I sent them to people like Matt Reedy, like Christie, like the teacher who told her students that glitter was for girls, like the athlete who didn't put her hand on her heart for the national anthem, like Jazmyn, like Richard, like myself. Almost every day I heard of a new person who had misstepped, misspoken, acted carelessly or selfishly or small-mindedly and was now paying for it. So almost every day, I wrote to them. I wrote, and I wrote, and I wrote. It became my version of Repentance. And in between writing those, I wrote a new college essay, about The Incident and what had become of me since. And I researched new schools to apply to. There were so many of them out there. And I kept volunteering. Because when I stopped, it turned out I missed it.

(Not yoga, though. Turned out I didn't miss yoga.)

And then one morning, I woke up and my first thought was not about what I'd done wrong.

I still thought about it, of course. But not first.

"Aren't you sad?" Emerson asked me one day.

"About which part?" I replied.

"You used to have this whole *plan*. This *identity*. You were a spelling champ, and you were going to Kenyon, and you were going to be a writer, and all of that. You knew exactly who you were and what you were going to do, and then it suddenly got stolen out from under you. How does that not just *devastate* you?"

Of course it *did* devastate me when I thought about it like that. But I also knew I wasn't alone. Abe used to have a plan—to go to UConn and travel the world—and it didn't involve living in a wheelchair or having a father in jail. Jazmyn used to have a plan—to be a big-deal musician—and it didn't involve getting slut-shamed by everyone she knew. Richard used to have a plan—to have a loving home—and it didn't involve losing both his wife and his daughter.

To Emerson, I replied, "Look, it sucked to lose my old life. But I still get to make a new one."

And I don't think it's a coincidence that the day after that, my sister mustered her courage and told our parents that she wasn't going to be a theater major anymore. She was going to stay at the University of Oklahoma, but switch to a different course of study. She didn't know which one.

They were pretty shell-shocked. Like me, they hadn't seen it coming. "You can't quit something just because it's hard," Mom told her. "If you really, truly want something, it's up to you to keep fighting for it. What do you need from us to keep going?"

"Nothing," Emerson said. "I just really, truly don't want this anymore."

"So then what *do* you want?" Mom asked, and I could see her already mentally preparing to move on to the next thing that Emerson was going to be extraordinary at.

"To be happy," my sister answered. "I want to be happy."

Mom turned to Dad for help. Dad looked way out of his depth. He tangled a Slinky around his arm and said, "Okay, well . . . what do you need from us to be happy?"

And we went from there.

Mom was the last one of us to cling to her old identity, to continuously try to squeeze herself into it, even though it clearly no longer fit. She took out advertising for her services, and hired an image consultant, and hounded her publisher to repackage her books. She could not accept that no amount of effort would bring back the life she'd loved. She saw me heading off on my new path of being an advocate for the victims of online shaming, and she saw Emerson heading off on her new path (whatever it was going to be), but everywhere my mother looked, she saw only blockades. "There's only *one thing* I can do really well," she told me and Dad, "and now I can't do it anymore."

"But that's not true," I pointed out. "Weren't you a strategy analyst for, like, a decade?"

"And a good one," Dad agreed. "Darlene, don't you remember how much you agonized over your decision to stop working?"

I honestly think she had forgotten.

So in the summer, a year after The Incident, she got a job, for a company, in an office, as a strategy analyst once again. "It might make sense, actually," she said. "I have two grown daughters. If there's anything I knew about parenting, I've probably already said it by now."

This is how you begin again.

People wrote back to me sometimes. They thanked me, or asked me for advice, or told me to mind my own business. They wanted to know what I had learned from it all, and if there was anything I could pass on to them so they could learn it more quickly, and with less pain and loss. "What would you say is the moral of your story?" asked one victim, and at first I thought it didn't have one, but now I imagine it does. And maybe I won't ever know the answer for sure. Or at least not until I'm very old, with miles of perspective, and this crime I committed is just a far-off memory, like a star that died eons ago but whose light we still see.

But for today, I think the moral is that we can do bad things and not be bad people. That we can make mistakes and do better next time. That we can hurt those who love us, and lie to those who trust us, and criticize those who are trying their hardest— and still our lives do not end. That no matter how many times we do wrong, we still have it within us to do right. That no matter how far off course we wander, we can always, if we try, turn ourselves back toward the sun.

Acknowledgments

Ideally in these pages I would acknowledge pretty much everyone I spoke to over the past couple of years, including my hairdresser and strangers who were unlucky enough to wind up next to me by the cheese platter at a party. There was nobody whom I was too proud or too shy to ask for advice on this book, and unfortunately I can't get all their names in here (especially some of those cheese platter companions, whose names I may never have known), but here's an abbreviated overview:

Thanks to Joy Peskin and Stephen Barbara for believing that I had something important to say here, and for their patient wisdom as I tried to figure out what my something important was.

Thanks to everyone who brainstormed with me, and who kept being friends with me even when I had no topics of conversation other than this book, including but not limited to Clare Hawthorne, Emily Haydock, Emily Heddleson, Kendra Levin, Brian

Pennington, Alix Piorun, Allison Smith, the Type A Retreat writers (Lexa Hillyer, Lauren Oliver, Jess Rothenberg, Rebecca Serle, and Courtney Sheinmel), and Camp Emerson's Bunk I from the summer of 2015.

Thanks to Naeem King, Candace McManus, and Joseph Visaggi for their insightful feedback on my early drafts.

Thanks to the Scripps National Spelling Bee for letting me watch some of the competitions (and for some of Winter's words!).

Thanks to Simon Boughton, Elizabeth H. Clark, Lucy Del Priore, Molly Brouillette Ellis, Nicholas Henderson, Kathryn Little, Venetia Gosling, Bea Clark, Heidi Gall, Michelle Weiner, Claire Draper, Jennifer Sale, and everyone else at my publishers and agencies who work so hard to make my writing career what it is. Thanks also to Kate Hurley for her always wise copyedits.

Thanks to the writers, YouTubers, and podcasters who informed the ideas that appear in this novel, especially Jon Ronson—without his book *So You've Been Publicly Shamed*, I would not have written this one.

I'd like to acknowledge the countless people out there who have had experiences similar to Winter's, some of whom I know personally, most of whom I don't. I won't list their names here, because they are too vast in number and because many of them I'm sure would rather be forgotten; however, I would be remiss not to acknowledge the particular inspiration that I derived from Monica Lewinsky's life. Furthermore, I acknowledge that issues of privilege, microaggressions, and culpability are nuanced and complicated, and that I did not get everything right.

I want to thank the teachers, librarians, and booksellers who have helped get my books into readers' hands, and of course I want to thank my readers themselves: you guys are the best.

Finally, thank you to my parents for their boundless love and belief in me.